# Love & Ghosts

### Crescent City Ghost Tours

# CARRIE PULKINEN

Love & Ghosts

Contact Information: www.CarriePulkinen.com

First Edition, 2019
ISBN: 978-0-9998436-5-9

CHAPTER ONE

"What about a one-night stand? Or a series of them?" Trish asked.

Emily Rollins cast a sideways glance at her friend. "I think I need to swear off men altogether." She gathered her billowing crimson skirt in her hands and climbed the stairs toward the hotel entrance, placing each step with precision. Practicality wasn't on the list of requirements when she selected her costume for the Masked Movie Character Ball, and the last thing she needed was to trip on a layer of satin and tulle and tumble down before she even got inside.

Trish adjusted her mask. "You can't punish yourself forever, Em. You promised you'd try to have fun tonight."

She sighed and peered out over Canal Street, the dividing line separating the French Quarter from the rest of New Orleans. An October breeze raised goose bumps on her arms, and she shivered as she turned and drifted up the stairs.

"I'm not punishing myself. I'm just…" She swallowed

the sour taste in her mouth. "It doesn't feel right to have fun so soon."

As they stepped inside the Maison Des Fleurs, soft classical music replaced the roar of outside traffic, and green carpet squished beneath her stilettos.

Trish touched her elbow. "It's been more than a year. It's time to move on."

"I know." She drew her shoulders toward her ears and wrapped her arms around her middle. "But after Jessica died…"

"Well, tonight you're the Queen of Hearts, darling, and you're smoldering. Every hot-blooded man who's passed through this lobby has checked you out."

Emily rolled her eyes, but her friend's abrupt change in subject did help loosen the vise-grip squeezing her chest. Now the damn corset was the only thing keeping her from breathing properly. "Trish…"

"Seriously. At least ten different men have given you a once-over in the five minutes we've been standing here."

She laughed. No one was checking her out, and she'd prove it. She whirled around to face the room, daring someone to look at her. A Captain Jack Sparrow look-alike wearing a simple black eye mask bowed formally, wiping the smug smile right off her face.

Trish nodded. "Look, babe. All I'm saying is you're new in town. It's a masquerade, so the whole point is mystery. You can be anybody you want to be tonight, and no one will know the difference. Let me teach you how to have fun for a change."

She crossed her arms. "I know how to have fun."

"Sure, if you like wet blankets and cold showers. Come on." Trish linked arms with Emily and dragged her toward the ballroom.

Emily stopped outside the door and yanked her arm free. Her friend's teasing words stung. She'd come to New Orleans for a fresh start—to get away from the guilt that had been chewing her to bits and spitting out the pieces— and she had moved on, hadn't she? She'd done plenty of new things.

An indoor skydiving place opened near her apartment a month ago, but she hadn't worked up the nerve to check their prices. Iconic street cars chugged along the tracks every ten minutes in front of the urgent care clinic where she worked, but she'd never hopped on one. Hell, the only reason she'd been to Bourbon Street was because Trish dragged her there. Aside from her occasional walks through Jackson Square, she hadn't explored the city she now called home. Her throat tightened. Maybe she hadn't moved on at all.

"All right. If I'm a wet blanket, what do you suggest? Should I make out with the first guy I see? Dance on the tables?"

"Just let loose. Relax. Maybe hook up with a bad boy for once in your life. That's what you need. A sexy New Orleans man to show you the city, get your mind off things."

"I've dated bad boys before."

Trish laughed and pulled her away from the door as a couple dressed as Princess Leia and Han Solo stepped past them. "Who? Phillip?"

"He rode a motorcycle once."

"He's an actuary, Em. You can't get any more boring than that."

She chewed the inside of her cheek. "He cheated on me. That makes him bad."

Her friend wrapped her arm around her shoulders.

"That's the wrong kind of bad, babe. And anyway, that jackass cheating on you turned out to be for the best. If he can't stick by you through the tough times, good riddance."

"It was quite a wakeup call, wasn't it?"

"And now you're here with me, learning to live the life Jessica would have wanted for you."

She chuckled. "From the authority on having fun."

"You got that right." She led her through the double doors into the ballroom.

Emily gasped. Thirty-foot ceilings soared above with two massive chandeliers dripping with crystals, hanging side by side in the center of the room. A polished wood dance floor took up most of the space, and a band on a raised platform belted out a smooth rendition of Frank Sinatra's "Fly Me to the Moon." A generous buffet complete with shrimp cocktail, boudin, and oysters on the half shell sat against the wall, and an open bar stood catty-corner to the food. Hundreds of masked people in elaborate costumes representing characters from all genres of movies milled about the ballroom, mingling, dancing, laughing…having fun.

"Drinks first." Trish led the way to the bar.

Maybe her friend was right. Maybe she did need to let loose tonight. It had been a year since her sister's death. That fresh start needed to begin sometime; she'd been stagnant long enough.

If a masquerade ball wasn't the perfect opportunity to elicit change, what was?

Trish handed her a gin and tonic. "So, what's the plan?"

Emily grinned. "Dare me."

"What?"

"Like when we were kids. Dare me to do something outrageous, and I'll do it."

Trish sipped her gin fizz. "Seriously? I know you can't see my eyebrows through this mask, but I am arching one in disbelief."

Her pulse quickened, and she swallowed before the lump could form in her throat. "Yes. I mean it. I promised I'd have fun, and you're going to teach me how."

Her friend slammed her hand on the bar. "Two shots of tequila, please." The bartender poured the drinks, and Trish handed Emily the tiny glass. "All right. I dare you to kiss a stranger."

"That's it? Just kiss someone?"

"Not *just* kiss. One: it has to be on a man's mouth. And two: there has to be tongue."

She chewed her bottom lip and stared at the liquid courage in the glass. A kiss. She could do that, couldn't she? Taking a deep breath, she tossed back the shot and set the glass on the bar. The tequila burned as it made its way down her throat and into her stomach. "Kiss a man, with tongue. Done."

Trish downed her shot and grinned. "And you are not, under any circumstances, to give him your number."

"Why not?"

"I don't want you getting all goo-goo-eyed over the first guy you meet. This city is a living, breathing entity, and it has to be experienced fully before you settle down. Get your fill of fun before you do anything else."

"Yes, ma'am." Emily gave her a mock salute and ordered another gin and tonic. She was going to need it.

"Another beautiful party, Momma. Well done." Sean LeBlanc kissed Madeline on the cheek and tousled the purple feathers adorning her sequined mask. Her floor-length black dress curled up in eight places on the hem—Ursula the Sea Witch's tentacles. And every time he took a step, he nearly tripped on one and busted his ass on the dance floor. All those years of dance lessons as a kid hadn't prepared him for waltzing with an octopus.

"Thank you. I do know how to throw a party, don't I?" Her satisfied gaze swept the room before landing on him.

"You always have." He twirled his mom across the dance floor, carefully avoiding her tentacles and hoping to evade the question he could tell she'd been biting back all evening. At least she was making an effort tonight.

"Tell me, Son. There are so many beautiful women here, but the only one you've danced with is your mother. Why?"

And there went her self-restraint. He faked a smile. "I don't know. I guess I'm not in the mood to deal with a woman tonight."

"When will you be?"

Grinding his teeth, he tried to quell his irritation and come up with an answer that would appease her. "I date every now and then, Momma. Nothing to worry about."

"First dates don't count. Unless you've had a second date I don't know about?"

"You know I haven't." He sighed. "I know what love feels like, and I'm not going to waste my time on someone it could never happen with." If it *could* ever happen again.

She narrowed her eyes. "Have you heard from Courtney lately?"

He stifled a groan. She knew the answer to that too.

"It's been almost two years since her spirit made contact. I don't want to talk about this."

"Sweetheart, she's been dead for three. Even her ghost has moved on. Don't you think it's time you did too? She would want you to be happy."

He pressed his hand into her back and eased her into a fast spin. "I'm dancing with the most beautiful woman at the ball. I am happy."

She playfully swatted him on the shoulder. "Your charm won't work on me, young man. I taught you everything you know."

The song ended, and he led her to the bar. Madeline wouldn't be happy until he was married with a kid or two, and he'd get there eventually. Maybe. But he wasn't going to force it. If he ever found the right woman, he'd know. Why would he waste his time with anyone else?

His mom had done nothing but worry about him since the day his wife died. Hell, he'd worried about himself for a while, but he really was ready to move on…if the right woman came along. That's what he told himself anyway.

Still, he had to do something to get her off his back tonight, or she'd be throwing women at him every time he turned around. "I'll make you a deal. I'll dance with the first person who recognizes my costume."

"Hasn't anyone gotten it right yet?"

"It's a classic eighties movie. Someone will recognize it." He picked up a Scotch on the rocks and took a sip.

His mom grinned. "It would be more convincing if you had a Buttercup."

"Maybe I'll find her tonight."

"I hope you do." Mint julep in hand, she patted his cheek and sashayed into the crowd to mingle.

The chances were slim. He'd been called Zorro seven times already, and he certainly couldn't see himself dating a woman who didn't recognize the main character of one of his favorite movies. His mother was right though. Courtney had only come back to console him the first year after her death. He hadn't heard from her since, so she had obviously moved on. It was time he did too.

"Mr. Sean." A tiny cold hand tugged on his.

He smiled at the little girl, and her blonde ringlets bounced as she giggled and pointed to a large, framed sketch hanging on the wall.

"That's me." She vanished and reappeared next to her brother across the room. Sean and his team had investigated this building many times. He knew all the ghosts that resided here, and most of them were friendly. The portrait of the children was his donation to the charity. This ball and every event his mom planned this year benefited the local animal shelters. A hotel the size of this one would pay thousands for a sketch of the spirits that haunted it, and he was more than happy to donate the proceeds to a good cause.

He still hadn't figured out how or when the siblings died; they didn't do much more than play and giggle. Her name was Alice; her brother was Jonathan, and that was the most they'd been willing—or able—to share so far. That they'd shown themselves to him tonight was a good sign, though. He'd have to get his team back for another investigation.

But now, he had a promise to keep. He scanned the crowd, searching for friendly faces. No need to waste his time on a woman who couldn't have fun at a party like this. If the food and free-flowing alcohol weren't enough, the band was on fire. But all these damn masks made it hard to see people's eyes. He'd have to go for smiles.

A blonde and a redhead sat at a high table near the dance floor. The Red Queen and the White Queen from *Alice in Wonderland.* Nice choice. Red laughed heartily at something the blonde said. Her crimson lips curved into a smile that lit up her whole face. She was definitely having a good time.

He ambled closer to their table to get a better look, and damn, did he like what he saw. Fiery red hair flowed over her shoulders and down her back. Her creamy breasts nearly spilled out the top of her tight-laced corset, and her shiny red high heels peeked out from beneath a flowing skirt that unfortunately blocked his view of her legs. Something about all that red had him burning inside.

The Lone Ranger escorted the White Queen to the dance floor, and Red's smile didn't fade. She sipped on a clear drink and swirled the ice in the glass. His pulse quickened.

Maybe he was in the mood to deal with a woman tonight after all.

———

Emily laughed as the Lone Ranger dipped Trish on the dance floor and nearly dropped her on her head. The bartender wasn't stingy with the alcohol, and after the shot of tequila and her second gin and tonic, her head spun in a delightful way. She pushed the glass away. Any more, and it might affect her judgment. She was on a mission. But not just any guy would do. If she was going to kiss a stranger tonight, she wanted to *feel* something.

Passion. Her life had been devoid of that emotion for nearly a year. Of course, she was mostly to blame for the downward spiral her last relationship had fallen into, but she could change. Trish only asked for a kiss. Emily would one-up her friend and make sure the kiss made her burn.

She scanned the ballroom. Plenty of men appeared attractive, but the costumes and masks made it hard to be sure. Captain Jack Sparrow looked cute, and she'd always had a thing for pirates. But he'd blackened his teeth to go with the costume, and the thought of kissing that made her skin crawl. A wolf-man character looked big and muscly, but she couldn't tell if the blanket of hair peeking out of his shirt was real or part of the costume. This was going to be harder than she thought.

She picked up her drink and downed the contents as a man in all black approached her. He wore knee-high boots and black pants that hugged his muscular thighs. His Renaissance-style shirt revealed a smooth, sinewy chest, and a long sword sat sheathed at his hip.

So far, so good.

A black cloth wrapped around his dark eyes acted as a mask, and another cloth covered his head, concealing his hair. Her gaze traveled up and down his body, and when she met his eyes, he smiled.

Her pulse quickened. She could definitely burn for this guy.

He sauntered toward her with a cocky gait—completely in character—and his playful grin and full, kissable lips sent her stomach flipping.

"What's the Queen of Hearts doing all alone at a party like this?"

Emily sat up straighter. "I could ask the same question of you, Dread Pirate Roberts. Where is your Buttercup?"

"I'm currently interviewing for the position. Would you like to apply?" His devilish grin widened; her heart pounded harder.

"And how many applicants would I be competing with? It must be a coveted position."

He chuckled. "So far tonight, ma'am, you're the only candidate." He cleared his throat and whisked her glass from the table. "Your drink is empty, and that's a shame. Let me get you another one." He examined what was left of the contents. "Gin and tonic?"

"Yes, but..."

"I'll be right back."

He strode to the bar, and she got a view of his backside as he moved. *Nice.* Everything about the man was scrumptious. She inhaled a deep breath to calm the swarm of butterflies in her stomach. What on earth was she thinking agreeing to a dare like this? She didn't go around kissing strangers.

"One gin and tonic for the beautiful queen." He slipped into the chair next to her and set the drink on the table.

"Thank you." She could do this. It was just a kiss, and he was just a man. An incredibly sexy pirate tonight.

He leaned an elbow on the table. "You know, you're the first person who's gotten my costume right."

"Really? *The Princess Bride* is a classic. I can't believe people don't recognize you."

"I know. It's one of my favorites."

"And you look so authentic. You've got the mustache and everything. Is it real?"

He smoothed the thin strip of hair above his lip. "Of course. But everyone thinks I'm—"

"Zorro?"

"Nailed it. By the way, my name is—"

"Westley." She stirred her drink and swallowed before raising her gaze to his. "Your name is Westley tonight."

"Oh, we're being mysterious?"

She shrugged. It was better if she didn't know his name. Trish was right: she didn't need to attach herself to the first man she met. And this guy was way too magnetic.

He smiled. "I get it. It's a masquerade. We can reveal our identities at the stroke of midnight."

She tilted her head. If she was still talking to him at midnight, she'd be in trouble.

"Okay. Westley, it is. Can I call you Buttercup?"

Covering the tip of the straw with her finger, she brought the other end to her lips and released the contents into her mouth. "I'll let you know."

He laughed and downed the rest of his drink. "I promised our hostess I would dance with the first woman who didn't call me Zorro." Standing, he offered her his hand. "Would you care to join me on the dance floor, my queen?"

"I would be delighted." She took his hand and let him lead her to the center of the floor. The band played Billy Joel's "Just the Way You Are," and Westley pulled her close. Though their bodies didn't touch, an inexplicable magnetism held her. His masculine scent, the warmth radiating from his skin—she couldn't have pulled away if she'd wanted to.

One hand on her hip, his left hand cradling her right, he led her around the floor with the grace of a professional. His strong arms guided her into moves she didn't know she had in her dance repertoire. He spun her, releasing his hold to twirl her under his arm and pull her back into a firm embrace.

She gazed into his eyes, unable to quell the butterflies flitting their way into her chest. "Wow. You're an amazing dancer."

His cocky grin returned as he twirled her. "All those years of cotillion finally paid off."

"What's cotillion?"

"Dance and etiquette classes my mom forced me to take as a kid. I hated every second of it."

"And now?"

"No regrets at all." He gave her one final spin and dipped her so low, her head nearly touched the ground. As he brought her back up, she stumbled into him, and he caught her in his arms. "You okay?"

"Yeah. I think it's the alcohol. I'm not usually this clumsy."

His gaze lingered on hers, and though she was steady on her feet, he still held her close. The feel of his firm body pressed to hers sent warmth flooding through her limbs, and as he started to let her go, she held on tighter.

"I love this song. Can we dance again?"

A slow smile curved his lips. "As you wish." He kissed the fingers of her right hand then traced his thumb across the tiny butterfly adorning the inside of her wrist. "That's a nice tattoo. What does it mean?"

Instinctively, she wanted to jerk her hand away, but she forced herself to hold contact. "It means I like butterflies."

"I like them too."

Her heart fluttered as he slid his hands to the small of her back and held her with firm yet gentle pressure. Cheek to cheek, she clutched his shoulders and tried to slow her breathing. His woodsy scent filled her senses, making her head spin, and as the slow, sultry music played on, she melted into his embrace.

She lost track of how many songs ended, how many new ones began as they held each other on the dance floor, softly swaying to the rhythm. She could've held on to this mysterious man all night. His strong arms. His intoxicating scent. The way his breath tickled her ear when he turned toward her.

He slid his hands up and down her back, his gentle touch raising goose bumps on her arms. His heart pounded against her breast as she glided her hands across his shoulders to cup the back of his neck. It was time. She was going to kiss him.

Her cheek brushed against his masculine stubble as she pulled away to look in his dark brown eyes. He inhaled deeply, dropping his gaze to her mouth. Her eyes fluttered shut as he leaned in. Something vibrated against her hip, and she opened her eyes. His gaze lingered on her lips.

"Westley?"

"Hmm?"

"Your pants are vibrating."

He chuckled. "They can leave a message."

"It might be important."

He pressed his forehead to hers and slid his hand up her neck, into her hair. "Nothing is as important as dancing with the most beautiful Queen of Hearts I have ever seen."

Heat flushed her cheeks. "I'm sure you say that to all the ladies."

"I can assure you I don't." He twirled her around the dance floor and stopped close to the edge.

Emily wasn't the type to swoon, but something about

Westley made her knees weak. "You really are a fantastic dancer."

"It's all part of my diabolical plan."

"Your plan?"

He smiled. "To keep you here until midnight, when the masks come off, and the identity of the most beautiful woman in New Orleans is revealed."

Her heart slammed into her throat. She wanted to know this man. More than his identity, she wanted to know *him.* But she couldn't. Trish was right. She shouldn't latch on to the first hot guy she met.

She needed to kiss him and walk away.

His phone vibrated in his pocket again, and he let out a disappointed grunt.

"You should answer that. It's probably important if they're calling again." She released her hold on his shoulders, but he tightened his grip around her waist.

"You're not getting away so easily." He fished the phone out of his pocket. Checking the screen, he sighed and pressed the device to his ear. "This had better be important, Jason."

He closed his eyes and listened. "You have got to be kidding me. Did you call Syd?" He stroked his fingers down her cheek and mouthed the word *sorry.* "How many over are we? Twenty-five? No, I'll be there in fifteen... Yeah. On my way."

He mashed the screen with his thumb to end the call and shoved the phone into his pocket. Wrapping his arms around her, he pulled her into a tight embrace and pressed his lips to her ear. "I have to go."

She fought the shiver running down her spine. "I figured as much."

"Can I see you again?"

She bit her lip to keep from saying yes. "Tonight, for me, was about learning to live again. To enjoy life, and I've enjoyed every second I've spent with you. But this is all I'm able to give right now."

He pulled back, disappointment evident in his eyes. "How about this? I'll give you my number, and if you ever decide you have a little more to give—and I'm not asking for much…just a little of your time—then you can call me."

The temptation overwhelmed her. She couldn't form an appropriate answer, so she did the only thing she could.

She crushed her mouth to his.

A deep groan rumbled in his throat as he parted his soft lips to let her in. He tasted sweet, like honey laced with warm whiskey, and when his tongue brushed against hers, fire shot through her veins. He tightened his arms around her, and she allowed herself to get lost in his embrace. They were the only two people in the world, and being in his arms was all that mattered. The kiss slowed to a gentle brush of the lips, and she had to get away before she gave in.

She took a step back and rested her hand on his cheek. "Thank you, Westley, for a lovely evening I will never forget."

His gaze was heavy and filled with longing. "Can I at least know your name?"

"My name is…" She shouldn't. The moment with Westley was ending, and sharing names would only quell the mystery. She stepped toward him and placed a soft kiss on his cheek.

"Call me Buttercup."

He chuckled and lowered his chest into a formal bow,

his heated gaze never straying from her eyes. "As you wish." He lingered for a moment as if hoping she'd change her mind.

"Goodbye, Westley."

"Farewell, Buttercup." He nodded and walked away.

CHAPTER TWO

*S*ean shook his head as he trudged up Chartres Street toward Jackson Square. The crisp fall air nipped at his cheeks, but it did nothing to cool the slow burn that woman had ignited inside him. The taste of her mouth—sweet lime and passion—lingered on his tongue. Was her face as gorgeous as her tall, sexy body? If he'd hung around long enough, he might have found out.

Damn job. Damn responsibility.

Christ, she'd felt good pressed against him, kissing him. Making him want more for the first time in years. Stirring up emotions he thought he'd never feel again. Buttercup had said she needed to *learn* to live, but with the way she was able to get him so worked up with a simple kiss…she was doing a fantastic job of living already.

The crunch of aluminum under his boot pulled him out of his thoughts. He picked up the flattened can of Coors and tossed it in a trash bin. He could fantasize about the things he'd never get to do with Buttercup later. Now, he had a job to do.

Jackson Square bustled with activity, as it usually did on Saturday nights. Though the park gates closed at dusk, and most of the artists had taken their wares home for the night, people still flocked to the cathedral plaza for the evening activities. A dozen psychics—some real, some fake —set up tables and offered readings for a small fee. Some used crystals, some tarots or runes, but they all focused on one common theme: giving people a glimpse into their futures. Sean smiled and nodded a hello to one of the mediums.

The old woman lifted a gnarled hand to wave. "I see a change coming for you, Sean."

"And I don't want to know about it." He hurried past the psychic. She'd offered to give him a reading several times, but he always declined. The future was best left unknown. Especially when there wasn't a damn thing he could do to change it.

"Hey, Zorro," someone called from a restaurant balcony.

He flashed the man a tight-lipped smile and waved. That was the eighth Zorro reference tonight, but it didn't matter. Buttercup knew who he was, and that was good enough for him. He shoved his hands in his pockets and made his way toward the church.

Swarms of people huddled around tour guides from various companies, preparing to be wowed by the sordid history of the city. Of course, most of these tours weren't historically accurate. "Fantastical exaggerations of legends" was a better description, but the tourists didn't care. They wanted to be entertained, and this late in the evening, most of them were drunk anyway.

Jason already had the overflowing tour group split in two, waiting on the steps in front of the St. Louis Cathedral. The massive white church towered over the square, providing the perfect backdrop for the haunting excursion he was about to lead. It had taken years to finagle Crescent City Ghost Tours into this spot, and earning the title of Most Reputable Tour Company five years in a row ensured him first choice of meeting spaces.

"Hey, man." Jason jogged toward him, clutching two iPads to his chest. "Sorry to pull you away from your mom's party. I didn't know what else to do. Most of the spots were prepaid so I couldn't send them away."

Sean took one of the iPads. "You did right. But I think you set a record for the most epic cockblock of all time."

Jason furrowed his brow and ran a hand through his dirty-blond hair. "Oh, shit. I am so sorry. You got her number though, right?"

He wasn't about to share the details of his failed attempt at landing a date with the sexy redhead with his employee. "You ever get ahold of Anthony? Why'd he no-show?"

"He finally picked up the sixth time I called. Said he didn't want to do it anymore. He quit."

"Shit. Figures he'd pick the busiest time of year to leave us high and dry."

"Syd will be back in town tomorrow. She and I can split his shifts until you hire someone."

Sean clapped him on the shoulder. "I appreciate that. C'mon. We've kept our customers waiting long enough. You claim a group yet?"

"I'll take the one on the left." Jason led him to the group that would be his captive audience for the next hour and a half.

A man in a Dallas Cowboys shirt stumbled forward. "You brought Zorro to be our tour guide?"

*Fantastic.* He was starting the night off with a heckler.

Jason switched to his tour guide voice, extra loud and filled with energy. "You guys are in for a treat. Sean here isn't just a tour guide. He's the owner of the company… and he's the one who collected all the evidence we'll be showing you along the way."

A hushed murmur fell across the group as the Cowboys fan shrank back into the crowd.

Sean tapped the iPad screen and brought up a photograph of a dark shadowy figure in the alley next to the cathedral. "That's right, ladies and gentlemen. Every story you'll hear on this tour is true. The hauntings are real, and we'll show you the proof. Our tour starts here in Pirate's Alley."

---

"All right, babe. Spill." Trish clutched Emily's arm and dragged her toward the bar. "Gin fizz and a gin and tonic, please," she said to the bartender.

"Actually, make mine a Scotch on the rocks." She had a warm whiskey taste on her tongue, and she wasn't ready to let it go. Her lips, still tingling from that amazing kiss, curved into a smile as the bartender filled her glass.

"Who was he, and when are you seeing him again?" Trish handed her the drink.

"I don't know, and I'm not." She sipped the Scotch and cringed at the bitter liquid. It tasted better on Westley's lips.

Her friend set her glass on a table and crossed her arms. "I'm not buying that for one second. You just ordered Scotch. You don't drink whiskey."

She took another sip of the unpleasant drink. The

sharp liquid burned its way down her throat, and she pushed the glass away. "I know. It tasted good on his tongue, so I thought I'd give it a try."

"And?"

"It's horrible." She took a swig of gin fizz and swished it in her mouth to wash away the rancid flavor. Westley must've been drinking a different brand.

Trish laughed. "So…tell me what happened."

"I did just what I said I would. We danced. He didn't tell me his name, and I didn't tell him mine. Then we kissed, and he had to leave." She shrugged and traced the rim of the whiskey glass with her finger.

"Where did he go?"

"I don't know. It sounded work-related, but I didn't ask."

"You really don't know anything about this guy?"

She let out a long sigh. "I know he's charming. He has this woodsy, masculine scent that makes my head spin; he's an amazing dancer, and he tastes like honey and whiskey—but evidently *not* the kind I ordered."

"And you wish you got his number."

*Yes.* "No. It's better this way. You're right. It was fun, and I'll always remember it that way. At least now I won't find out he's an asshole later. He'll always be charming Westley to me." Dipping her finger in the drink, she put a drop of the golden liquid on her lip. She flicked her tongue out to taste it and wrinkled her nose. It still didn't taste like him.

"Emily? Is that you, dear?" The most glamorous octopus she'd ever seen approached her from the bar. Her black, sequined gown had eight tentacles curling up from the floor, and purple feathers adorned her sparkling mask.

"It's me, Madeline LeBlanc. I'm so glad you could make it."

She shook the woman's hand. "Trish, this is my real estate agent, Madeline. She's the one who gave me the tickets for tonight."

Trish shook her hand. "Thank you so much, Ms. LeBlanc. It's a beautiful ball."

"Oh, you're welcome. It's my pleasure, really." She turned to Emily and flashed a knowing smile. "I see you and the Dread Pirate Roberts hit it off. Where did he run off to?"

Tongues of heat crept up Emily's cheeks to lap at her ears. How many other people had noticed her escapade with Westley? "He, umm…had to go. I don't know where."

"How odd of him to run off on you and not say where he was going. Well, I'm sure he'll call you tomorrow."

She glanced at Trish before focusing on the floor. "I don't think so."

Madeline touched her shoulder. "He will, dear. He's a gentleman."

Emily cleared her throat and met her real estate agent's gaze. "I don't even know his name."

"His name—"

"Is best left unknown." Trish wrapped her arm around Emily's shoulders. "Tonight was an experiment. A reminder that Em's still got it, and she doesn't need to attach herself to the first man she meets."

Madeline's gaze cut between Trish and Emily. "You don't want to see him again?"

"Oh, I do. And I'm sure if it's meant to be, we'll run into each other somewhere."

Madeline pursed her lips and stirred the melting ice in

her drink. "Are you sure you don't want me to work some Sea Witch magic for you? Give you a strong pair of legs so you can go after your man?"

"I'm sure, Madeline." Her legs weren't the problem. What she needed was a stronger heart, because the one she had still wasn't fully recovered from the last time someone smashed it to bits. Between her sister and then Phillip, she'd lost too much already. As much as she longed for her mysterious pirate, she was better off not knowing him. "I'll leave it up to serendipity. If I see him again, I'll know it was meant to be."

"Hmm…" She flashed a small, unconvincing smile. "Do you ladies like art?"

"Sure we do." Trish clutched her arm and cast her a sideways glance, curling her lip with a *what is this crazy lady talking about now?* look.

"Come with me. I want to show you the piece that was donated to our cause tonight." Madeline turned and motioned for them to follow, her tentacles swishing as she sashayed through the crowd.

Emily looked at Trish and shrugged. Madeline was supposed to be the best real estate agent in New Orleans and the go-to person for anything and everything social. She seemed to know everyone…and their business. She'd already offered to play matchmaker for Emily on several occasions, and it wouldn't have surprised her if Madeline knew the mystery man's identity.

But Emily didn't need to know. She wanted to, but she certainly didn't need to.

Madeline gestured to a large charcoal portrait. "The hotel paid five thousand dollars for it, and the artist generously donated the proceeds to our charity. What do you think?"

Two children in period clothing sat on the grand staircase in the portrait. The girl's blonde ringlets hung down to her shoulders, and her eyes sparkled with mischief. The boy was younger, and he clutched the girl's arm and angled his chin down in a timid smile.

"Five thousand dollars?" Emily stepped closer to examine it. The artist definitely had talent. Each stroke of charcoal was precisely placed, creating an exquisitely realistic image. The artist had captured the children's personalities on paper as if he knew them personally. "It's a beautiful drawing. Who are the children?"

Madeline smiled wistfully at the portrait. "Their names are Alice and Jonathan. No one knows where they came from or why they're still here."

"Still here? Are they orphans?"

"No. They're ghosts."

Emily scoffed and stepped away from the picture. "There is no such thing."

Trish grimaced. "That's a touchy subject, Em. New Orleanians take their spirits very seriously."

"You live in the most haunted city in the country," Madeline said. "If you aren't a believer yet, you will be."

A pang shot through her chest, and she had to force a whisper over the lump in her throat. "The belief in spirits isn't logical, and it does more harm than good."

Madeline clasped her hands in front of her. "It sounds like you're speaking from experience."

"I…" She inhaled deeply and let her breath out slowly. No matter how much she liked the woman, she wasn't about to share the pain the so-called spirit world had brought into her life. Better to walk away now than get involved in a useless conversation. "It was a lovely party,

Madeline. Thank you for inviting me. I should be going, though. I have a long day at work tomorrow."

"Of course. I'm so glad you made it."

Hiking up her skirt, she hurried toward the exit. Ghosts weren't real; she'd convinced herself of that a long time ago. She'd tried to convince her sister too, but Jessica's obsession with the spirit world ended up killing her. No one could see ghosts, and Emily would make damn sure she didn't get involved with anyone who thought they could. Whoever made that portrait was a scam artist; there was no other explanation.

"Emily." Trish rushed to her side and followed her toward the door. "Are you okay?"

"I'm fine. I think I'm going to head home though. I have to work in the morning."

She let out a heavy sigh. "I know you don't want to believe in ghosts—"

"I *can't*, Trish."

"I know. But most of the people in this city do, and you're going to run into it all over the place. Just about every building in the French Quarter has a story about a haunting, and lots of people pay to hear about them. It's big money here, so you're going to have to learn to take it all with a grain of salt."

"I know. And you warned me about it before I moved here." She shook her head. "I should've taken that job in Dallas."

Trish pursed her lips. "Dallas is far less exciting than New Orleans."

"With far fewer believers in the paranormal."

"Maybe so, but your BFF doesn't live in Dallas, does she?"

"No, you don't." And the fact that her childhood best

friend lived here did tip the scales in New Orleans' favor. She'd have been completely alone if she'd gone to Dallas, her life even more boring than it already was. If that were possible.

"Don't act like you regret moving here. If you'll just get out and explore, I'm sure you'll fall in love with this city like I did. Give it a chance."

"You're right. This was my first encounter with a believer. I guess it caught me off guard."

Trish shrugged. "And it probably won't come up that often if this was the first time in three months. Still, it wouldn't hurt to learn about the legends. At least you won't be so shocked next time it happens."

"I'll think about it." Listening to a bunch of ghost stories was the last thing she wanted to do. Ghosts were nothing more than products of people's overactive imaginations. Anyone with a logical, analytical mind knew hauntings weren't possible, and until she saw some believable proof, she would continue to only believe in things she could see. That's what she told herself, anyway.

"I'm going to head home. You coming?" She gave Trish a hug.

"Nah. I'm going to hang around a bit longer. See if I can find myself someone as exciting as your mystery man."

A fresh flood of warmth washed through her body. "Good luck."

Emily stepped outside, and the crisp night air raised goose bumps on her bare arms. She called for an Uber and climbed into the backseat. Her apartment was only six blocks away, but her high-heeled Mary Janes were already rubbing her toes. She'd be on her feet all day tomorrow, and she didn't need the blisters a walk home would cause.

Hiking up her skirt one last time, she climbed the

stairs to her apartment. Peaceful silence greeted her as she opened the door and stepped inside. She unlaced her bodice on the way to her bedroom and inhaled the first truly deep breath she'd taken since she put the damn thing on. The costume was silly and extravagant, and she still wasn't sure why she'd let her friend talk her into wearing it.

She yanked off her mask and dropped the dress on the floor. Tiny flakes of red glitter rained down around her legs as she stepped out of the garment and smiled. Extravagant, yes, but the effect it had Westley was well worth the hassle. She shivered.

Now there was a man who'd be occupying her dreams for a while. But as much as she wanted to see him again, it was definitely better this way. No one was as charming and perfect and seemingly handsome as he appeared to be. Now she could hold on to that vision of him and never be disappointed. Of course, she could only envision him with that stupid mask and head covering. His eyes were a deep goldish-brown, but she had no clue what color his hair was, or if he even had any.

Blond. She'd imagine him blond like the Westley from the movie. Dark eyes. Light hair. Tanned skin. Oh yeah, he was welcome in her dreams. She slipped on a blue cotton nightshirt and poured a fresh ring of salt around her bed. Hopping over the trail, she climbed into the sheets and peered over the side. The ring was intact. No breaks anywhere. No nightmares would be invading her sleep tonight.

---

Sean stepped through the double doors of the empty ballroom and found his mother admiring his portrait of the ghost children. Her mask lay on a table, and she rubbed at her smudged eye makeup and turned around to greet him.

"Where did you run off to in such a hurry?"

"Sorry, Momma." He gave her a hug and a kiss on the cheek. "One of my employees up and quit on me, so I had to run a tour."

"Let me guess. The young Anthony?"

He nodded. He'd have to hire someone else and quick. October was far too busy for Jason and Sydney to handle on their own.

"Kids these days have no manners. No respect for others."

"I know, Momma. I'll try to hire someone older next time."

She pressed her lips into a line and stared at him. "I noticed you found a Buttercup tonight."

"You saw that, huh?" An image of those perfect red lips curved into a seductive smile flashed in his mind, and his chest tightened. He couldn't wait to put pencil to paper and immortalize the gorgeous queen.

"And then you let her go."

He shoved his hands in his pockets. "That was her choice, not mine. She doesn't want to see me again."

She crossed her arms and shook her head. "Bless your heart. Men can be so stupid."

"Momma!"

"I'm sorry, but that girl does want to see you again. She was crazy about you."

He glared at her. Madeline LeBlanc was famous for her meddling, and he could see exactly where this conversation was heading. "And how would you know that?"

"Because I know her, and I spoke to her after you ran off."

His heart thumped against his chest. "What did she say?"

"She called you charming, perfect…I think the word 'amazing' may have been mentioned."

He laughed. "Well, if she felt that way, why wouldn't she even tell me her name?"

His mom shrugged. "Something about not attaching herself to the first man she meets. She just moved here a few months ago. And she also mentioned if she ran into you again, she'd be happy about that. Serendipity, she called it. She sounds like a hopeless romantic to me… kinda like someone else I know."

"I am not a hopeless romantic. I'm waiting for the right girl." Why didn't anyone understand that? Just because he was a man, it didn't mean he had to chase after everything with boobs and a pair of legs.

Madeline arched an eyebrow. "She could be the one, and I can arrange that serendipity for you."

His chest squeezed even tighter. Could she be the one? He hadn't felt that alive since Courtney died. And his mom knew how to get in touch with her. Temptation gnawed at his gut, and he had to bite his tongue to keep from agreeing to her suggestion. Buttercup had said all she could give him was tonight. He wouldn't ask for more.

"No, I'll respect her wishes. And who knows? Maybe I will run into her again, and we can have that serendipitous moment after all. It'd be a nice story to tell your grandchildren one day, wouldn't it?"

She fisted her hands on her hips. "Don't play the grandchildren card on me unless you're serious, young man."

He winked. "I would never tease you about that."

"Love at first sight is a real thing. I knew your father was the one the second I laid eyes on him."

He sighed. "Goodnight, Momma. Are you okay to drive home? You didn't have too many mint juleps, did you?"

She waved a hand dismissively. "I'm fine. But you let me know when you change your mind."

"I won't change my mind."

"Yes, you will."

"Goodnight." He turned and strode away. Pausing in the doorway, he opened his senses, searching for any lingering spirits that might want to show themselves before he left. They must have sensed his brooding mood; no one appeared to him. Just as well. He couldn't focus on much but that fiery red hair and soft, pale skin. Even though she'd worn a mask, he'd recognize her anywhere. And the tattoo on her wrist would be confirmation enough he'd found her again if he ever ran into her.

# CHAPTER THREE

*S*ean sipped his coffee and put the finishing touches on yet another sketch of the beautiful redhead, who'd been starring in his dreams the past three nights in a row. He'd managed to capture the playful sparkle in her eyes perfectly, even through the mask, and his pencil lingered on the delicate curve of her smile the way his lips had days before. He shouldn't have been so hung up on a woman he hardly knew, but if he couldn't get her off his mind soon, he might have to take his mom up on her offer of scheduled serendipity.

He dropped the pencil and slammed the sketchbook shut. *Don't be an idiot.* He'd had his chance at love, and he should consider himself lucky for getting to experience it once. What made him think it could happen again?

He dumped the rest of his java down the sink, grabbed his keys, and headed for the office. Climbing into his silver Tesla Model S, he started it. Sometimes he missed the sound of a gas-powered engine rumbling to life, but the soft hum of the electric motor provided a gentle reminder of the pollution he wasn't spouting into the air every time he accelerated.

A canopy of live oaks covered his driveway, dappling the morning sunlight into intricate patterns of light and shadow on the concrete. He pulled onto St. Charles and rolled through the Garden District, admiring the scenery. His artist's eye would never tire of the lush gardens and grand antebellum homes that made up his neighborhood, homes that had stood for hundreds of years, many of them still belonging to descendants of the original owners.

He grew up in a mansion three streets over that had been in the LeBlanc family from the beginning. His mom still lived there, and one day, he probably would again.

As he headed toward his French Quarter office, the quaint, old charm of the Garden District gave way to the modern feel of the Central Business District. The buildings grew taller, their exteriors blander. He drove past Trinity Memorial Hospital, and his chest gave a little squeeze as it did every time he passed the place where Courtney spent her final hours of life. But she was in a better place now, and he still had a life to live. She'd told him that herself, many times when she came to him in his dreams.

His dreams. The only face he'd seen in his dreams lately was that of a living, breathing redhead. He shook his head to chase Buttercup's image from his mind. He was ready to move on. He had been for some time, though he didn't think he'd ever meet another woman he could burn for. Until now.

He turned down a side street in the French Quarter and punched the button to open the security gate on the alley near his building. Pulling into a parking space, he killed the engine and headed to the office. Sydney sat at the computer, her fingers flying over the keys as she updated the tour company's website. Her jet-black hair was sheared short in a lopsided pixie cut, and an intricate sleeve of tattoos covered her left arm from her shoulder to her wrist. He closed the door behind him, and she waved a hand in the air.

"Hey, boss. I'm almost done updating the calendar. I think we'll be able to keep our full schedule after all. The new guy is awesome." She turned around, and her almond-shaped eyes twinkled with her smile. "Where'd you find him?"

He peered at the screen over her shoulder. Two tours per night, every night for the rest of October. Three on Saturdays. He'd better be awesome, or Sean was going to be leading a lot of tours this month. "A friend in the investigative side of the business recommended him. Seems to really know his stuff. Theater major too."

"He's really good. I think he's ready to go solo."

"Eric? So soon?" He stepped around the desk, and Sydney moved from the computer so he could sit. He'd intended to hire someone older and hopefully more responsible after the last college student quit without notice. But Eric was so enthusiastic, and he seemed to know everything about Sean's investigations and the evidence he'd collected.

She drummed her unpolished nails on the desk. "He's done four tours with me the past two days. He's ready."

He closed the calendar and eyed Sydney. She'd been twenty-one when he hired her four years ago, the same age as Eric now, and she was his most trusted employee. Of course, she grew up in his neighborhood, so he'd known her all her life. She handled the schedule, designed the company website. Hell, she even ran all the tech equipment on investigations. She was indispensable.

His mother's words rang in his ears. *Kids today have no respect.* Not all kids. "Call him and let him know he's on the eight o'clock tour alone. I'll follow in the crowd tonight in case any emergencies arise."

"Okay." She traced her finger over the wood pattern in the desk. "He's been asking about going on an investigation too. Got anything scheduled?"

He leaned back in the chair and linked his fingers behind his head. "I'm working on something for Halloween. You in?"

"Sounds like fun. Who else is coming?"

"Just the four of us, I suppose."

"Oh." She chewed her bottom lip and averted her gaze.

"Why do you ask?"

"No reason." She busied herself checking the charging cables on the iPads. Finding a loose one, she pushed it in with a trembling hand and nearly knocked it off its base. She caught it before it could fall, and she let out a nervous giggle.

Uh-oh.

He scrubbed a hand over his face as a sickening feeling formed in his gut. "If you saw something, I don't want to know about it." Sydney was one of the psychics who actually could see glimpses into the future. Occasionally. Uncontrollably.

She dropped her arms by her sides and turned to face him. "I never said I saw anything."

"Good."

The door chime dinged at six fifty-five, and Emily cringed. No one had walked through the clinic entry since six-fifteen, but of course her last patient would arrive five minutes before closing time. So much for actually getting to leave at seven.

The mother eased her son into a chair and strutted toward the reception desk. Her heels clicked across the tiles, echoing through the building. "My son is sick. He needs to see a doctor."

Trish handed the woman a clipboard. "If you'll fill out this form and give me your ID and insurance card, we'll get you right back."

She reached a manicured hand across the desk and snatched the clipboard, her pointy, hot pink nails scratching across the plastic. "This can wait. He needs to see a doctor *now.*"

Emily backed into the hallway, out of sight. It figured her last patient of the day would be a difficult one. She glanced at the sick child through the window. He sat curled up in the chair, his forehead resting against his knees. Well, the patient wasn't the difficult one.

"We need some basic information and a signature on the consent for treatment form. It only takes a minute." Trish's voice never lost its cheerful tone.

"Isn't this an emergency room? My son could be dying."

"This is an urgent care clinic, ma'am. If your son is dying, I'll call for an ambulance to take him to an emergency room." The sound of a dial tone buzzed in the air. Emily imagined Trish's finger hovering over the nine button. She offered to call for an ambulance at least five times a day, but one was rarely needed.

"No, no. He just has a sore throat and a fever. I don't

want to deal with a hospital." The clicking of her heels receded as she made her way to her son and sat next to him. The boy reached for his mom, but she pushed him away and focused on the form.

Ten minutes later, Emily opened the door to patient room number three. "Hi there." She made eye contact with the child first, then focused on the mom. "I'm Emily Rollins, the nurse practitioner at this clinic. How can I help you today?"

The woman flipped her fluffy blonde hair off her shoulder. "Where's the doctor?"

"We don't have a doctor on duty today, but she's only a phone call away if we need her. Nurse practitioners are licensed to treat the same injuries and illnesses as doctors." She handed her a pamphlet explaining her occupation.

The woman snatched it from her hand and scoffed. "My son needs a doctor."

Emily took a deep breath. "He needs medical care, yes. Unfortunately, at seven o'clock on a Tuesday night, your only options are an urgent care clinic or an emergency room. If you'd like to take him to the hospital…"

"No." She fisted the pamphlet in her hand. "He has a sore throat. His fever won't go below 103, even with ibuprofen."

"May I?" She held up her light and a tongue depressor.

"Please." The mom motioned toward the little boy.

"Can you open really big for me?" She peered into the boy's mouth. Large, white puss pockets covered his swollen throat, and his lymph nodes had enlarged to twice their normal size. She listened to his heart and lungs and checked for any more abnormalities before entering her findings into the computer.

"Did the nurse swab his throat already?"

The woman nodded.

"I see. Here it is." She clicked on the link for the test results and pulled up the information. Of course, it was positive. "He has strep. Lots of rest. Lots of liquids. I'll send in a prescription to your pharmacy. Make sure he finishes all the medication, even if he feels better."

The printer spit out a release paper, and she handed it to the mom. "Take this to the reception desk, and Trish will get you checked out." She handed the boy a lollipop. "I hope you feel better soon."

He flashed a small smile and took the candy.

Emily let out a heavy sigh and cleaned up the room. She'd been warned in nursing school that some people had a hard time accepting care from a nurse rather than a doctor. She'd gotten used to having to explain her qualifications, but sometimes it still irked her when people gave her that doubtful look. She flipped off the light and stepped into the hallway.

"Will you tell her I'm sorry I doubted her?" The woman and her child still hadn't left. "And that I appreciate her help?" She must have read the pamphlet.

Emily waited for the door to chime their exit, and she turned off the hall lights and locked the interior door. "I heard what she said." She pulled her purse from a drawer behind the reception desk.

"I guess she gave you a hard time?" Trish shut down the computer and gathered her things.

"Nothing more than usual. But it's irritating when they walk in five minutes before closing time, wait no more than fifteen minutes to see me, and then they act like that. She would've waited hours at an ER." She followed Trish out the door and waited for her to lock up.

"At least she changed her tune and apologized. Even if it wasn't to your face."

"True. Well, I'm off till Saturday."

"I work tomorrow."

"Okay. I'll see you later. Stay safe." She walked up Canal Street and started to make her usual left on Dauphine to head home, but she hesitated. She'd done nothing but work three twelve-hour shifts since the night of the ball and hadn't had a lick of fun since that kiss. Her fresh start had gone stale, and it would be too easy to slip back into her stagnant routine. She needed to shake things up.

Sure, she was exhausted and her feet hurt, but maybe a stroll through the French Quarter in the crisp evening air would energize her. At least she'd get to see a little more of the city she now called home.

The streets bustled with activity. Especially Bourbon Street, which she hurried across to avoid the crowds. Trish had taken her bar hopping when she first arrived, and she didn't remember much of the night. The excruciating headache she'd endured the next day had tried to remind her, but she was probably better off not knowing.

After that night, she'd done nothing but work, eat, and go to the gym. It was time she lived, and the best way to do that was on a full stomach. She made her way to Jackson Square and ambled up to her favorite food cart.

"How's it going, Maury?" She grinned at the vendor as he used a pair of tongs to place a hot dog onto a bun.

The old man's eyes crinkled as he smiled. "Never better, Ms. Emily. How are you this lovely night?"

"I'm good. Thanks for asking." Her stomach rumbled as she squirted mustard across the all-beef frank and returned the bottle to the cart. Biting into her favorite guilty pleasure, she reveled in the deliciousness of the smoky flavor dancing on her tongue and downed the whole sandwich in two minutes. She bought a bottle of water and said goodbye to Maury.

He waved. "See you soon."

"You know it."

She walked deeper into the square toward the church. Most of the artists who set up shops along the fence had packed up and wouldn't be back until daylight returned. But plenty of fortune tellers and supposed mediums had tables set up throughout the pedestrian mall. She passed an old woman with sagging skin and gnarled hands, who looked up at her with a toothless grin.

"Tonight's an important night for you, princess. Sit down, and I'll tell you what your future holds."

"No, thank you." She hurried past and avoided making eye contact with any of the other scam artists. That woman couldn't tell the future any better than a coin-operated fortune telling machine. She'd make some broad, general statements that could be applied to any person, in any aspect of their lives, and then she'd ask for twenty bucks. They were all the same. Bogus.

She made her way toward the towering cathedral, where a crowd had formed on the front steps. It was probably one of those haunted history tours Trish had suggested she take to familiarize herself with the ghost stories of the city. While the ghosts couldn't possibly be real, the sordid history of New Orleans had always fascinated her. It wouldn't hurt to learn a little more about her home.

She found the tour guide, a young man in his early twenties, wearing a top hat covered in an array of steampunk contraptions. He wore a long trench coat and an ascot tie. He seemed so comfortable in the attire, it was hard to tell if he was dressed up for the job or if this was part of his normal wardrobe. Halloween was more than a week away, but the French Quarter seemed to celebrate the holiday all month long.

She tapped his shoulder to draw his attention away from the swarm of giggling girls surrounding him. "Excuse me, sir. Is there any room left on your tour?"

He turned to her and tipped his hat. "You're in luck. I've got one spot left, and it's yours for thirty-five dollars."

"Thirty-five dollars? How long is the tour?"

"Hour and a half. Can I sign you up?"

She'd been on her feet thirteen hours already today. Could she handle another two? The temptation to head back home and curl up in bed was overwhelming, but what good would that do her? She was already here, so she might as well stay. Besides, maybe the tour would surprise her. It could be fun.

"Sure. Sign me up."

---

Sean would've recognized that fiery red hair anywhere, even if it was pulled back in a ponytail tonight. And those perfect lips were pale pink as opposed to crimson, but he'd memorized the way they curved into a seductive smile. Her crystal blue eyes reflected the streetlights as she handed Eric her credit card and waited for him to finish the transaction. She lifted her right hand to sign the iPad with her finger, and her sleeve slipped up to reveal the pink and teal butterfly adorning the inside of her wrist.

Hot damn. Buttercup was joining the ghost tour tonight.

He took a deep breath to slow his heart as he eyed her from afar. She wore black slacks and a pale yellow sweater with a scoop neck that didn't scoop nearly low enough. Sensible black flats replaced her red high heels, and a similarly sensible black bag hung from her shoulder.

So this was the alter-ego of the gorgeous woman who'd set fire to his soul with a simple kiss. She was every bit as beautiful in her practical clothes. And even more sexy, if that were possible. This was the woman who was learning to live, and he was on a mission to be the man who taught her how to let go.

Buttercup skirted around the crowd and settled into a spot at the back. Sean needed to pay attention to Eric's performance—to make sure he delivered the correct information and entertained the group as well as Sydney claimed he could. The back row was as good a place as any to observe his new employee. Eric straightened his hat, winked at a blonde in the front row, and began his speech. Sean strolled up next to Buttercup.

"Good evening." He clasped his hands behind his back and grinned.

She flipped a switch on the side of her phone and dropped it into her purse. "Hello." She glanced at him and dropped her gaze to the ground.

"Nice night for a ghost tour."

She raised her eyes to meet his and quickly looked away. "The night is nice. Yes."

"But not for a ghost tour?" Did she not recognize him? Or was she pretending not to?

She let out a sigh and wrapped her arms around herself. "I honestly don't know what I'm doing here. I don't believe in ghosts."

"Maybe you will after the tour."

"I don't think so."

He'd heard that line many times, but more often than not, after ninety minutes on this tour, the skeptics turned into believers. He could turn Buttercup into a believer too. "You never know."

Her gaze met his and traveled down to his lips, where it lingered a second too long. His heart gave a squeeze as the urge to lean in and taste her pooled in his chest. She narrowed her eyes and gave him a once-over as if she might recognize him.

"I haven't lived here very long. I'm just getting acquainted with the city."

She really didn't recognize him. He could have some fun with this. "So you're not a tourist then?"

"No. Well, tonight I guess I am. I haven't been out much since I moved here. What about you?"

"Oh, I live here too. I'm Sean, by the way." He held out his hand.

"Emily. It's nice to meet you." She placed her palm in his, and a tingling sensation shot through his body. Parting her lips, she sucked in a little breath. She must've felt it too. The spark from the ball was still there, whether or not she knew who he was.

Eric motioned for the group to follow and led the tour into Pirate's Alley. He pulled up a big QR code on his iPad and held it out to the crowd. "I'm going to be showing you actual evidence of the hauntings at several locations on this iPad. But if you want to scan the QR code now, you can also watch the live presentation on your phone."

Perfectly delivered. And just as he'd been trained, Eric walked around the group letting the customers scan the code. A symphony of beeping sounded as people's phones connected to the tour presentation site, and the blonde

Eric had been eyeing giggled as he whispered something in her ear. He'd have to have a word with his new employee about picking up women on the job. Only *he* was allowed to do that.

Emily laced her fingers together and left her phone in her purse.

"Aren't you going to scan the code?" Sean asked. "You'll miss out on all the evidence if you don't."

"I'm sure if it's that convincing, I'll be able to see it on the iPad."

"I'll scan it then. You can look at mine." He pulled his phone from his pocket and scanned the code. She needed to see it up close to get the full effect. This was the only tour in the city using this type of technology to deliver vivid proof of the ghosts haunting the French Quarter. He was proud of his operation, and for some strange reason, her approval mattered to him.

Eric maneuvered to the front of the group and played a series of still photos of the alley. A dark mass appeared in shot after shot, moving closer to the camera with each image. Sean held out his phone so Emily could see, and she pressed her lips together and blinked at the screen. Stepping closer, he rested his hand on her back, and her breath caught. She swallowed and moistened her lips with her tongue. She may not have been interested in the images, but she had to be feeling the chemistry.

Should he tell her who he was? If he did, she might turn tail and run. And the night was going well so far. Better to let things play out and see how it went. He leaned in closer and whispered in her ear. "Pretty amazing evidence, isn't it?"

He purposely lingered near her neck, breathing in her clean, sweet scent. Soap and lilies. She shivered as if his breath tickled her ear, and her own breathing grew shallow.

She cleared her throat and stepped away. "I'd hardly call it amazing. That can be easily faked in Photoshop."

He stiffened. Plenty of skeptics had chalked the evidence up as fake, and it never bothered him before. Some people didn't want to believe, and that was fine. The unknown could be scary, especially in regards to life after death. But Emily calling his evidence fake *did* bother him.

He hardly knew the woman. Her opinion on the supernatural shouldn't have mattered any more than the next person's, but it did. And he knew exactly why. He liked her, and he wanted her to like him. All of him.

"This tour guarantees none of their evidence has been retouched." He followed next to her as the tour moved on to the next stop.

"I don't have much faith in a company that makes its money spreading rumors and lies."

*Ouch.* He stopped walking and crossed his arms.

"And even if they aren't retouched," she turned and stepped toward him, "they could have been fabricated on the spot with a play on light and shadow."

He arched an eyebrow at the stubborn woman.

She shrugged and curved her lips into that seductive smile that weakened his knees. "I'm a skeptic. I can't help it if I have an analytical mind."

"Analytical, huh?" They walked side by side toward the tour group. "What about passion? And art?"

"Those things are nice, but there's not much room for them in my job. *Com*passion, yes. But I have to be rational."

"Where do you work?"

"At an urgent care clinic." She stepped backward off

the curb and nearly landed on her ass. But he caught her by the shoulders and pulled her to his chest.

She fit in his arms exactly like he remembered. Perfectly. The fresh scent of her shampoo wafted through his senses, and he fought the urge to press his nose to her hair and breathe in her essence. "Are you okay?"

She pulled from his embrace, but her right hand lingered on his chest. Her gaze traveled down to his lips again, then returned to his eyes. She narrowed her own eyes as if trying to put the pieces together. She remembered him, but her "analytical" mind wasn't allowing her to accept it.

"I'm sorry. I'm not usually clumsy."

"Aren't you?" She'd said those same words to him on the dance floor at the ball. Surely she'd remember.

She stiffened, yanking her hand from his chest. "No, I'm not."

Eric played another piece of evidence, this time of a coat hanger flying across the screen inside a hotel room.

Sean showed her his phone. "You can't tell me that was faked. You can see the hanger the whole time. No one touches it."

She rolled her eyes. "No, but that doesn't mean someone didn't tie a piece of fishing line to it before they started filming. There are plenty of ways to fake all of this evidence. Ghosts aren't real, and the people who believe in them are...Well, it's not good for them."

"Not good for them?"

"I'm sorry. I shouldn't have come here. It was nice meeting you, Sean, but I have to go." She turned and marched across the street.

"Wait. Emily, where are you going? The tour isn't finished." He darted into the road and collided with an oncoming pedal cab. Sean grabbed the handlebars as the driver slammed on the brakes. The front tire skidded between his legs, narrowly missing the important parts.

The driver rang his bicycle bell and grumbled, "Watch it."

"Sorry." He maneuvered around the cab and caught up to her. "Please don't go. I'm sorry if I upset you."

She sighed and rubbed her arms. "You didn't upset me. This tour…the ghost talk…it's…" She shook her head.

"Hey, Sean?" Eric called from across the street. "Can you help me with something?"

"Oh, you know the tour guide?" She arched a delicate eyebrow. "No wonder you've been talking it up so much."

"Sean?" Eric called again.

He groaned. "Can you wait here for a second, Emily? I need to see what he wants, but I'm not done talking to you."

"There's really nothing more to say. I need to get home."

He looked at her. "Please? Give me five minutes? It'll be worth it, I promise."

"Sean?" Eric again.

She gestured for him to go.

"I'll be right back. Please." He looked both ways before crossing the street this time. Eric met him on the curb. "This better be important."

Eric glanced across the road, and Sean followed his gaze. Emily still stood there, her arms crossed, shifting her weight from foot to foot.

"The presentation froze." Eric shoved the iPad in his face. "It won't restart."

"This happens occasionally." He turned to address the group. "Sorry, folks. We're having a bit of technical difficulty." He lowered his voice to Eric. "Hold these two buttons down until it restarts. Then everyone will have to rescan the QR code to get back in sync with the presentation. Didn't Sydney teach you this?"

Redness spread across Eric's cheeks. "Right. Reset, rescan. I'm sorry, my mind blanked. I really am ready to do this on my own."

"I know you are. You're doing a great job." He patted him on the shoulder and started across the street, but Emily was already gone.

---

Emily flung open her door and trudged into her bedroom. What was she thinking going on a ghost tour? She knew they'd present the stories as if they were real, but she didn't expect so many people to buy it. She'd seen firsthand how a belief in the supernatural could turn into a deadly obsession, and she wanted nothing more to do with it.

Just stop engaging. That's what she'd have to do. Smile and nod and let people believe what they wanted to believe. Just because her sister went nuts trying to prove ghosts existed, it didn't mean everyone would. And it wasn't her responsibility if they did.

No more arguing. Especially not with hot guys like the one she met tonight. She yanked the cord to turn on her ceiling fan and climbed into bed. On her hands and knees, she traced her gaze along the line of salt surrounding her bed.

When she'd lived with Phillip, she'd learned the hard way the trail had to be complete to keep the nightmares at bay. He had a tendency to step on the salt when he climbed into bed, breaking her circle of protection. She'd tried filling a water hose with the granules and wrapping that around the bed, but the gory nightmare that left her gasping for breath proved that experiment a failure. It seemed the only way the salt would work was if she applied it directly to the floor.

Luckily, the low speed of the fan didn't stir up enough wind to disturb the granules. The line was intact, so she could rest easy tonight.

If she could get her mind off that gorgeous hunk of a man called Sean. If she could've kept her mouth shut about the "evidence," he might have asked her out. He seemed interested, anyway. His dark brown eyes smoldered when he looked at her, and his crooked smile reminded her of her mystery man from the ball.

For a moment, she thought it was him, but their similarities began and ended with the smile. Westley had a mustache, and Sean's face was smooth. His dark hair was thick and wavy, and Westley had to be a blond. Sean couldn't have been Westley, anyway. Surely he would've said so if he was. If she tried hard enough, she could think of a thousand reasons why they had to be different men, the most important one being she didn't want them to be the same.

Embarrassing herself in front of Sean was enough. She couldn't allow the memory of her night with the mysterious Westley to be tarnished too.

She pulled the covers up to her chin and squeezed her eyes shut. It didn't matter if it was the same man or not. She'd never see either of them again. Sean had asked her to wait while he talked to the tour guide, but she was too humiliated to hang around. Had she been aware he knew the guide, she might have held her tongue instead of condemning the supposed evidence. As it was, she'd made an ass of herself, and the best way for her to save face was to walk away.

One of these days she'd learn to keep her mouth shut and not embarrass herself in front of every good-looking guy she saw. In her defense, she was exhausted, and it had been two and a half years since she'd been on the dating scene. She'd forgotten what it was like to be single. The awkwardness of meeting someone new.

There was one way to get over that. Next time she met a man who made her heart race, she was going to ask him out. Why not? She was a strong, independent woman. If she wanted a man, she should be able to go after him. No more rules. No silly games. She was going to do things her way.

CHAPTER FOUR

"So, everyone's good with the schedule for the rest of the month?" Sean turned his laptop around to show his employees the screen. Their weekly lunch meeting at Dat Dog on Frenchman Street was one of the highlights of his week. There was nothing better than an alligator sausage hot dog smothered in crawfish etouffee, and a "work meeting" was the perfect excuse to have them on a regular basis.

"And *everyone* works Halloween. The only reason you can call in sick is if you're on your death bed or you lose a leg. Understood?" He narrowed his eyes at his employees.

"What about an arm?" Eric grinned as his leg bounced up and down.

"You can still walk without your arms."

"Yes, sir." Sydney gave him a mock salute.

Eric sat up straighter. "I'll be there."

"So, Junior's going to work out after all?" Jason mussed Eric's hair, and Eric knocked his hand away and punched him on the shoulder.

"Shut up, man. I'm only four years younger than you."

"I'm kidding. We're glad to have you aboard, assuming you're going to stick around." Jason stole a French fry from Sydney's plate, and she slapped his hand.

"I'm not going anywhere," Eric said. "This is my dream job." He grabbed the last fry off Sydney's plate.

"Hey! I was going to eat that!"

"Sorry." Eric held the half-eaten fry toward her, and she snatched it from his fingers.

Sean closed his laptop. "Gentlemen…"

Sydney cleared her throat and crossed her arms.

"And lady. Can we focus, please? I have somewhere to be at three o'clock." He tapped his Rolex and shook his head.

"You have a date with that redhead from the other night?" Eric wiggled his eyebrows. "She was smokin'."

"Redhead? Y'all went out to pick up chicks without me?" Jason crossed his arms.

Sydney straightened her spine and gave him a quizzical look.

Sean dragged a hand down his face. How did this work meeting morph into a discussion about his personal life? "No, not the redhead." Only in his dreams.

"Someone else, then?" Eric asked. This kid fit in with the crew like he'd worked there for years. That wasn't such a good thing at the moment.

"Yes. I have a hot date with a pit bull named Roxy. I'm walking her through the Quarter to advertise an adoption special at the shelter. Satisfied?"

"So you're using the dog to pick up chicks?" Resting his hands on the table, Eric leaned forward like he was seriously interested in Sean's dating techniques.

"I'm not trying to pick up chicks." His voice sounded

exasperated, even to him. This meeting had gone way off track.

"Calm down, guys." Sydney tossed her trash in the can behind their table and patted Sean on the arm. "You know Sean doesn't date."

"I do date. I just…" He closed his eyes for a long blink. "C'mon, Syd. You too?" He'd known Sydney his entire life. She'd known Courtney and everything he went through when she died. He didn't need this shit from her too.

He let out a heavy sigh and looked her in the eyes. "You know I'm trying."

"I know." She focused on her hands and picked at her fingernails. "I'm sorry."

"I'm sorry too." Eric punched his shoulder. "The way she was looking at you during the tour, I thought surely you were going to hook up."

"Well, we didn't. Can we move on now?"

His employees nodded.

"So we all work on the thirty-first, and immediately after the eight o'clock tour, you need to gather up your gear and meet me in the lobby of the Maison Des Fleurs. I managed to secure the ballroom for the evening, and we're going to have a little Halloween investigation."

"Awesome," Sydney sang. "I can't wait to try out my new spirit box."

"Count me in." Jason grinned, and they all stared at Eric.

"Wait…I'm invited too? I thought I was just a tour guide."

Sean shoved his laptop into his bag. "You're one of us now. Consider it your initiation. Welcome to the team." He rose from the table and slung his bag over his shoulder. "Now if you'll excuse me. I have a date with a pretty little pit bull, and if I'm lucky, she just might kiss me."

---

Trish clutched Emily's arm with a freshly manicured hand and led her out of the salon. "How's the fresh start going? Anything exciting happen since the ball?"

"Ugh. Not good." They walked up Royal Street, and she stopped to admire a black and red vintage-style dress in a boutique window. "I've been working so much. I haven't had much time."

"What'd you do yesterday, then? You had the whole day to yourself."

They ambled farther up the street and stepped into an art gallery. "Laundry. Cleaned my apartment. Went to the gym."

"Em…" Her voice held a disappointed tone. "I'm going to have to see about rearranging my schedule so we can have more time off together. We need to sync up our shifts so I can help you live."

"I am trying, okay? I went on a ghost tour Tuesday night." She clutched her purse strap on her shoulder and stared at a giant painting of a cartoonish blue dog.

Trish raised her eyebrows. "How did that go?"

"Horribly." She crossed her arms over her stomach. "I made an ass of myself in front of this really hot guy. I insulted his friend."

"But you got his number, right?"

"What? No, I didn't get his number. C'mon." She jerked her head toward the exit and led her friend out onto the street. "I was so embarrassed I ran away. Besides, what happened to not getting serious with the first guy I meet?"

Trish shrugged. "This wasn't the first guy. He was the second. Why'd you run away?"

"I told him the company was spreading lies and all their evidence was faked. I didn't know he was friends with the tour guide."

"Ouch. I guess he didn't take it well?"

"I don't know. He wanted to talk to me more, but I ran away while he was distracted. I was too mortified to face him."

They walked in silence toward her apartment, and she mulled over the conversation in her mind. With his heated gaze and the way his lips lingered near her ear when he whispered to her, he'd seemed genuinely interested. At least, she assumed that was the way a man would act if he were interested in a woman. It had been so long since she'd been on the dating scene, she'd forgotten how to flirt. She shook her head. Apparently, she'd forgotten how to talk to men altogether. When was she going to learn to keep her mouth shut?

Trish sighed and wrapped her arm around Emily's shoulder. "Babe, we're going to have to work on your dating skills."

"I know. I suck."

"You don't suck. You're just getting warmed up. Did you at least get a name this time?"

"Sean." A tiny sigh escaped her lips with the name, and a warm shiver ran down her spine. "It's such a sexy name, don't you think? Sean."

"Very sensual."

"It just rolls off your tongue like a melody. Sean. Hello, Sean."

Trish laughed. "Oh, Sean. Right there. Oh, yes. Oh, Sean."

She glared at her friend. "It sounds better when I say it."

"Relax." She rolled her eyes and swung open the door to the bakery downstairs from Emily's apartment. "What's he look like?"

"He's about six foot two, wavy dark hair, dark brown eyes, sexy smile. You know…his smile reminded me so much of the Dread Pirate from the ball, I almost asked if he was him."

"Why didn't you?"

"It couldn't have been him. He would have said something, don't you think? I mean, my costume wasn't *that* much of a disguise." She shuffled forward as the line moved toward the counter. "Anyway, with the amount of alcohol I drank that night, maybe I'm not even remembering him right."

"True. What do you want?"

"Chicken salad on a croissant. And anyway, Sean didn't look anything like how I imagined the guy from the ball looking without his mask and head cover."

Trish ordered the sandwiches and handed her a paper cup. "No one can compete with your imagination. That's not fair."

"Actually, Sean was better. All that wavy dark hair…" Heat crept up her cheeks, and she fanned herself with a napkin.

"And let me guess: when you fell off the curb, he caught you in his arms and held you as he gazed into your eyes." She clasped her hands beneath her chin and batted her lashes.

The heat in Emily's cheeks spread to her ears. "How did you know that?"

Trish giggled. "You always turn into a klutz around hot guys, and they have to catch you when you fall. It's kinda your thing."

"It is not my thing."

"Anyway…you ran away from him." She handed her the sandwich.

"Like I said, I suck. Let's go upstairs to eat these." She led her friend out of the bakery and up the side stairway to her apartment above.

Trish followed her onto the landing. "Living so close to a bakery this good could wreak havoc on your waistline."

"Tell me about it. And my apartment smells like fresh-baked bread every morning. It's amazing." She bent down to look at the label on a large box sitting outside her door.

"What did you order?"

"I don't remember ordering anything, but it's addressed to me." She handed her food to Trish and pushed open the door. Lifting the box, she stumbled inside. "Jeez, this is heavy."

She slid the package onto the table and peered at the return address. No name. The address wasn't familiar, but the box had come from Houston.

Trish plopped into a chair and unwrapped her sandwich. "Who's it from?"

"I have no idea."

"Open it."

Her stomach tightened. She hesitated as a wave of wariness rolled through her system. "I don't know. It's kinda creepy."

"It's just a box." Trish took a bite of her lunch.

"You're right. I'm being silly." She grabbed a pair of scissors from the drawer and cut through the tape. The flaps popped open, and a packing peanut floated to the floor. She brushed a layer of Styrofoam aside and reached her hands into the package, sliding her fingers down a smooth piece of wood. "It feels like another box."

"A box inside a box. How mysterious."

She lifted the object from the package, and packing peanuts rained onto the table and all over the floor. "I hate these things." She tossed a few into the carton and peered at the box she received.

Her heart gave a thud. She recognized the two-foot rectangular cherry-wood chest instantly. It belonged to her sister. She ran her hand across the lid, feeling the contrast of the smooth wood against the rough carvings etched into the top. They were letters, though she didn't recognize the language. And as far as she knew, her sister never figured out what it said either. She lifted the lid, but it didn't budge. A copper keyhole nestled in the center of the front panel kept it locked tight.

"Is there a key in there?" She nodded toward the packaging, and Trish dug through the peanuts.

"I don't see one. What is it, Em? Where'd it come from?"

She slid her hands across the top and tried the lid again. Still locked. Of course. "It belonged to Jessica. She bought it at an estate sale a few months before she died." Pressure mounted in the back of her eyes. She hadn't cried over her sister's death in months. She wasn't about to start now.

"Maybe Robert sent it to you?"

"Maybe. Is there anything else in the box?" She fished her hand through the Styrofoam and found an envelope in the bottom of the package. Pressing it to her chest, she squeezed the paper, hoping to feel a key inside. Aside from the letter, it was empty. Her disappointment must have been evident in her eyes because Trish put a hand on her shoulder.

"Are you okay? Do you want to be alone?"

"No." Being alone was the last thing she wanted right now. If she were alone, the tears might fall, and she was through crying over a woman who chose to take her own life—even if she was partially to blame.

"Do you want me to read the letter to you?"

She nodded and passed the note to her friend.

Trish pulled the single sheet of paper from the envelope and scanned the contents. "It's from Robert. You ready?"

She inhaled a deep breath and lowered herself into a chair. "Yeah. I'm ready."

"'Dear Emily, I hope this package finds you well. I know it's been a while since we've spoken. I've met someone. And, well, it's been more than a year. I hope you don't mind that I'm moving on. I was going through Jessica's things, and I found this box. She didn't have it long, but she was very attached to it. I couldn't bring myself to throw it out, but I also don't feel right taking it into my new home. I think she would've wanted you to have it.'"

Trish looked up from the letter. "Sure you're okay?"

A heaviness settled in her chest, the most weighted emptiness she'd ever felt. "I'm fine. Does it say anything else?"

Trish reached across the table and gave her hand a squeeze. "There's a little more. It says, 'I know she had a key for it. I locked it myself after she passed, but I've misplaced it. If I find it, I'll send it your way. I hope you're enjoying New Orleans. Your mom said you moved there for a fresh start. I hope you understand that's what I'm doing too. Take care, Robert.'"

Folding the letter, Trish slid it back into the envelope. She placed it on the table and stared at her friend intently. "How do you feel about that? Him moving on, I mean?"

She opened her mouth to speak, but she paused. How did she feel about it? At the moment, she wasn't sure she felt anything at all. "Am I supposed to feel a certain way?"

Trish lifted her shoulders.

"I didn't expect him to stay single forever. I guess it's about time he moved on. A year is more than enough time to mourn."

"You're right. It is. Good for him." She flashed an unconvincing smile.

"Good for Robert." Emily scooped up the rest of the loose Styrofoam and dropped it into the box.

"What are you going to do with it? It's kinda pretty."

The finish of the wood was faded, and the rough edges could use a little sanding. But with a coat of fresh varnish —or maybe even a cheerful paint—the piece could be eye-catching on her shelf. She looked at the butterfly tattoo on her wrist, and the hollow heaviness in her chest lifted. It wouldn't hurt to have another reminder of her sister around. They'd been best friends her whole life—up until Jessica's obsession with the spirit world made her crack.

"I'll keep it. It'll look nice once I clean it up." She picked up the heavy box and gave it a shake. The wood was so thick and solid, it was impossible to tell what was in it. Robert didn't mention locking anything inside, but he also didn't say the box was empty. "Do you think a locksmith could open it without breaking the lock?"

"It's worth a shot. Maybe she hid a million dollars in the lining."

"Yeah, right. I doubt Robert would've locked it away and sent it to me if that were the case." She slid the box onto the counter and positioned it against the wall.

"Maybe he didn't know."

"Maybe, but I—" The theme song from *The Princess Bride* sounded from Emily's purse, and she rushed to grab the phone.

Trish grinned. "No…you're not hung up on Westley at all."

"Shut up." The urgent care clinic's number lit up the screen, and her heart sank. That could only mean one thing. "Hello?"

"Hey, Emily. It's Sarah. The school just called. Presley has a fever, and she's vomiting. Peter's out of town, and I can't get ahold of my mom. I have to go get her. Do you think you could come in today?"

She glanced at the clock. Two p.m. "For the whole evening?"

"Yeah. I'll need to stay home with her. If you'll do this for me, I'll work the first half of your Saturday shift this weekend."

She closed her eyes for a long blink. Only working half the day on Saturday sounded nice, but she *so* wasn't in the mood to deal with patients today. "Yeah. I'll be there in half an hour. Go take care of your little one."

"Thank you so much, Emily."

She hung up the phone and tossed it into her purse. "That was Sarah. I have to go in."

"Okay." Trish picked up her purse and stepped toward the door. "Call me later, and let me know if you get the box open. I'm curious what's inside it."

She eyed the hunk of wood, not wanting to leave with the mystery unsolved. Something about the box called to her, but she didn't have time to answer it now. "I will. See you later."

---

Sean jogged behind the pit bull along the raised bank of the Mississippi River. He slowed his stride, trying to get the bundle of energy to relax, but all the dog wanted to do was run. "Calm down, Roxy. You're never going to get adopted if you don't let anyone meet you."

He tugged on the leash and slowed to a walk, waving as he passed a young mother with two small children. A little boy with sandy blond hair reached toward the dog, but his mother ushered him away.

Poor pit bulls. They got such a bad rap.

Roxy sat in the grass, her tongue lolling from her mouth, and he scratched her behind the ear. The LeBlanc family chose a new charity every year and spent the next three hundred sixty-five days organizing dinners, auctions, and other fundraisers to provide much-needed supplies and cash to the recipient.

Walking the shelter dogs wasn't part of the package, but he enjoyed doing it so much he planned to keep it up after the year ended. The shelter overflowed with pit bulls, dobermans, and other "aggressive" dogs that really just needed to be loved. He'd helped get six adopted so far, and hopefully, Roxy would make number seven.

He pulled the leash tighter to keep her walking by his side, rather than running, and crossed the street into Jackson Square. Hundreds of people milled about, stopping to take photos of the giant Andrew Jackson statue with the St. Louis Cathedral as a backdrop. Couples cuddled under trees, and children ran in circles around the park benches. A woman with long red hair stepped into view, and his heart nearly stopped beating. He started toward her, but as she turned, he caught a glimpse of her face. Definitely not Emily.

He stopped and bent to pet Roxy, hoping his hasty approach hadn't been obvious. While she was an attractive woman, Paisley Monroe was nowhere near as drop-dead gorgeous as Emily. He'd memorized every curve of Emily's perfect features, down to the tiny freckle beneath her bright blue eyes.

Paisley's eyes held all the brightness of a dead fish, and her voice grated in his ears like the high-pitched squeal of a dental drill. If he kept his head down, maybe she wouldn't recognize him. He scratched the dog behind its ears and imagined what he would have said to Emily had it really been her.

He should've told her who he was on the ghost tour. Maybe then she wouldn't have run away. Or maybe she still would have. She was dead set against believing in anything supernatural, and that was a shame. If he'd had more time, he could've changed her mind. He still might. He could always call on his mom for that scheduled serendipity she'd promised. The real kind obviously wasn't working out for him.

"That's a cute dog. What's his name?" Paisley stood over him, beaming a smile. *Damn.*

"Her name is Roxy. She's up for adoption at the shelter. They're offering half-price adoption fees this week." He smiled back and rose to his feet, taking a step away.

"Oh?" She twirled her red hair around her finger. It wasn't nearly as vibrant as Emily's. Nor was it natural. In fact, now that he saw her up close, he couldn't believe he'd mistaken her for his Buttercup, even if it had only been for a second. "Is Roxy the only woman in your life right now?"

He chuckled. "She's, uh…no. I'm seeing someone." It was only a tiny lie. He was seeing Emily every night…even if it was just in his dreams.

Paisley frowned. "Oh. That's too bad."

"But Roxy is looking for a companion." He rubbed the dog's head, knocking loose a string of gooey saliva that oozed from her maw to the ground.

She crinkled up her nose. "I'm more of a cat person." She flipped her hair, wafting the overpowering scent of designer perfume into his face, and walked away.

That confrontation wasn't so bad. At least she didn't beg him for a date this time. He knelt down eye to eye with the dog. "I'm sorry, Roxy. We'll find you a home."

Her eyes locked on something behind him, and a low growl resonated from her chest. An icy hand gripped Sean's shoulder, and every hair on his body stood on end. The dog stepped back and whimpered. It had been ages since a spirit had initiated contact with him. He did his best to block them out until he was ready to communicate. He'd either let his guard down today, or this spirit had something extremely important to tell him.

He gazed up at the woman and tried not to react to her gruesome appearance. Tangled blonde hair hung down to her shoulders, and her brown eyes, ringed with black, bulged from their sockets. Her lips were swollen and purple, and the rope burns and bruises from the noose that killed her were still fresh on her neck.

She moved her lips as if she were speaking, but no sound came from the spirit. She was either freshly dead, or this was her first time trying to cross over, and here in Jackson Square, with all the noise and bright sunlight, it was impossible for him to tell. She tried to speak again, but still the words wouldn't come. Her lips were too swollen for him to read, but the last word she said could have been "please."

When the spirit released her grip on his shoulder and faded away, Sean let out a breath. Roxy's gaze locked on something else behind him, and he swiveled his head to see what had caught the dog's attention now.

"Please don't let it be another ghost."

He'd barely uttered the words when she barreled into him, knocking him flat on his back and using his chest as a springboard. The breath whooshed from his lungs as the dog darted over him and plowed toward a hot dog cart across the street.

"Roxy, no!" He scrambled to his feet and gave chase, but the damn dog was too fast. She lunged for the vendor, and Sean snatched the end of her leash in time to be yanked into the cart. His shoulder slammed against the rusty edge, and the entire contraption toppled over, spilling wieners and buns onto the street. As his head knocked against the metal, he bounced off, rolling onto the ground.

Piercing agony shot through his left arm, and when he reached toward the pain, he found himself skewered by a pair of hot dog tongs. Moisture stung his eyes, so he squeezed them shut and yanked the utensil from his arm. Blood poured from the crescent-shaped wound, dripping down to dot the mess of buns littering the ground.

"Damn dog."

"Are you okay?" The vendor, a slight man in his mid-sixties with leathery skin and cracked lips, offered him a dirty rag and a hand up.

Sean accepted both, wrapped the leash around his wrist, and pressed the cloth against his left arm. His right arm burned from the scrapes extending from his shoulder to his elbow. Scrapes from a rusty piece of metal. *Fantastic.* "I'll be fine."

The hot dog stand was ruined. Roxy had lapped up every wiener the vendor had, and now she was working on the buns. The rusty edges of the cart had splintered with the impact, and it lay in three mangled pieces on the ground. The food stand was probably this man's livelihood. Without it, he wouldn't be able to feed himself or his family, if he had one.

The small crowd that had gathered around the accident dissipated, and the man looked at the mess in the street and pressed his lips into a hard line. His eyes shimmered, and he shook his head. "You'd better get that arm looked at. You're bleeding through." He shuffled toward Sean and pulled the bloody cloth from his hand. Then he took a clean rag from his pocket and tied it tightly around the wound. "That oughta hold ya until you can get it sewn up."

"Thank you." Sean's chest tightened at the man's compassion. He'd just lost his only form of income, but he was more concerned about Sean's injuries than where he was going to get his next meal.

Sean pulled his wallet out of his pocket and handed the man five hundred dollars. "That should cover the food and paper products." He passed him his business card. "And here's my number. Call me tomorrow, and I'll see about replacing your cart. Maybe with something a little less rusty."

The man's eyes widened, and the corner of his mouth twitched. "This is too much. I didn't have five hundred dollars' worth of food in there." He held the money toward Sean, but he waved it away.

"The rest is for the hassle. I'm sorry about all the trouble." He bent to pick up a piece of the broken cart and winced at the pain shooting through his arm. Roxy sat on her rump, staring up at him with the big, innocent eyes of a puppy. A giant splotch of ketchup covered the letters on her "I'm adoptable" vest, making it read "I'm a table" instead. He shook his head.

"You go get that shoulder taken care of." The old man took the piece of rubble from his hand. "I'll take care of this."

"All right. But I'm serious about replacing your cart. Please call me tomorrow."

The man smiled to reveal a three-tooth-wide gap. "Will do. Now get on outta here."

Sean managed to keep Roxy under control long enough to return her to the shelter and explain why she was covered in ketchup and mustard. Blood had already soaked through his makeshift tourniquet, and little bits of rust flaked from his shoulder as he stretched the soreness from his other arm.

"You probably need stitches." The shelter receptionist nodded to his arm.

"I know." But spending the rest of the afternoon in a hospital was not on his agenda. "Do you think that new urgent care clinic could take care of this? I don't want to go to the ER."

She keyed in something on the computer and nodded at the screen. "It says they treat most illnesses and mild to moderate injuries. I don't see why not. It's over on Canal."

Emily had said she worked at an urgent care clinic. With any luck, he could turn his injury into another bit of that serendipity she'd been asking for. "Is that the only one in the area?"

"There's a few in the CBD. This is the only one in the Quarter."

She didn't explicitly say she worked in the French Quarter, but the fact that she ended up on a walking tour that night made it probable. It was worth a shot. This was the first time he'd felt more than an inkling of attraction to anyone since Courtney, and he'd be damned if was going to let it slip away.

CHAPTER FIVE

*E*mily shuffled down the hall to the next patient room and nearly ran into Becca as she darted out the door and yanked it shut behind her. The nurse giggled and handed her the patient's folder.

"What's so funny?" Emily took the folder and hesitated to open it. "Please tell me someone didn't 'fall' on a beer bottle and have it break off in an unspeakable place again."

"Oh, nothing like that." She glanced down the hall and stepped closer, lowering her voice. "He's a hottie, and he asked for you by name."

"Me?" She opened the folder and read the name. Sean LeBlanc. The only Sean she knew was the one from the ghost tour. Surely it wasn't… Her throat tightened. What if it was?

Becca grinned. "You're probably going to need some assistance with this one."

She took a deep breath and rested her hand on the doorknob, hoping the cool metal would chill the warmth already spreading through her body. "I'll let you know if I do."

She slipped through the door and pressed it shut, keeping her back turned to the man on the table. She could get through this without making a fool of herself again. She had to.

"Hello, Emily."

She slowly turned around and tried to smile, but as soon as she saw his condition, her nursing instincts took over. He was a mess, with blood dripping from a dirty rag tied around his left arm and dirt and who-knew-what kind of stains all over his dark blue shirt. She stepped closer and found a bloody scrape on his right arm extending from his elbow into his shirtsleeve. A knot the size of a golf ball protruded from his hairline, yet somehow, he managed to smile.

She scanned his chart. His vitals looked normal, aside from the elevated blood pressure she'd expected to see. "What happened to you?"

"I got in a fight with a hot dog cart."

She stifled a giggle and shined a light into both of his eyes. The pupils constricted like they should, and the little flecks of gold in his irises sparkled in the light. "Looks like the cart won."

"Oh, I don't know. I did a number on it."

"I'm not sure I want to know." She brushed his hair away from his face and ran a finger across the welt. He sucked in a sharp breath through his teeth and locked his gaze on hers. The moment lasted no more than a second, but something inside her melted just a little. She yanked her hand away and turned to the computer to enter her findings.

And her findings were that she was feeling things she

shouldn't be feeling about a patient, and she needed to get her act together. "Have you experienced any dizziness, sudden fatigue, or sleepiness?"

"No. My head will be fine. I think I might need some stitches, though." He reached for the cloth tied around his arm and grimaced. She slipped her hands into a pair of latex gloves.

"Here. Let me." Lifting his shirtsleeve, she untied the rag and peeled it away from his arm. Congealing blood oozed from a crescent-shaped incision about an inch and a half long on his deltoid. A trail of dried blood led her gaze down his very muscular bicep and ended in the crook of his elbow.

She chewed her bottom lip and stepped around the table to examine his other arm. If he were just any patient, she'd call the nurse in to clean him up, and she'd return to do the sutures. But the way his gaze never left her face as she lifted his sleeve and assessed his injury had her glued to the spot. A wave of possessiveness washed over her. She needed to take care of him. And, after all, he had asked for her by name.

She flicked her gaze to his and turned to the computer. The dark intensity of his eyes made it impossible for her to look too long without quivering. Maybe she should leave and let Becca take care of him. And she could take a cold shower in the process.

"A few sutures in your left arm will close that right up. I'll clean up the scrapes on your other arm, and you should be good to go." She opened a few drawers and cabinets, clanking supplies in her trembling hands.

"Are you okay? You seem a little nervous." There was that smile again. So familiar, yet so foreign at the same time.

"I'm fine." She placed everything on a metal tray and wheeled it closer to the bed. "I need you to take your shirt off."

He arched an eyebrow. "But we haven't even had our first date."

Warmth spread from the bridge of her nose across her cheeks. She had to gain control of this situation before she turned into a pile of putty on the floor. "That's highly inappropriate, Mr. LeBlanc. You are a patient in this facility, and I am your caregiver." She sounded way more uptight than she planned, but at least she got her point across.

His smile faded. "You're right. I'm sorry. That was inappropriate."

Change the subject. She needed to change the subject before she melted. "LeBlanc. Is that a common name in New Orleans? I've heard it before."

"Very. LeBlancs have been in New Orleans since the seventeen hundreds."

"Are you all related?"

He chuckled. "I suppose it's possible, from way back when. But not closely enough to claim each other anymore."

"That makes sense." The tightness in her chest released, and she could breathe again. Her hands weren't shaking anymore. "Well, let's get started."

He lifted his shirt halfway up his chest and winced. "I, uh…might need some help."

"Would you like me to cut it off?"

"Then I'd have nothing to wear when I leave. Could you help me get it over my head?"

*Holy moly.* Okay, she could do this. She was a nurse practitioner with years of experience. She'd seen plenty of half-naked people in her practice and removed dozens of articles of clothing. Some of them on good-looking guys too. This shouldn't be any different. Her gaze darted about the room, looking at anything and everything but the beautiful man before her. Maybe she could do it with his shirt still on. But she needed to sterilize the area, and the scrapes extended far up into his sleeve.

The shirt had to go, and she had to remove it.

She sighed and reached for the hem, pulling it up toward his right arm. The backs of her fingers brushed against his stomach, and she bit her tongue to keep the whimper from escaping her lips. He bent his right arm, and she worked the sleeve over his elbow, carefully lifting the fabric over his shoulder. He grunted and ground his teeth. Obviously, she wasn't being careful enough.

"I'm sorry. Did I hurt you?"

"It's okay. How bad is it?"

"There's some rust embedded in your skin, but I can clean it out. You're going to need a tetanus shot though."

"I figured as much."

"It's a doozy of a shot. Think you can handle it?" She made the mistake of looking in his eyes again, and she melted a little more.

"As long as you're the one to give it to me."

This time she couldn't stop the whimper, but she tried to hide it with a nervous laugh. "Okay. Let's get this shirt off so we can get started." She worked the garment over his head and pulled it off his left arm, being extra careful to avoid irritating the gash. He straightened his spine as she stepped away and admired…no, not admired…examined his torso for more injuries. He was all smooth, tanned skin and rippling muscles.

"Your chest is flawless." Even to herself, she sounded breathless. She really needed to get her act together.

His mouth twitched like he was trying not to smile. "Why, thank you."

"No. That came out wrong. I mean..." She took a deep breath and composed herself. "How did you manage to tear up both arms, get a huge knot on your head, and not have a scratch anywhere else?"

"Lucky, I guess? I hit the cart with my right arm and my head, apparently, and landed on a pair of hot dog tongs with my left."

She giggled.

"It's not funny."

"It is, actually. It's kinda funny." And funny was good. Funny would distract her from those washboard abs and amazing pecs.

He smiled. "Yeah, okay. I guess it is a little funny."

"Lie back, and I'll get you stitched up, okay?"

"Yes, ma'am."

She numbed the cut and cleaned it out. "So, what exactly were you doing when you got into this scuffle with a hot dog cart?"

"I was walking a shelter dog. A...something distracted me, and I dropped the leash about the same time the dog got a whiff of the hot dogs. I caught up to her and grabbed the leash, but I was too late. Strong dog. I tumbled. You know the rest."

"A *something* distracted you. Do I want to know?"

He glanced at her and looked at the ceiling. "I'd rather not say."

Probably a woman. A man this attractive probably had a different woman in his bed every night.

"And no, I wasn't checking out a woman." His gaze caught hers, and she swallowed.

"I didn't say that."

"But you were thinking it."

"I wasn't… I'm going to close you up now." She tied the first suture, acutely aware of his dark gaze on her face.

"You didn't tell me you were a doctor."

She tied the second suture. "I'm not. I'm a nurse practitioner."

"Oh? Are you sure you're qualified to be giving me stitches? I thought only doctors did that."

"I am highly," she yanked the last suture closed, and he winced, "qualified." She cleaned the wound and bandaged it. She heard comments like that daily, and she always shrugged them off. It shouldn't have been any different coming from him, but his words cut deeper than most. "All done. I'll send Becca in to clean up your other arm, and you'll be on your way."

"What about the tetanus shot? You promised you'd give it to me."

"I made no such promise. Becca can administer it." She tossed the soiled gloves, gauze and equipment into the proper bins and rose to her feet.

"I'm sorry. Please don't go."

Fisting her hands at her sides, she turned to look at him. His dark brow furrowed over his intense eyes as he rose into a sitting position.

"I shouldn't have said that. It was out of line. I'm familiar with nurse practitioners, and I know you're highly qualified. It was a joke. A terrible, poorly executed joke."

She inhaled deeply and fought the urge to roll her eyes. Damn, he was good at apologies. "Okay. I forgive you. Lie back again." She rolled the tray around the other side of the table and placed a towel beneath his right arm. "This might hurt a bit. I can try to numb it if it's too much to handle, but it's a big area."

"I can handle it."

She squirted the sterilized water on the scrape, and he winced. "Are you sure?"

"Yeah," he said through clenched teeth.

She finished cleaning the wound and bandaged it.

"I am sorry about what I said earlier." He sat up and watched as she cleared away the mess.

"It's okay."

"But we are even now."

She stopped and turned to face him. "What do you mean even? I never insulted your profession. I don't even know what you do."

He grinned and started to run a hand through his hair, but grimaced as he lifted his arm. "On the ghost tour, you said all the evidence was fake and the tour guide was spreading lies."

"I said I was sorry about that. I didn't know the tour guide was your friend."

"He's not my friend. Well, I guess he is my friend now, but he's also my employee."

Her mouth fell open, her stomach twisting as his words set in. "Your employee?" She forced the words out in a whisper.

"That fake, untruthful tour you took? I own the company."

Her stomach dropped to her knees, and her ears burned like she'd stuck her head in an oven. He simply sat there smiling, his hands folded in his lap, his feet dangling from the table, his bare chest in all its gloriousness taunting her.

If she could've found a hole, she'd have crawled into it and died. "I…oh. I am so sorry, Mr. LeBlanc."

His grin widened. "It's Sean. And it's okay. We both apologized. We're good. Right?"

Her mouth hung open again, so she snapped it shut and nodded. Could this situation get any more awkward?

"So, how about that tetanus shot?"

Oh, yeah. Way more awkward.

"Umm…right." She picked up the syringe and filled it with the vaccine. "Usually, this shot is given in the deltoid. But because of your injuries, I don't think that's a good idea. You're already going to be sore for a few days, and this will make it much worse."

"What do you recommend?" The sly tone of his voice told her he knew exactly what she'd recommend. He wanted her to say it.

"Well, the other place this vaccine is administered is in the…uh…in your…" She'd turned into a babbling idiot. She was a professional. She did this every day. But twenty minutes with a half-naked Sean LeBlanc, and her brain had forgotten how to string words into sentences.

"In my ass?"

Did he wink when he said that?

"Glute. In your gluteal muscle. That's where I recommend you get the vaccine." Finally, her brain was working again.

He reached for the button on his jeans. "Are you sure you're not just trying to get me naked?"

She shouldn't have looked. She didn't need to see his long fingers slip the button through the hole. His left hand held the fabric aside as his right hand slowly slid the zipper down, the teeth coming apart one by one to reveal the dark gray waistband of his underwear.

She dropped the syringe on the floor.

"Oh, shoot." She scrambled to pick it up and toss it in the trash. Putty. She was turning into putty. "Maybe you should put your shirt on first. Here."

She picked the shirt up off the counter and carried it toward him. As she stepped toward the bed, her ankle twisted, sending her tumbling into him. She caught herself with her palms flat against his bare chest as he threw his hands to her waist to catch her.

Her fingers splayed against his chest, her hands so pale against his warm, tanned skin. He was soft and hard at the same time, and he didn't move his hands from her hips. She dared to raise her gaze to his and was met with his dark, intense stare. Her knees felt like jelly, but she managed to step away and hold herself upright.

"I'm sorry."

"You're not usually so clumsy?" He arched a brow.

"No, I'm not." It was an accident. It was not her *thing*. She didn't have a thing.

He slid his arms into his shirtsleeves and held them out shoulder level. "Could you help me get it over my head?"

*Dear lord.* Anything to cover up that incredibly, amazingly distracting body. She pulled it up over his head and slid the hem down to cover his stomach. Her gaze lingered a little too long on his unbuttoned jeans before she stepped back to retrieve another vaccine.

"You don't have to remove your pants. If you'll stand up and turn around, you can pull them down just enough for the vaccine." Because if he pulled them down completely, there would be nothing left of her but a blob on the floor.

He stood and turned to face the table. "Is this how

you want me, Emily?" Her name rolled off his tongue like music, sending goose bumps chasing down her arms.

She filled the second syringe and turned around to find him grinning at her over his shoulder, half his ass exposed as he leaned against the table. Her bones felt like rubber. She wiped an alcohol swab against his skin. His backside was round and firm, and she had to stop thinking about him like this. What was wrong with her? She'd never had such inappropriate thoughts about a patient before. And his flirtatious smile and charming words weren't helping one bit.

"Your hands are shaking. Do you need a minute? Seeing me half-naked seems to have done a number on you."

"I've seen plenty of naked men." She jabbed the needle into his ass and depressed the plunger.

"Ow. A little rough, don't you think?"

"Most men can take it." She tossed the syringe into the receptacle.

He buttoned his pants and stepped toward her.

"You're free to go." She handed him the folder. "Take this to the receptionist, and she'll get you checked out."

He took the folder and caught her hand in his, rubbing his thumb across the butterfly on the inside of her wrist. "That's a nice tattoo. What's it mean?"

Her breath caught at the gesture. He'd done the same thing Westley had done at the masquerade. But he couldn't be. She refused to let him be… "It means I like butterflies."

"I like them too." The corner of his mouth pulled into that familiar crooked grin.

Her stomach fluttered like a dozen butterflies had been turned loose inside her as her hand slip from his grasp. It wasn't possible. She would not believe it. "Do you have someone at home who can watch you tonight? Wake you up every two to three hours to check for a concussion?"

"I'll stay at my mom's. She'll take care of me."

"Good. Ibuprofen will help the pain and swelling." It was a coincidence. This was not the same man she met at the ball. *Please don't let it be him. I've embarrassed myself enough.*

"Emily." Becca opened the door and stuck her head inside. "We need you in room two."

She tore her gaze away from Sean's, welcoming the relief of the distraction. "I'll be right there." She turned to him. "Put some ice on your shoulder."

He dropped his chest into a low bow and looked up at her. "As you wish."

Her heart stood still for a beat or two before slamming into her breastbone like it was trying to break free. "Westley."

He rose to his full height and smiled that familiar smile. "It's good to see you again, Buttercup."

"Emily," Becca called from the hallway.

She didn't know if she wanted to throw herself into his arms or turn tail and run, but her feet instinctively led her through the door toward her next patient. "I'm sorry. I have to…I have to go."

Her thoughts scattered in a million different directions. Sean was Westley. And he knew she was Buttercup. Did he know who she was on the ghost tour? Had he just figured it out? Had he known all along?

She stepped into the next patient room, and seeing the swollen man lying on the table collected her thoughts into pinpoint focus. His clothes were covered in red splatters, but the sharp tinge in the air told her it wasn't blood. Several angry, red welts adorned his arms, and his face had swollen to the point she could hardly see his eyes.

She picked up a syringe of epinephrine and swabbed his skin with alcohol. "Paintball?"

"Mm-hmm."

"Let me guess. You're allergic to red dye?"

He nodded.

She gave him the injection, and within minutes, the swelling subsided. But what had started out as a slow Thursday afternoon turned into a chaotic evening. Patient after patient poured through the clinic with everything from broken bones to strep to colds. The last patient left at seven-fifteen, and Becca locked the door.

Emily took a deep breath for the first time that evening, and a sick feeling formed in her stomach. She stepped behind the reception desk and scanned the counter for any notes that might have been left for her. Nothing.

"Becca, that man who was in earlier, the one who needed stitches…Sean LeBlanc… Did he, uh… Did he leave a message or anything for me? A note or something?"

She arched an eyebrow. "That good-looking guy with dark hair?"

"Yeah, him."

"No. He paid his bill and left."

Her chest deflated. "Oh. Okay."

Becca shuffled through a stack of papers and pulled out a registration form. "But all his info is right here if you need to contact him. I'm sure he wouldn't mind." She flashed a mischievous grin.

"Oh, no. I couldn't."

"He did ask for you specifically. It wouldn't hurt to

give him a call. You know…check on him. See if he has any questions…like if he wants to ask you out to dinner."

She chewed her bottom lip and eyed the form. It was tempting. "No. It wouldn't be ethical to use a patient's information for personal use." She balled her hands into fists to stop herself from reaching for the paper.

"Okay. But you know where it is if you change your mind."

---

Sean slipped his key into the front door of the Garden District mansion and pushed it open. The scent of roses wafted into his senses as he stepped into the foyer beneath the ornate crystal chandelier and closed the door. He'd never noticed the overwhelming floral scent when he lived here, but if it was always this strong, he probably smelled like a pretty girl his entire childhood. Fantastic.

"Momma? You home?" He hung his jacket on the coat rack and carried his backpack into the sitting room, dropping it on an off-white chair. An old woman in a high-necked dress from the 1900s lifted a translucent hand to wave.

"Good evening, Lenore. Is Momma home?"

The ghost nodded and pointed toward the kitchen.

"Thank you, ma'am. Have a good evening." He pushed through the swinging door into the kitchen. "Hey, Momma."

She sashayed toward him and cupped his face in her hands, turning his head as she examined the knot on his forehead. "How are you feeling?"

"I'm okay. A little sore." He shrugged off her concern

and sat at the table. "Lenore's fading. I don't know if she's going to be around much longer."

His mom smiled wistfully and nodded. "I haven't heard her moving around much lately. She will be missed."

His great-great-grandmother had probably haunted the house since the day she died. She'd been there his entire life, and when his dad had figured out Sean could see ghosts too, he'd enlisted Lenore to help him learn to control his ability. Sometimes spirits sought him out specifically if they needed to pass on a message or just wanted to be acknowledged, but Lenore was tied to the house she'd grown up in.

"So she's crossing over?" His mom lifted his shirt sleeve and clucked her tongue.

"A little bit at a time, apparently."

"If you had a good woman at home, she could be taking care of you tonight instead of your momma."

He grinned. "A good woman did take care of me this afternoon, until she had to move on to her next patient."

She set a plate of food in front of him. The savory scents of slow-cooked roast beef and carrots filled the air, and his mouth watered. She sat in the chair next to him and sipped a mug of spiced cider. "Oh?"

"Her name is Emily, but you already knew that."

A warm smile spread across her face, deepening the fine wrinkles around her eyes. "You found your Buttercup."

"Twice. She went on my ghost tour, and she sewed up my arm."

"And when are you seeing her again?"

He shoved a bite of roast into his mouth and let the tender meat fall apart on his tongue. Juicy, with oregano and a hint of garlic, the flavors reminded him of his childhood. This had been his dad's favorite dish before the cancer took him. "I was hoping you could help me with that."

She raised her eyebrows as if urging him to continue.

"I didn't exactly get the chance to ask her out either time."

Her eyes narrowed. "Why not?"

"It's a long story. But remember when you offered that scheduled serendipity? I think I'd like to take you up on that now."

Her entire face lit up as she stood and carried her mug to the sink. She shuffled back to the table, giggling like a school girl. What had he gotten himself into?

"You be here Saturday at ten-thirty for brunch. I'll take care of everything else."

## CHAPTER SIX

*S*ean wrapped his hands around the brown paper cup, hoping the hot coffee inside could warm more than the chill in his fingers. A cold front blew through Louisiana last night, dropping the temperature to an unseasonably cool fifty degrees. He hadn't dressed for the weather, which made his two-block walk to the coffee shop unpleasant enough as it was. The ghost that had been following him all morning didn't make it any better.

He turned the corner to head to the tour office and stepped right through the specter. Her frigid energy ripped through his body, raising goose bumps on every inch of his skin. A shiver ran from the top of his head down to his toes, and he ground his teeth together. The spirit dissipated, but as soon as he opened the office door, she reformed inside.

She was still having a hard time coming through; her bloodshot eyes bulged, and her swollen lips couldn't form words. If he tried hard enough, he could block her from his consciousness. But the desperation in her eyes called to him. He wanted to help the poor woman.

"You're going to need to build some more energy to communicate with me. I can't hear you."

The spirit tilted her head and stared at him without blinking. Most spirits didn't blink—they didn't need to—but the way her eyes bulged from her head unnerved him. She'd come through clearer in his dream last night. Her face had appeared as it probably did when she was alive, but the bruises and rope burn around her neck had been vibrant and disheartening. Had she been murdered or was it suicide? Her insistence in trying to communicate made him think murder.

He'd checked with the police this morning for any recent hanging victims who matched her description, but his search came up empty. If she was recently deceased, she either wasn't from close by or her body hadn't been found.

"I want to help you, ma'am. I really do. But you're not coming through all the way."

The spirit's shoulders slumped, and she dissolved.

Sean sighed and sipped his coffee. The bitter liquid warmed him from his tongue down to his stomach, but his arm hairs stood on end as the electric charge the spirit left behind danced in the air around him. He yawned and stared bleary-eyed at the computer screen. Between his mom waking him every few hours to check for a concussion and the ghost haunting his dreams, he'd gotten maybe three hours of sleep in total.

Luckily, the guest load was light for a Friday night in October, and it looked like Jason, Eric, and Sydney could handle the tours tonight. Saturday was another story though, and he'd definitely have to lead an eight o'clock group. Possibly six o'clock too, but he wasn't concerned about Saturday night. The anticipation for Saturday morning was driving him insane.

Why did he get his mother involved? He could have asked her for Emily's number and called her. But he wanted to see her again. To ask her out in person. Her reaction when he'd called her Buttercup was one of pure surprise. She really had no idea he was the man she'd kissed at the masquerade, and their encounters had a habit of ending way too soon. A simple phone call would be too easy for her to walk away from.

It had been too damn long since he'd felt something… anything…for a woman. The rolling, nauseating sensation in his stomach had to be a good sign. He was going to ask her on a proper date, and he was going to do it in person.

Emily had lunched with his mom on several occasions since she'd move to New Orleans, and Madeline assured him the beautiful redhead would think nothing of being invited over for brunch. Hopefully his mother was right. Saturday morning couldn't get here fast enough.

---

Emily's phone chimed as she walked through her front door. She had half an hour to change out of her yoga clothes and get ready for lunch. Tossing her keys and purse on the table by the window, she glanced at her sister's mysterious box. She needed to call Robert and thank him for sending it to her. Or at least send him a text letting him know she'd received it. She hadn't talked to her brother-in-law in months. Maybe a text would be better.

She pulled a stool close to the counter and sat there, contemplating the container. Surely Robert had emptied it of anything valuable before he locked it, but the thought didn't squelch her curiosity. It could still have something inside: old letters, photographs, some kind of memento

Jessica had held on to that Robert wouldn't have found valuable. She needed to know what was inside that box.

Maybe whatever contents it held would explain her sister's attachment to the old hunk of wood. Jessica had to haggle with the estate planner to even convince her to sell it. Her sister had wandered into a closet during the sale and found the box hidden behind a stack of blankets. The planner insisted it wasn't for sale, but Jessica had dipped into her savings account, and her generous offer was too tempting for the planner to refuse.

She ran her hand across the top of the box. What was it about this thing that had intrigued her sister so?

Maybe she could pick the lock. She rushed to her bathroom and dug through a drawer in search of a hairpin. She didn't know the first thing about lock-picking, but hairpins always seemed to work on TV. Grabbing a handful, she headed back to the kitchen. Straightening out a pin, she jabbed it into the lock and swirled it around, hoping to connect with whatever mechanism held the lid shut. She didn't feel anything.

She tossed that pin aside and tried one without straightening it. Maybe both ends needed to go inside the lock. She twisted the pin around, and the sound of metal connecting with metal sent her heart racing. She jiggled the hairpin and tried lifting the lid. It was still stuck shut.

"Damn it. There's got to be a way to get this open."

A loud *thunk* and the sound of glass breaking drew her attention away from the box. A photo of Jessica taken a year before she died had fallen off the table. She probably jostled it when she put her purse down. Sliding off her stool, she tossed the broken glass into the trash and set the frame on the table.

Focusing her attention on the box, her fingers trembled, and she fumbled with the make-shift key, dropping it on the floor. She wiped her sweat-soaked palms on her leggings and tried again. Hairpin number three bent in the lock, and she fought to remove it. A faint knocking on the door only distracted her from her task for a second. She had to get this box open.

Eye level with the lock, she slid pin number four into the keyhole. A cold draft wafted into the room, blowing her hair into her face. She dropped the pin and cursed.

"What are you doing, Em?" Trish stepped into her apartment and closed the door. "I was knocking for five minutes before I let myself in. Sorry I'm late."

Emily picked up the hairpin and stared at it. What *was* she doing? She glanced at the pile of pins on the counter and pushed Jessica's box against the wall. "You're not late. You texted me ten minutes ago."

"I texted you forty-five minutes ago. Why aren't you ready? I'm starving."

Had it been forty-five minutes? She'd only just sat down to play with the lock when Trish arrived. Surely she hadn't lost track of time that easily. "I was trying to open the box."

"Any luck?"

"No."

"There's an antique shop in Metairie that specializes in old locks. The owner's a retired locksmith. Why don't we have lunch out that way, and we can swing by the shop and see if he can open it for you?"

A flood of relief washed through her, and she relaxed the tension from her shoulders. "How did you find out about him?"

Trish shrugged. "Google. I'm curious what's inside too."

"All right. I'm going to get changed."

"Mind if I get some water?"

"Sure." Emily went to her bedroom and changed into jeans and a navy blue sweater. She slipped on a pair of brown suede ankle boots and wrapped a cream-colored scarf around her neck. Cold October days in New Orleans were rare, and she planned to make the most of it.

When she returned to the living room, Trish held the picture of her sister and had a puzzled expression on her face. She handed the frame to Emily. "It fell off the table all by itself. I was in the kitchen."

She took the picture and examined the frame. "There must be something wrong with the stand. It fell off earlier today too. Maybe I can buy a new one while we're out." She pulled the picture out and slipped it into a drawer, then she tossed the frame into the trash.

She slung her purse over her shoulder and heaved the box onto her hip. "Where's this antique shop located?"

"I can map it on my phone, but can we please go eat first? I skipped breakfast."

She sighed and looked at the box. Taking an hour for lunch first wouldn't hurt anything. "Okay. I'll lock it in the trunk while we eat."

———

Emily pushed a green bean around on her plate and glanced out the window for the umpteenth time since they'd entered the restaurant. No one was going to break into her trunk and steal the stupid box, but she couldn't help herself. Hopefully once she got it open and saw what —if anything—was inside, she could forget about the damn thing. Her thoughts had been so consumed with the chest, she'd forgotten about the confession she needed to make to her friend.

"Do you remember that guy I talked about? Sean?"

"The sexy guy from the ghost tour with the sensual name?"

Her body warmed at the image of him sitting shirtless on the patient bed. She shivered. "Yeah. He came into the clinic last night. I had to give him stitches."

She raised her eyebrows. "It figures it would happen on my day off. Why didn't you call me?"

"I was in shock. But it gets more…well, interesting." She drummed her nails on the table.

"How so?"

"Trish, Sean is…he's Westley. From the masquerade."

Trish choked on her dirty rice and dropped her fork on her plate. She took a big gulp of sweet tea, set the translucent red cup on the table, and wiped the condensation off with her finger. "And you just found out who he was at the clinic?"

"Yeah. He told me right before an emergency came in."

She pressed her lips together and nodded. "And you let him walk out the door, didn't you?"

Emily lifted her hands. "What was I supposed to do? The next patient was in anaphylactic shock, and I was in regular shock."

Trish narrowed her eyes. "I suppose I can forgive you. At least you're telling me now, eighteen hours after it happened."

"Gee, thanks." She leaned back in her seat and crossed her arms.

"So you've randomly run into the 'perfect' man you made out with at the ball twice now?"

Emily nodded.

"Talk about your serendipity, Em. And you didn't give him your number this time either, did you?"

She sucked on her straw and stared at her friend, hoping her silence would answer the question.

"You didn't."

She shook her head.

"Are you nuts? You said yourself you'd know it was meant to be if you ran into him again. And now it's happened twice."

She sat up straight. "I got busy. I couldn't leave another patient to die while I gave some guy my number. By the time I finished helping all the patients, he was checked out and long gone."

"But he put his number on his registration form, right? You could still call him."

She sighed. "I'm not going to use his private information for personal use. Not only is it unethical, it's illegal."

"I doubt he'd press charges."

"That's not the point. Besides, I don't know what I would say. I'm too chicken to call him." She finally ate the green bean she'd been pushing around for the last fifteen minutes. It was cold and flavorless.

Like her love life was turning out to be.

"Remember Madeline, my real estate agent?"

"Yeah."

"It sounded like she knew him, didn't it? Maybe I could ask her to give him my number. Then if he's really interested, he can call me."

Trish grinned. "I think that's a fantastic idea. Call her right now."

"I'm having brunch with her Saturday. I'll ask her then. Let's go get that box opened."

The antique shop had a small storefront tucked away in the corner of a run-down, L-shaped strip center in a questionable part of town. The word *open* handwritten on a plank of wood hung in the door, and a middle-aged man sat behind a counter tinkering with a wooden clock.

When Trish pulled the door open, a bell chimed, but the man didn't look up. Holding his tongue between his teeth, he used a tiny screwdriver to pry open a metal covering on the back of the clock.

Emily set the box on the countertop and cleared her throat. The man still didn't look up.

"Excuse me, sir."

No response.

"Sir?" She waved her arms, hoping to get his attention.

He glanced her way and sucked in a breath like he hadn't seen a customer in a long time. He ran his finger up the back of his ear, apparently turning on a hearing aid. No wonder he didn't notice them come in.

"How can I help you, young ladies?" His gaze darted back and forth between Emily and Trish like he hadn't seen a woman in a long time either.

"I have this old box, and I was wondering if you could open it."

He adjusted the glasses on his nose and ran a hand across the top of the box. Emily winced. In the short time since the artifact arrived, she'd grown attached to it. She wanted to yank it away and tell him not to touch it, but she needed his help. She also needed to get a grip.

It was just a box.

Turning the chest around, he peered at the lock. "Do you have the key?"

She ground her teeth to stop herself from spouting off a sarcastic comment. Of course she didn't have the key. "No. I was hoping you could maybe pick the lock or something."

"Hmm…" He picked it up and moved it to a shelf behind the counter. "I'll look at it. Write down your name and number, and I'll call you when it's done." He offered her a pen and paper.

She bit her lip. She wasn't about to leave it here and walk away. "Actually, it's a family heirloom. I was hoping you could work on it now?"

He cut a sideways glance at her and went back to working on the clock.

"I'll pay double your fee."

He snapped his head toward her and narrowed his eyes. "My fee is fifty dollars."

"I'll pay a hundred if you'll do it now. Cash."

He let out a heavy sigh like the job was putting him out, but the corner of his mouth quirked as he picked up the box and set it on his workbench. Unfolding a black velvet pouch, he ran his fingers over what must have been his lock picking tools. Deciding on an instrument to use, he picked up a silver scalpel-looking device and slid it into the lock.

Emily held her breath. It had to work.

A round woman with curly gray hair entered from the back room and beamed a smile. "Good afternoon. How are you today?"

The locksmith turned to the woman and set his tool on the counter. Emily tried to hide her annoyance with a smile. The curiosity was killing her. She needed to know what was inside that box like she'd never needed to know anything in her life. "We're good. Thank you."

"What are you working on, Ed?"

He straightened his posture and gestured to the box. "This young lady is paying a hundred dollars to get this box opened immediately. Must be something really important inside."

The woman peered over Ed's shoulder and froze. Her expression went flat, unreadable. She shook her head. "Get that thing out of my store."

He scratched his head. "But I haven't got it open yet."

"Good. Take it away." She snatched the box from the work table and shoved it toward Emily. "And don't ever bring it back."

Emily clutched the box to her chest. "I don't understand."

"There's evil in that box, and I want nothing to do with it."

"But it's just a hunk of wood. It's—"

"Get out!" The woman marched around the counter and flung open the door.

Emily followed Trish outside, and the woman slammed the door shut and locked it. She stood on the sidewalk and watched as the woman lit a bundle of herbs with a lighter and waved it around, filling the small store with smoke.

"Sage," Trish said. "That's odd."

She put the box in the trunk and climbed in the car. Trish slid into the passenger seat and buckled her seatbelt. "Maybe you should get it checked out before you open it. That was an odd reaction for that woman to have."

She pulled onto the highway and headed toward the French Quarter. "Checked out by whom? It's just a box."

"But she said there was evil in it. Maybe a priest? Or someone who knows Voodoo?"

Emily scoffed. "You can't be serious, Trish. There is no evil in that box. It's just a box."

"It wouldn't hurt."

"It would be a waste of time."

"So, what are you going to do?"

Determination creased her brow as she merged into the fast lane. "I'll text Robert. Maybe he can still find the key. If not, I'll try another locksmith. Or break it open, I don't know. I have to know what's inside. It's driving me crazy."

"I can tell. You should call Madeline too. If she can put you in touch with Dreamboat, maybe he can get your mind off the box."

# CHAPTER SEVEN

*S*ean flipped his sketchbook shut and laid it on the nightstand. The blonde ghost finally came through fully in his dreams last night and was even able to utter a word. Though "help" wasn't the most helpful thing she could've said. Of course she wanted help. At least now he had a good sketch of what she looked like when she was alive. He could give it to the police if she wanted help finding her killer or her body. But it didn't seem like that was the kind of help she needed. A nagging feeling in the back of his mind told him the spirit wasn't recently dead, which made her appearance to him even more mysterious.

He slipped on his shoes and shuffled into the dining room. His gaze landed on another sketchbook, and he couldn't fight the smile tugging at his lips. While the other book contained mostly images of spirits he saw in his dreams, this one was filled with portraits of Emily. She'd been on his mind constantly all week, and he was finally going to see her again. In a private place, where they'd actually have time to talk.

He ran his finger across his latest sketch of her in her

white lab coat, stethoscope hanging around her neck, a timid smile curving her lips. He still had a little pain in his ass where she jabbed the needle in so hard, but that was his own fault for taunting her. She was just so damn sexy when she got all worked up.

He closed the book, slid it on a shelf behind the table, and glanced at his watch. If he was going to make it to his mom's by ten-thirty, he needed to leave. Turning, he stepped away from the table and smacked right into a frigid ball of energy. Ice seemed to claw through his body, ripping its way from front to back as he passed through the spirit. A sickening feeling formed in his stomach, and his entire body trembled and shivered as the energy dissipated from his system. He fisted his hands at his sides and pressed his lips together. He'd opened himself up to this, and it was time to shut it down.

He turned around to find the blonde ghost standing in his dining room, her bulging eyes and rope-burned neck vibrant as ever. Her face still held the same strangled expression, but this time she managed to raise an arm to reach for him.

He took a step back and a deep breath to quell his frustration. "This." He gestured to her and then to his house. "Is not okay. You can't follow me inside my home."

She lowered her arm and stared at him.

"And I can't help you while you're in this condition. You're too weak to communicate."

The spirit opened her lips and mouthed the word help.

"Yes, I know you want help. But until you can build up enough energy to tell me what you need help with, there's not much I can do. I can't help you cross over. That's not in my skill set, so if that's the kind of help you need, you'd best look somewhere else."

She stood there and stared.

"Showing yourself to me all the time is draining what little energy you have." He let out a frustrated sigh. "I didn't want to do this, but I'm going to have to block you for a while. You need to leave my house, go do whatever it is spirits do to gain more energy, and come back when you can tell me what you need."

He stepped toward the door, and the ghost floated in front of it, blocking his exit. If he could get the spirit out of his home, he could block her from his consciousness. At least for a while. "Please leave. I don't want to force you out."

She didn't move. He glanced at his watch. Ten twenty-five, and he still had to pick up the champagne for the mimosas. "I have somewhere to be, and I do not want to step through you to get out my door."

The spirit only tilted her head.

"All right. You asked for it." He opened a drawer and grabbed a bundle of sage. Lighting one end, he waved the burning herbs in the air, wafting the smoke toward the spirit. "I asked you nicely. Now I'm ordering you. Leave my home."

The spirit's expression contorted with even more pain, and she disappeared.

"Finally." He extinguished the burning herbs and clamped down on the channel the ghost had used to communicate with him. He'd open himself up to her again in a few days. Hopefully by then, she'd either be stronger, or she would have found someone else to help her with whatever she needed. Now he could focus his attention on the living.

"Thanks for inviting me over for brunch, Madeline. I appreciate it." Emily set her purse on a table in the foyer and followed Madeline into the sitting room.

"It's my pleasure. Please, have a seat. Can I get you something to drink?"

"No, thank you. I'm good." She looked at her seating options. Two straight-backed, cream-colored chairs sat across from a pale-yellow loveseat. She walked toward one of the rigid-looking chairs, but she thought better of it and opted for the sofa.

Madeline held a hand over one of the chairs and smiled. Then she moved to the other and sat down, crossing her legs at the ankles. "Have you had any luck running into your Dread Pirate?"

Warmth spread through her chest, and she gazed at her hands in her lap. "About that. The way you talked about him at the ball, it sounded like you knew him."

"Oh, I know him very well."

She cleared her throat. "Do you know him well enough to… I mean, would you mind giving him my phone number and asking him to call me? If you think he'd be interested in seeing me again?" What was she doing? She felt like a shy teenager trying to convince a friend to talk to a boy for her. She might as well write "Do you like me? Circle yes or no" on a sheet of notebook paper and slip it under the desk.

"I think he would be very interested." An amused grin lit on Madeline's lips, and Emily couldn't bear to hold her gaze.

Instead, she focused on a portrait on the wall behind Madeline. The woman wore a burgundy high-necked dress reminiscent of the early 1900s, and her dark hair was piled on top of her head with shiny ringlets hanging down to frame her face.

Madeline followed her gaze and rose from her chair. "Do you like it? Come have a look."

Emily stepped closer to the portrait and admired the artistry. The smooth lines and careful attention to light and shadow reminded her of the picture from the masquerade. The signature in the bottom right corner confirmed her suspicion. The initials SPL were barely discernable from the rest of the portrait.

"This is by the same artist who did the one that went for five thousand dollars at the ball, isn't it?"

"Yes. He's very talented, isn't he?"

She had to agree with her there. The artistry was incredible. Almost lifelike. "Yes, but the picture at the ball was supposedly of ghosts. Is this…?"

"She was my husband's great-grandmother, Lenore."

"Oh." Cool relief washed through her system. "So the artist based it off an old photograph or painting?"

Madeline laughed. "The only portrait we had of Lenore was done when she was fifteen years old."

"Where did this come from?" The woman in the picture appeared to be in her early forties.

"This is how her spirit showed herself to him."

Emily clamped her lips together and refrained from making a comment. Too many people in this city believed in ghosts, and she'd have to talk until she turned blue before she could convince them their beliefs were based on nonsense. It had taken her long enough to convince herself. "How much did you have to pay to have it commissioned? If you don't mind my asking."

"Nothing, of course."

"Of course?"

"I'd be offended if my own son charged me for a portrait of our ancestor."

"Your son drew this?" Her gaze landed on the signature. SPL. SP LeBlanc.

"He did. And I hope you don't mind, I invited him to brunch with us today."

S LeBlanc. Sean LeBlanc.

The front door opened.

Her stomach dropped.

Madeline clasped her hands beneath her chin. "He's here."

"Momma?" Sean called from the foyer.

"In the sitting room."

His footsteps echoed on the polished wood floor, and Emily rested a hand against the wall to steady herself.

"Hey, Momma. Here's the champagne."

Madeline kissed her son on the cheek and took the bottle. "You're late."

His gaze locked with Emily's, and a familiar smile played on his lips. "Hi, Emily."

She tried to speak, but her voice came out as a squeak. Clearing her throat, she tried again. "Hello." She cast her gaze to the floor. Sean LeBlanc was Madeline's son. How could she be so stupid? She'd touted herself as being an analytical mind, but she'd quickly dismissed any notions that connected Sean to his mother or the man she met at the ball. And she knew exactly why. Every time she looked at him, her thoughts scattered like light hitting a prism. She couldn't form a coherent sentence around him, much less a logical thought. That had to stop.

"A LeBlanc is never late," Sean said to his mom. "Everyone else is just early."

"That line only works for this LeBlanc." She pressed a hand against her chest. "You are late."

"Sorry, Momma. What'd I miss?"

"I was just showing Emily your portrait of Lenore, but she doesn't believe you drew her spirit."

He followed Madeline to a wet bar in the corner of the room. "It's okay. She doesn't believe in ghosts."

Emily shuffled to the loveseat and lowered herself onto the cushion. Her heart threatened to beat right out of her chest. She didn't have much faith in her knees at the moment either.

Madeline filled three flutes halfway full with orange juice, and Sean popped open the bottle of champagne. "Would you like a mimosa, Emily?"

If he didn't stop saying her name like that, she would go into cardiac arrest. "Just orange juice, please. I have to work later."

"As you wish." He handed her a glass and settled onto the loveseat next to her. Angling his body toward her, his knee brushed against hers, shooting a tingling sensation right to her chest.

She started to pull away, but she stopped herself. She was acting like a shy teenager again. What was wrong with her? She'd wanted to see him, and here he was. She might as well make the best of it.

"How's your arm?"

"Still sore, but it's getting better. I didn't count on my ass hurting this long, though." He raised his eyebrows accusingly and sipped his drink.

"It can take three or four days for the pain to go away completely. Is it bruised or swollen?"

"I don't know. Do you want to check?"

She held his challenging gaze. "You'd like that, wouldn't you?"

"Maybe."

Holy moly, she was turning to putty again. She couldn't tear her gaze away from those intense dark brown eyes.

Madeline sat in the chair across from them. "I woke him up every two hours, like you ordered, and let me tell you, Sean is a grump when he doesn't get enough sleep."

He glanced at his mom. "You're one to talk, Momma." He turned to Emily. "She's more grizzly bear than human before she has her coffee in the morning."

"Hush, Son. That's not true, Emily."

A bell chimed in another room, and Madeline rose to her feet. "I'm going to check on the quiche. You kids talk amongst yourselves for a bit." She sashayed out the door.

Emily stared straight ahead. Her body hummed with electricity. A static charge seemed to build around her, making her arm hairs stand on end. Her thigh still rested against Sean's, and the heat radiating through their clothes sent more heat pooling in other parts of her body. But a chill ran down the back of her neck.

Sean cleared his throat and shook his head. The electric feeling dissipated, leaving only the warmth behind. What a strange sensation. She sucked in a deep breath and looked at him. She would not let this man scatter her thoughts to the wind again. She wanted answers.

"You knew all along, didn't you?"

He stretched his arm across the back of the sofa. "What did I know?"

"Who I am. That we met at the masquerade."

A smile played on his lips. Those soft, kissable lips. His kiss would be even softer now that he'd shaved the Westley mustache. *Oh no.* She was staring at his mouth. His smile widened, and she forced her gaze to his eyes.

"I did. And I'm a little offended you didn't recognize me."

She shifted in her seat. "I suspected, but I thought you'd be blond."

"Blond?"

"Your head was covered. I imagined you with light hair like the character."

"Oh." His shoulders slumped. "Sorry to disappoint."

"I'm not disappointed." Quite the opposite. "But why didn't you tell me who you were?"

He took a deep breath as his gaze traveled over her face to linger on her lips. Was he replaying that magical kiss in his mind like she was? "I was going to at the ghost tour, but then you ran away."

"Sorry about that."

"And your hands were shaking bad enough at the clinic. Would you have been able to sew me up if I dropped a bomb like that on you?"

She straightened. "I'm sure I could have."

"Well, you know now, and that's what's important." His gaze met hers, and she felt her body drifting toward him. She fought the urge to lean into his side and rest her head on his shoulder. Setting her glass on an end table, she folded her hands in her lap.

Sean set his glass down and put his hand on top of hers. "Have dinner with me."

"Umm…" A *yes* tried to escape her lips, but she bit back the answer. His hand was warm and soft and strong. An artist's hand. She'd never dated an artist before. She normally went for the intellectual type. For routine. Stability. Dating Sean would certainly be an adventure.

But he thought he could see dead people, and she would not allow herself to get involved in *that* again. She couldn't. He seemed sane enough…but so had her sister in the beginning.

"I don't know, Sean."

He squeezed her hand. "Just dinner. That's all I'm asking for."

She took a deep breath and shook her head. Well, maybe one dinner wouldn't hurt. It would give her a chance to gauge his sanity, at least. To see how far his obsession with the so-called spirit world ran.

"I know what the problem is." He picked up her hand and laced his fingers through hers. "You've forgotten how attracted you are to me."

She laughed. Like that could happen.

He tugged her arm toward his body, tucking his elbow inside hers, securing his hold as if afraid she'd run away. "I think you need to kiss me again."

Her body involuntarily drifted toward his as she arched an eyebrow and tried to play it cool. "Oh, you do?"

"Yeah. Before you say no to dinner, kiss me. If you don't feel fireworks, we don't have to go out."

She didn't need to kiss him to feel that kind of burn. Just looking at him lit her fuse. But if he thought they needed to kiss, she'd play along. "Fireworks, huh? That's asking a lot."

"I wouldn't accept anything less." He leaned toward her, his masculine, woodsy scent drawing her in, holding her captive. "What do you think?"

Oh, yes. She was going to kiss him. But first, she'd make him work for it. She leaned away. "Here? In your mom's house?"

He pursed his lips and glanced at the empty chair.

"You're right. That's weird. Let's go outside." He tightened his grip on her hand and pulled her through a doorway into the kitchen. Madeline leaned against the counter, sipping her mimosa and grinning.

"I'm going to show Emily your garden, Momma."

"Okay. You kids have fun. I'll let you know when the food's ready."

She had a hunch the food had been ready for some time, but Madeline was too busy playing matchmaker to bother with it.

---

Sean pulled Emily through the back door and led her down the porch steps into the yard. Her hand slipped from his grasp, and she turned a circle on the stone path.

"Wow. This is so pretty." She stepped toward a stone fountain bubbling by the fence. A mermaid sat atop a rock, pouring a bucket of water into the basin below. Towering oak trees created a canopy over their heads, and vines of ivy climbed up the metal fence behind the fountain. He'd sketched that setting dozens of times, always in awe of the way the sculptor had captured the splendor of the scene. But it paled in comparison to the beauty standing before it.

He stepped back and watched her admire the surroundings. She was dressed for work in tan slacks and sensible brown shoes. A pale blue sweater hugged her curves, the shallow V-neck giving him a modest peek of the soft flesh beneath. She'd tied her red hair into a knot on top of her head with two chopsticks sticking out at opposing angles, exposing the delicate curve of her neck. The sunlight glinted in her eyes, shone in her hair. She was the most beautiful woman he'd ever seen, and he'd have been happy to just look at her all day.

She turned and stepped toward him. "This garden is amazing."

"You should see it in the spring when everything's in bloom." He moved toward her and brushed the backs of his fingers down her cheek.

"I bet it's beautiful."

"Very." He glanced over her shoulder, where a silhouette of his mom darkened the window. He could've handled kissing Emily in the sitting room, in front of the ghost Lenore. But having his mother watching through the window… That wasn't going to work.

"Come with me." He took her hand and led her to a gazebo near the back fence. A thick magnolia tree stood between the small structure and the house, blocking them from his mom's curious view. He stepped into the gazebo, but Emily hung back, taking in the scenery.

"This is cute. It's—oh!" She stumbled over the step and fell into him, her hands landing flat against his chest.

He caught her around the waist and grinned as she looked up at him. "I think that's the fourth time you've thrown yourself into my arms now. Are you trying to tell me something?"

"I did not throw myself." She smoothed the wrinkles out of his shirt, but she didn't pull from his embrace. "I missed the step."

"And you aren't usually clumsy?"

"No."

"Hmm…" With his arms around her waist, he pulled her deeper into the shade of the gazebo.

Her light blue eyes were almost the same color as the sky, and a glint of mischief sparked in her gaze as she focused on his lips and slipped her tongue out to moisten her own. A tiny smile lifted the corners of her mouth. "What 'hmm'?"

"You're shorter than I remember." Why was he stalling? She'd agreed to kiss him. All he had to do was press his lips to hers. His nerves were getting the better of him. She was obviously interested, or she wouldn't still be standing here in his arms.

"Patent leather high heels aren't exactly practical when I'm on my feet all day." She ran her hands up his chest and rested them near his neck. Definitely interested.

"Maybe not practical, but they were damn sexy."

"You're not blond. I don't wear three-inch heels all the time. It seems we've done nothing but disappoint each other today."

"Oh, I'm not disappointed, sweetheart. You could make a muumuu look sexy."

"You think so?"

"I do."

She snaked her hands behind his neck. "Are we going to stand here talking all day, or are you going to kiss me?"

That was all the invitation he needed. He took her mouth with his, and she parted her velvet lips with a gasp. His tongue brushed hers, and his body burned. She was sweet and soft, and she melted into his arms like she was made to be there.

She slid her hands up and down his neck, gliding them across his shoulders and down to squeeze his biceps. Piercing pain ripped through his arm, and he instinctively jerked away.

"Careful with the stitches." He cradled his injured arm in his hand, silently berating himself for being such a wuss. Damn, he was enjoying kissing her.

"I am so sorry." Her lips were swollen from the kiss, and he wanted nothing more than to feel them against his skin again.

"I'm fine." He rotated his shoulder to ease the pain.

"Let me make sure I didn't pop a suture." She lifted his sleeve and peeled the bandage away from the wound. She brushed her fingers over the incision and pressed the bandage to his skin. "It looks good. Healing fast."

"I don't know. I think you might need to kiss it and make it better."

A seductive smile lit on her lips. "Are you sure that's where you want my lips? On your boo boo?"

"Hmm…no. But I do think I need a do-over on that kiss. It ended entirely too soon."

She slid her hands behind his neck and pressed her body to his. "I promise I'll be more careful this time."

The feel of her soft curves against him, her tongue tangling with his, had him hardened with need. She must have felt his arousal, because she pressed into him, sliding her hands into his hair. Good lord, this woman was hot.

"Soup's on, kids," his mom called from the porch, and he groaned inwardly. She really needed to work on her timing.

He cupped Emily's face in his hands and ran his thumb across her swollen lips. "Dinner?"

"I'm free Wednesday."

"Wednesday works for me. We better get inside before my mom comes looking for us." He took her hand and led her out of the gazebo.

She hesitated on the step, biting her lip and furrowing her brow.

"What's wrong?"

"I don't normally do this sort of thing. I don't want you to think poorly of me."

"What sort of thing?"

"Sneak into gazebos and make out with men I hardly know."

"Hey." He pulled her into a hug. "I don't think poorly of you. And for the record, I don't normally do this sort of thing either. You're the only person who has this effect on me." He rubbed her arms and laced his fingers through hers.

Emily was quiet. Practical. Reserved. But she had an adventurous side, and the fact that she was letting him experience that part of her had him aching to pull her back into that gazebo to explore some more.

"Sean?" His mom called again.

"Coming." He sighed and looked at Emily. "Are you hungry?"

She smiled. "Starving."

As they entered the kitchen, his mom eyed their entwined hands and flashed him her classic "I told you so" look. "Did you enjoy the garden, Emily?"

An adorable blush spread across her cheeks, and she glanced at him before speaking. "It's a lovely garden. I especially like the gazebo."

Madeline made her famous Quiche Lorraine, and Emily scarfed down every bit she was served. She wasn't kidding when she said she was starving. She took seconds on the cinnamon rolls, and she looked like she was considering thirds when a *thunk* sounded from the foyer.

"I wonder what that was?" His mom looked at him. Of course she wanted him to investigate.

He reached under the table and gave Emily's hand a squeeze. "Be right back."

His high school senior portrait lay face down on the foyer floor. Unfortunately, the glass didn't break, so he had no reason to throw the god-awful photograph away. As he hung the frame on the wall, the air temperature in the small room seemed to drop ten degrees, and goose bumps rose on his arms.

He scanned the area, but no spirits showed themselves to him. He was still blocking the blonde ghost, but it was possible she'd followed him here. If she was able to knock a picture from the wall, she had more energy than he'd thought. But he wasn't about to let a dead woman interrupt his life. He'd learned to control his gift years ago, and only he decided which spirits to communicate with.

He shuffled into the dining room, and both women looked at him expectantly. "Picture fell off the wall. I put it back."

"Is Lenore being mischievous again?" his mom asked.

Emily shifted in her seat and gazed at her plate. The subject of spirits was a touchy one with her, and he wasn't sure why. Most nonbelievers would laugh off a comment like that, or if they were assholes, they'd scoff and make a rude retort. Emily's reaction puzzled him. It was something more than nonbelief, and he intended to figure out her problem with ghosts. Eventually.

"I think it came loose. Probably from the door opening and closing over time. The draft or something." He wasn't about to explain that Lenore had been sitting in the chair across from him the entire time.

The tension in Emily's shoulders eased, and she raised her head. He took her hand under the table, lacing his fingers through hers. There was definitely something more to the ghost issue than an analytical mind.

They finished brunch, and when it was time for Emily

to leave, he walked her to the white Prius she'd parked along the street. A practical car for a practical woman. It suited her.

He stopped by the driver's side door and faced her. "I knew I could get you to go out with me if you kissed me again."

She leaned against the car, a playful smile curving her lips. "I didn't need to kiss you to know I wanted to see you again. I just wanted to make you work for it."

"Well, you let me know if there's any more work you need done. I'm happy to oblige." He leaned in to take her mouth, but she pressed her index finger against his lips.

"Don't press your luck."

He laughed and shoved his hands in his pockets. "Dinner Wednesday?"

"*Just* dinner."

"Text me your address. I'll pick you up at seven."

"Okay." Her eyes held his like she wanted to say something else. Then her gaze slid down to his lips and lingered there. She wanted to kiss him. The magnetic energy dancing between them pulled him toward her, but he fought it. He wasn't going to get shot down again. And if she wanted to play hard to get, he'd let her. The heated look in her eyes told him she'd felt every bit of the excitement exploding inside that gazebo this morning.

He cupped her cheek in his hand and ran his thumb over her smooth, porcelain skin. She leaned into his touch and closed her eyes.

"Have a nice day, Emily. I'll see you Wednesday."

CHAPTER EIGHT

*E*mily stared at the calendar on the wall, focusing on the square for Wednesday, the day of her date with Sean. The anticipation of seeing him again had twisted a knot in her stomach so tight she could hardly eat her breakfast. Between him and her sister's stupid box she still couldn't get open, her thoughts had been a whirlwind of anxiety.

Trish had the nerve to tell her she was getting obsessed with the box. She kept suggesting she take it to a Voodoo shop to have it checked out. It was a ridiculous notion, and if Robert would hurry up and send her the key, she could prove it. Though she doubted any kind of evil was trapped inside the box, maybe she wasn't meant to open it. Maybe she shouldn't try.

"Am I going to survive?" The patient's voice snapped her back to reality. Mr. Armstrong was pushing ninety, and his daughter rolled her eyes and helped him into his wheelchair.

"You drink half a bottle of brandy every night, Dad.

Swallowing two ounces of mouth wash isn't going to hurt you."

Emily handed the paperwork to his daughter. "You might experience some nausea, but you'll be fine. Just remember to spit next time, okay?"

"Sorry to waste your time." His daughter pushed him to the door. "Again."

"No problem."

As soon as the patient left the room, she fished her phone from her pocket and sent a text to Robert. Hopefully he hadn't forgotten about the key.

She glanced at the clock. One-thirty. If she was going to take advantage of the two o'clock lull, she needed to order lunch soon. She opened the breakroom door and found Becca touching up her makeup.

"I'm going to order lunch. Want anything?"

Becca shoved her makeup bag into her purse. "If you don't mind, I'm going to meet Andy next door. I'll keep my phone on me in case things get busy."

"No problem. It's been a slow day." She headed to the front desk and leaned against the counter.

Trish minimized the window she was browsing the web with and spun around to greet her. "You're not going anywhere, are you?"

"No. I was going to order something for lunch. Do you want anything?"

"Actually." She glanced toward the door. "I, uh… already ordered you something."

"What did you order?"

"It's, umm…" She picked up a pen and tapped it on the counter. "It's a surprise? I mean, you bought lunch last time, so I thought I'd take care of it today."

She eyed her friend. Trish wasn't a nervous person, but

the way her leg bounced up and down, she seemed like she wanted to bolt for the door. What was she up to?

"Bye, ladies. See you in a bit." Becca pranced out the door.

Emily crossed her arms and looked at Trish. "What's going on?"

"Nothing." Trish's eyes held all the guilt of a kid with her hand stuck in a cookie jar.

Emily's phone buzzed in her pocket, and she yanked it out to check the screen. Robert hadn't taken long at all to respond. She typed in her unlock code, and her heart sank. The text wasn't from Robert, it was from her cheating ex, Phillip.

*I miss you. Can we talk?*

She shuddered at the thought of talking to that creep again. She typed in her response: *Not a chance*, and hit send. The moment she walked in on his naked secretary straddling him in their bed, it was over. She didn't do second chances.

When the front door chimed, she shoved the phone into her pocket and looked up to greet the new patient. Sean walked through the door carrying a paper bag and a tray of to-go cups. He wore jeans and a dark blue, long-sleeve button-up shirt, and his dark hair was tousled from the wind. Her heart did this weird *thud…thud-thud-thud* thing, and she nearly tripped over her own feet as she rushed around the counter.

"Sean. What are you doing here?"

His smile could've lit an entire city block. "I heard you ladies might be hungry." He set the food and drinks on the counter and turned to her. "And I missed you." He cast a glance at Trish. "Did I time it right?"

She grinned. "Perfectly."

He reached in the bag, pulled out a sandwich wrapped in wax paper, and handed it to Trish. "Meatballs, extra sauce, and sweet tea."

She batted her lashes and widened her grin. "Perfect. Thank you."

"Thank *you* for the advice."

Was her best friend fawning over *her* man? Heat flushed her cheeks. He wasn't hers yet, and she needed to remember that. Still, it wouldn't hurt to get him alone. "Do you want to come back?" She gestured to the door leading out of the waiting area.

"Only if there won't be any needles involved this time. My ass is still sore."

Trish giggled.

Emily glared at her friend, grabbed the bag, and pushed open the door. "No needles. I promise."

He picked up the Styrofoam cup and followed her into the break room.

She took a deep breath to slow her sprinting heart. This was the fifth time she'd seen him. She'd made out with him twice. There was no reason to turn into a babbling idiot again. He obviously liked her, or he wouldn't be here.

She opened the bag and pulled out the contents. "There's only one. Aren't you eating?"

"I can't stay. I've got work to do. I just didn't want to wait until Wednesday to see you again."

She set the sandwich on the table next to the cup and stepped closer to him. Electricity seemed to sizzle between them, and she couldn't help but inch nearer. "This was sweet. Thank you."

"Tell me if I'm being too forward. I don't want to scare

you away." He closed what little distance remained between them, until they stood toe to toe.

Her breathing grew shallow. Was she afraid? If she stopped to think about it, she'd be scared to death. Her feelings for Sean were frighteningly intense for the short amount of time she'd known him. And then there was the ghost issue. But being near him felt so damn good, she wadded up her fear into a little ball and stuffed it into the back of her mind. She could deal with it later. Right now, the sexiest man she'd ever met had brought her lunch, and she wanted to show her appreciation.

"I'm not scared." She laced her fingers through his and placed a soft kiss on his cheek. "I missed you too."

"Good." He cleared his throat as if he were nervous. "Because it's been a long time since I've dated anyone, and I'm not familiar with all the rules."

"I'm not sure the rules apply in this case."

He grasped her other hand and brought her fingers to his lips. "I like you, Emily. A lot."

"I know." She felt like she'd been shot in the chest with a confetti cannon. His actions proved he liked her, but hearing him say the words sent her heart into overdrive. "I like you too, Sean. A lot."

"Would it be wrong for me to kiss you while you're working?"

"I think a little one would be okay." She linked her fingers behind his neck and pressed her lips to his.

He let out a satisfied "Mmm…" that weakened her knees, and he wrapped his arms around her waist.

She pulled away before the sparks he ignited inside her burned the building down. "What did you bring me?"

"Trish told me you like olives, so I got you a muffuletta."

"I love olives. What's a muffuletta?"

He balked. "Are you serious? How long have you lived here?"

"Three months."

"You haven't lived until you've had a muffuletta from Serio's. Have you seen that show *Throwdown with Bobby Flay?*"

"The cooking show?"

"Yeah. The owner went up against Bobby to make the best muffuletta."

"So he was on TV?"

"Yeah. And he beat Bobby Flay."

She eyed the sandwich. "Impressive."

"Try it."

"Right now?"

"Just take a bite. Then I'll go."

She slid her hands up his chest, and he wrapped his arms around her waist again. They fit together so easily, it felt like she'd known him forever.

But the ghosts.

The tiny ball of fear in the back of her mind tried to unravel itself, but she squashed it down. "And if I don't, you'll stay?"

"I would love to, but I have to get back to work. Just one bite? So you can tell me what you think?"

She sighed. "Okay." She unwrapped the sandwich and weighed it in her hands. It was heavy, with thick Italian bread surrounding three types of meat, cheese, and a chopped olive salad. The first bite was like a flavor explosion in her mouth. Ham, salami, and mortadella blended perfectly with provolone cheese, and the tangy zip of olives had her mouth watering for more.

His gaze never left her eyes as she chewed and swallowed the delicious treat. He looked at her expectantly. "And?"

She set the sandwich on the table and wiped her mouth on a napkin. "Where have you been all my life?"

He chuckled. "Me? Or the sandwich?"

"Both. It's delicious. And you're pretty tasty too."

His mouth quirked into a crooked grin. "I'm glad you like us."

The front door chimed, and she sighed. "That'll be a patient."

"You better eat fast then. I'll show myself out."

"Thank you for coming."

"My pleasure. I'll see you Wednesday." He slipped out the door, and she took another bite of the sandwich. Then, she braced herself for the onslaught of sweetness and sipped the tea he'd brought her. To her surprise, the drink was unsweetened, just the way she liked it. He must've drilled Trish with questions to figure out what to bring and the perfect time to arrive.

She'd convinced herself never seeing the mystery man from the ball again was a good thing, because no one could be so charming and wonderful in real life. It seemed she was wrong about that.

She finished the sandwich and attended to her patients for the rest of the afternoon. The evening lulled with long stretches of downtime, and the temptation to call him had her reaching for her phone. But she refrained. On her walk home, she wandered through Jackson Square, checking out the tour guides, but he wasn't there. As lunchtime approached the next day, she found herself hoping he'd show up to surprise her again.

Trish sat at the computer, filing an insurance claim for a patient. She hadn't flashed her any secretive smiles or smirks, so she didn't seem to know about any surprises today. Still, it wouldn't hurt to ask.

Emily leaned on the desk next to her. "Sean didn't happen to call today, did he? If not, I'm going to order lunch."

"No, he didn't. Why don't you call him?"

Her heart fluttered at the thought. "Oh, I couldn't do that."

"Why not?"

She opened her mouth to answer but paused. Why couldn't she? He'd surprised her with lunch yesterday, showing he obviously liked her. Maybe she should reciprocate. Let him know she was thinking about him. It was the logical thing to do. But was she bold enough to just call him up?

"You could always text him." Trish shrugged her shoulders and turned to the computer.

A text. That was more her style. She shuffled to the break room and pulled out her phone. *Thank you again for lunch yesterday. Are you busy?* Her finger hovered over the send button. She chewed her bottom lip and deleted the *Are you busy?* part. That sounded too desperate. She hit send before she could change her mind and scrolled through her other messages.

A text from Robert said he still hadn't found the key, and that bothered her more than she cared to admit. Last night she'd lost an hour staring at Jessica's box. Just staring at it. Her mind had wandered off somewhere dark and empty, and by the time she came back to coherence, she'd missed the latest episode of Law and Order. If Robert didn't find that key soon, she was going to break the damn thing open. She'd have to.

She deleted Phillip's latest text. Her ex kept begging

her to come back to Houston so he could see her. Her response to that had been a big *hell no.* Why on earth would she want to see that jerk again?

As she laid the phone on the table, it buzzed with Sean's reply. *I wish I could bring you lunch again today, but I'm in meetings all afternoon. Call you tonight?*

She sighed and typed in her response. *Sounds good.*

---

Sean parked his car in front of the clinic exit and leaned against the hood. He'd told Emily he'd call her tonight, but seeing her in person would be much more fun. She stepped through the door and stopped, tilting her head and lifting her eyebrows in a look of surprise.

She strutted toward him. "Nice car. Is that a Tesla?"

"It is. Would you like a ride home?"

"Can I drive it?"

He chuckled. It had been a long time since he'd been this interested in a woman, and he'd do almost anything to make her happy. But he drew the line at letting her in the driver's seat, especially along these narrow French Quarter streets. He shuddered as the image of Emily running his precious car into a hitching post flashed in his mind. "Maybe another time."

Her gaze flicked to the car for a second before traveling up and down his body. She was only looking at him, but her eyes held so much heat, he felt like he would spontaneously combust.

"Well, I would love to have a ride in your car, but it would be over in five minutes if you drove me home. It's a nice night. Feel like walking?"

"Walking's good." He pressed the remote to lock his car and offered her his hand.

She accepted and laced her fingers through his. "I didn't expect to see you tonight."

"I didn't expect to come, but when I finished work, I realized a phone call wouldn't do. I wanted to see you again." Though his insatiable need to be with her felt foreign, it was something he'd like to get used to. Just holding her soft, warm hand had his body buzzing.

"I'm glad." She paused at the corner of Dauphine Street. "We can turn here, or we can take the long way home."

"Hmm." He tucked a stray strand of hair behind her ear. "The long way would probably take longer."

"That's generally how it works."

"The long way it is then." He pulled her to his side and continued strolling up Canal Street. They hung a left on Chartres and headed toward the square. Was this the same path she'd taken the night she wound up on his ghost tour? "Where did you live before you moved here?"

"Houston. My parents still live there."

"Were you a nurse practitioner in Houston?"

"Yes. I worked at a clinic similar to this one."

"Why'd you move?"

She inhaled a long, deep breath and pressed her lips together. He'd hit a sore spot. "I was in a rut and needed a fresh start. I almost moved to Dallas, but Trish convinced me to come here. I had already accepted another job, but when she called and said there was an opening where she worked, it was a no-brainer. I needed a friend nearby after…" She dropped her gaze to the ground and chewed her bottom lip.

"After?"

She blew out a hard breath. "After I caught my boyfriend cheating on me."

"The bastard."

"Tell me about it. We were together for two years." She shrugged. "But he got tired of me. I…wasn't myself for a while. I don't know, maybe I'm boring."

He stopped and rested his hands on her hips, trying to catch her gaze. "You are anything but boring." How could any man get tired of such a beautiful, spirited woman? He sure as hell couldn't. She was all he thought about anymore.

"No. I'm pretty dull. That's another reason I moved here." As her gaze flicked to his, she took his hand and kept walking. "I thought the excitement of the city would get me living again, but I haven't done much since I got here."

"Well, we can change that. If, after our date, you'll agree to more than just dinner."

She smiled and squeezed his hand. "I'll let you know."

"I'm glad you didn't go to Dallas."

"Me too."

They entered Jackson Square and strolled toward the cathedral. Moonlight glinted in the puddles left over from an afternoon rain, and a guitar player stood on the corner, adjusting his instrument. The usual psychics had their tables set up offering tarot readings, and he quickened his pace as they approached the old fortune teller. Her gaze bore into his back as they passed, but thankfully she kept her mouth shut this time.

Sydney stood on the cathedral steps, preparing to give a tour to six customers. It was a small group, but Mondays were usually slow. He waved, and she grinned in return, giving him a thumbs up.

He turned to Emily. "Do you walk home this way every night?"

"A few times a week, depending on how tired I am. Why?"

"It's odd I haven't seen you before. I'm here a lot around this time."

She chuckled. "I tend to shy away from crowds. I prefer to blend in. Like I said, I'm boring."

"You have an adventurous side, though. I've seen it." And he planned to do everything he could to help her see it too.

"Maury's back!" Emily pulled him toward the hot dog vendor. "Nice cart, Maury. It's good to see you again."

The old man smiled. "Yes, ma'am. Mr. LeBlanc bought it for me. Look here. It even has a bun warmer."

"Wow. Who doesn't like their buns warm?" She looked at Sean. "You bought this?"

He shrugged. "Seemed like the right thing to do after I destroyed his old one."

She playfully poked his side. "Figures you'd choose my favorite vendor's cart to demolish. I was worried about him."

"I didn't choose it; the dog did. And I righted the wrong."

"That you did, sir." Maury prepared two hotdogs and offered them. "Here. On me tonight."

"Oh, thank you. But I couldn't take one for free." She reached into her purse.

"You're my best customer. I insist."

"Thanks, Maury." Sean took the sandwiches and handed one to Emily. "I'm glad the new cart is working out for you."

Emily took a bite of her hot dog and closed her eyes as she chewed. "Mmm…so good."

He grinned as he watched her savor the food. "You're his best customer? I didn't know you had a thing for hot dogs."

"Guilty pleasure." She took another bite.

They finished the food as they walked through the square and turned onto St. Ann Street. She slipped her hand into his and lightly brushed his bicep with her fingers.

"How's your arm?"

"Better every day."

"That's good." She chewed her bottom lip like she was thinking. "So, I have to ask. Did you and your mom have this whole thing planned out?"

"What do you mean?"

"The brunch. Your mom saw us dancing at the ball. Did you talk to her about it?"

"You mean did I use my mom to find you after you told me you didn't want to see me again?"

She flashed an apologetic half-smile. "Well, when you say it that way, it sounds bad."

"She offered. Hell, she all but insisted, but I told her no. I wasn't going to pursue someone who wasn't interested in me. But then you showed up on my ghost tour."

She cringed. "Ugh. That was a mistake."

He stopped walking and turned to face her. "Was it?"

"Not seeing you again. That wasn't a mistake." She slipped her hand from his grasp. "Just…going on a ghost tour in general. I don't believe in ghosts. I don't know what I was thinking."

"What is this aversion to spirits about?"

She shrugged and rubbed her arms. "I just don't believe in ghosts. It's not logical."

"I think there's more to it than that."

She sighed. "I had a bad experience with someone who believed in them, and I don't want to talk about it."

"Okay. We won't talk about it." Not now, anyway.

"Doesn't it bother you that I don't believe in ghosts? Your whole company is based on the paranormal." She shook her head and gazed at the ground, brow furrowed.

He was losing her. He could feel her pulling away, putting up a wall. Yes, her nonbelief bothered him, but not enough to stop him from pursuing her. It was an issue, but nothing they couldn't work through with time.

She shrank into herself and clutched her arms. He could almost see the second thoughts swirling in her mind, driving a wedge between them, and that would not do.

"Hey." He stepped toward her and lifted her chin, raising her gaze to meet his own. "It's okay." Before she could pull away, he lowered his mouth to hers. She stiffened at first, but as he stroked his thumb across her cheek, she leaned into him, parting her lips and accepting the kiss. A tiny whimper emanated from her throat and vibrated across her lips as his tongue brushed hers. Dear lord, the woman was sexy.

She rested her hand against his chest and pulled back to look at him. "You're very good at that."

"At what?"

"Making me lose my train of thought."

He pressed his forehead to hers and slid his fingers into her hair. "It's hard for me to think about anything but you lately."

She smiled and kissed him again. Crisis averted. Thank

goodness he was able to derail that locomotion of disaster. If she was that hung up on the existence of spirits, their relationship could've ended before it even began.

---

Emily closed the door and leaned against the frame. That man had her head spinning like a tilt-a-whirl, and she wasn't sure if she should jump off or go along for the ride. Every time the topic of ghosts came up, the ball of fear she'd wadded up in the back of her mind tried to untangle itself. And every time he kissed her, he managed to shove it back into the corner for her.

He didn't seem the slightest bit obsessed. In fact, he rarely mentioned the subject. As long as they didn't talk about it, she could pretend it wasn't an issue.

She pulled her phone from her purse and sat in a chair at the kitchen counter. She'd heard a text notification chime on her walk home, but she'd been more interested in the gorgeous man by her side than whatever the interruption could've been. She entered the unlock code and found a message from Robert.

*Found a key. Don't know if it's the right one, but it's in the mail.*

Her pulse quickened, and she ran a hand over the top of the box. "I'll get you open soon. Don't worry."

She set her phone down and rested her chin on her hand. The woman at the antique shop had said evil lived inside the box. That was the most ridiculous thing she'd ever heard. Even if spirits were real—which they weren't—an evil one certainly wouldn't be living inside a box. And if something evil did live inside this box—which it didn't—her sister definitely wouldn't have kept it to begin with.

Jessica was convinced ghosts were real and that she could communicate with them, but she wasn't a devil worshipper. She wouldn't have played with something she thought was evil.

Unless she didn't know it was evil. She ran her hand over the box again and shook her head. That was a train of thought she wasn't about to board. Emily was a sane, logical person. Now more than ever she needed to get this box open to prove—at least to herself—that it was just a box.

What would Sean think about it, though? He was so adamant his "proof" of the paranormal was real. Did he honestly think he could see ghosts? Did she want to get involved with someone like that?

She pulled the box closer and rested her chin on top of it. If Sean were anyone else, she'd walk away now while she still had her heart intact. But the red flag his belief in spirits threw up couldn't compete with the fire that raged in her soul every time their eyes met. She'd burned for him the moment she saw him, and the flames were only getting hotter.

"I don't know what to do." She rested the side of her face against the box, closed her eyes, and prayed for some sort of guidance.

An image of Jessica flashed in her mind. Her sister wore the same jeans and light pink t-shirt she'd found her in when she died. She raised an arm toward her and opened her mouth. "Don't." Her voice sounded strangled.

Sucking in a startled breath, Emily raised her head and rubbed her sore temple. She sat up and stretched, her back aching from the awkward position she'd been in. A dull pain stretched from the top of her neck up to her forehead. As she squinted her eyes, the glowing-red clock face came into focus. Midnight.

"I must've fallen asleep." She pushed the box against the wall and slid out of the chair. A wave of dizziness washed over her, and she squeezed her eyes shut, grasping the edge of the counter for support.

When her equilibrium steadied, she shuffled into the bedroom. She knew better than to fall asleep anywhere but her bed. She poured a fresh ring of salt around her mattress and crawled beneath the covers. She was lucky she'd only dreamed about her sister this time. It could have been worse. Much worse.

What had Jessica said in the dream? "Don't." What could that have meant? Was her subconscious trying to tell her not to go out with Sean? Maybe it meant "don't blow it with Sean." Or maybe it didn't mean anything at all.

# CHAPTER NINE

*E*mily sat on the edge of the reception desk, linking paperclips together into a chain. The two o'clock lull had turned into a long, quiet afternoon, which was fine with her. After passing out with her head on the box and dreaming about her sister, she'd hardly slept once she made it to bed. The busy morning hadn't helped her headache, but after two rounds of ibuprofen, it had finally subsided.

"I don't know, Trish. I'm having second thoughts."

Trish dropped her pencil and looked at her like she was crazy. "I don't know him, but any man who'll go to that much trouble to see you, bring you lunch, *walk* you home…is worth taking a chance on."

"It's happening so fast. I haven't had time to process everything."

"So what? He likes you. You like him. What's wrong with moving fast?"

She wound her paperclip chain around her hand and unwound it again. Trish had a point. In every other way, Sean was amazing. But… "He believes in ghosts."

"Lots of people do."

"I don't."

"So you say. And I still don't see the problem."

"You should. You know what happened with Jessica…"

"And you came here to move on from that. Whether or not ghosts are real, you have a life to live, babe."

She sighed and laced the chain through her fingers.

Trish arched an eyebrow at her hand. "You're going to unclip all those when you're done fidgeting, right?"

"His whole job revolves around spirits. He runs a ghost tour company, and he does investigations. I'm not sure I want to get involved in that."

"Who says you have to get involved in his job? I don't see him coming to work with you. Except the time he brought lunch, which was really sweet."

"I guess you're right."

"If I had a good-looking guy after me—who was also nice—I'd be all over him. I wouldn't let something silly like whether or not ghosts are real get in between me and that hot body. What happened with Jessica happened, and nothing you do now will change that. Do you like him?"

"I do."

"How much?"

"More than I should."

She took the string of paperclips from Emily's hands and unlinked the chain. "So, give him a chance. What have you got to lose?"

"You're right. I'm being too cautious. I need to stop overthinking it." As if on cue, her phone buzzed in her pocket. A message from Sean lit up the screen. "He wants to walk me home tonight."

"Type yes and hit send before you think of a reason to say no."

Overthinking things had always been a problem of hers. Whenever she was able to turn off her brain and just be with him, magical things happened. She needed to throw caution to the wind, and it needed to happen now. "I'll do better than that." She clicked the call button and pressed the phone to her ear.

Sean answered on the first ring. "Uh-oh. Is this the phone call to let me down easy? You already have a hot date tonight?" The smile behind his voice was evident, but a hint of uncertainty tinged his pitch.

"That all depends on you."

"Oh?"

What was she doing? They already had a date scheduled for tomorrow. She shouldn't be asking him for another one tonight. *Don't overthink it.* "Would you be interested in stopping somewhere on the way home and grabbing a bite to eat? I haven't been to the grocery store in a while, and I'm basically out of food." *Stop talking and let him answer.* "But if you already have dinner plans, I understand." She pressed her fingers to her lips to keep herself from babbling anymore.

Silence hung on the phone, and her racing heart sank into her stomach. Oh, god, what had she done? Things were going fine with him taking the lead. Maybe he was one of those guys who got offended if a girl asked him out. He did seem a little old-fashioned when it came to dating, what with all those dancing and manners classes he took as a kid. Old-fashioned was fine; she enjoyed his charm. But if he couldn't let her take the lead every now and then, it was better to find out now.

He inhaled deeply, the sound of his breath sending a

shiver up her neck. "I would love that." His voice was thick. Deeper than usual, and so sexy the phone nearly dropped from her trembling fingers. "Is there anywhere particular you want to go?"

"Umm." She cleared her throat. Holy moly, if the man could get her this worked up over the phone, she was a goner. "Anywhere is fine. I'm not picky."

"Okay. I'll see you at seven."

She ended the call, and the phone slipped from her sweaty hand. Catching it before it hit the floor, she shoved it into her pocket and took a deep breath. Not thinking was definitely the way to go with this. Everything about them seemed to click together and fall into place if she'd let it happen naturally.

No more worrying. No more second-guessing. She'd come to New Orleans to start a new, exciting life, and from now on, that was how she planned to live.

---

Sean pulled up to the clinic as Emily stepped through the door. She wore navy pants, a light blue sweater, and a smile that lit up the entire parking lot. As she walked toward him, she pulled the chopsticks from her hair, and it spiraled down, spilling over her shoulders like red satin. Dear lord, the woman was sexy.

He slid out of the car and met her at the sidewalk. "Hey, beautiful. How was your day?"

"Good. Kinda slow, which was good because I—"

Wrapping his arms around her, he pressed his lips to hers. He couldn't help himself. She smelled like springtime with a faint hint of antiseptic, and he couldn't get enough of her. Trailing kisses across her jaw, he nuzzled into her neck and breathed in her intoxicating scent. "Sorry, you were saying it was good that your day was slow?"

"Hmm?" She rested her head on his shoulder and inhaled deeply. "Oh, yeah. I didn't sleep well last night. I'm exhausted."

He took her hand and led her to the passenger side of the car. "Then let me drive you to dinner, and I'll get you home right after."

"Okay. But there's no rush."

He climbed into the driver's seat, pulled onto Burgundy Street, and headed deeper into the French Quarter. Emily blew a breath into her hands and rubbed them together.

He closed his hand around her frigid fingers. "Are you cold?"

"Yeah. I just got a chill. I don't know why." She rubbed the back of her neck with her other hand, and the coldness crept toward him.

He cranked up the heater, but it wouldn't help. The temperature drop wasn't due to the weather; a spirit had entered the car. The coldness was the entity gathering energy from the air around them, sucking the heat from the cabin. He clamped down on his channel, blocking the ghost from making contact. He wanted to tell it to leave, but he wasn't about to speak to a spirit in front of Emily.

The blonde woman's essence floated in the air, tingling his senses as the spirit tried to make contact. She was getting stronger, liked he'd asked her to do, but she'd have to wait. He was with Emily now, and she deserved all of his attention. The spirit must have realized his unwillingness to communicate, because the buzzing energy he'd felt a moment ago dissipated, the warmth returning to the car.

Emily stopped rubbing her neck and relaxed her

shoulders. "That was weird. My fatigue must be affecting my nervous system."

Weird indeed. But strange because she noticed the presence of the spirit before he did. The question was whether or not she really knew what it was. "Are you too tired for dinner? I can take you home."

"No, no. I'm fine. It was just a chill. I want to have dinner with you." She smiled and squeezed his hand. "Where are we going?"

He pulled into a parking lot and hurried around the car to open the door for her. "I know you love Maury's hot dogs, and I'm not trying to steal away any customers from him, but I think you're going to like this place."

They rounded the corner, and he motioned toward the blue two-story building with yellow windows and pink shutters. Dat Dog was his go-to restaurant for delicious food and great atmosphere. When he found out Emily liked hot dogs possibly as much as he did, he knew he'd have to bring her to his favorite restaurant.

"Wow. It's bright." She eyed the building skeptically. Strings of lights wound around the pink wrought iron railing of the second-floor gallery, and a neon sign glowed over the entrance. "Dat Dog?"

"They serve gourmet hot dogs. Way better than anything you'll find in a roadside stand."

"Nothing's better than Maury's."

"Give it a try? I think you'll be surprised." He led her across the street and into the restaurant. The pink and blue color palette from the outside spilled over into the inside, giving the entire establishment a cheerful atmosphere. It was impossible not to have a good time inside a place like this.

She stared up at the chalkboard hanging behind the counter. "That's quite an impressive menu."

"What would you say to an alligator sausage topped with crawfish etouffee?"

"I would say, 'Shut up and get in my mouth.' Are you kidding? Gimme."

"And you have to wash it all down with a beer."

"Of course you do."

Oh, yeah. This was a woman after his heart. He ordered two of each of his favorites, and they sat in a bright pink booth by a window. Emily tossed her hair behind her shoulders and used both hands to pick up the massive hot dog. She took a bite and inhaled deeply, closing her eyes as she chewed.

A soft *mmm* resonated from her throat as her lids fluttered open, and she returned the food to her plate. "Aren't you going to eat?"

Christ, this woman could turn dinner into foreplay. Did she have any idea how much she turned him on? "Oh, I am. But watching you enjoy the food is much more fun."

A flush of pink spread across her cheeks. "Don't tell Maury I cheated on him."

"Your secret's safe with me."

After dinner, he drove her home and walked her up the steps to her apartment door. The same buzzing spirit energy raised the hairs on the back of his neck, but he shut it out. This ghost was going to have to work on her timing.

Emily slid her key in the lock and turned to face him. "Thank you for having dinner with me."

"My pleasure." He stepped toward her and cupped her cheek in his hand.

She leaned into his touch and closed her eyes, covering his hand with her own. Inhaling a deep breath, she opened her eyes and fixed him with a determined gaze. "You should kiss me now."

"That will also be my pleasure." He pressed his lips to hers, intending to pull away after a gentle kiss. But she leaned into him, wrapping her arms around his neck and pressing her supple body to his. She held him tight, parting her lips and slipping her velvet tongue out to brush with his.

Heat pooled in his groin, and he glided his fingers into her hair, reveling in the passion of their kiss. God, it felt good to want someone again. She broke from his mouth to trail her lips across his jaw, down his neck, and up to his ear. "Do you want to come inside?"

Hell yes, he did. He put his hands on her shoulders and pushed her just far enough away to see into her eyes. They sparkled with passion and mischief, and he could have taken her right there on the landing if they weren't so close to the street. "Do you want me to come inside?"

Her tongue slipped out to moisten her lips, and his knees nearly buckled beneath him. She slid her hands down his chest and hooked a finger in the waistband of his jeans, pulling him toward her. "I wouldn't have asked if I didn't want you to."

She reached behind her, opened the door, and pulled him through the threshold. Kicking the door shut, she pressed him against it and turned the lock. Her hungry gaze traveled up and down his body as she slipped her hands beneath his shirt. The feel of her soft fingers against his skin had his core tightening, his entire body aching to feel her close to him, on him, with him.

"I want you, Sean."

He wanted to answer. To say he wanted her too. But hearing those words from her lips rendered him incapable of speech. He slid his hands down the small of her back, cupping her ass and pulling her close, trailing kisses up one side of her neck and down the other. He didn't just want this woman. He needed her.

She undid the buttons on his shirt and gently slid it down his injured arms, dropping it on the floor. With a playful smile, she pressed her lips to each bicep and rested her hands against his chest. "All better now?"

"I don't know. I think I might still need a nurse to take care of me." He reached for the hem of her sweater and tugged it over her head. Good lord, she was beautiful. He ran his hands over her light blue satin bra, cupping her full breasts in his palms. Her breathing shallowed, and her heart pounded against his fingers.

"That can be arranged." Her voice was breathless, her gaze heavy, and when she popped the button on his jeans, he couldn't help himself. He had to have her.

"Bedroom?"

"This way." She tugged him into the room and unhooked her bra, sliding the straps over her shoulders and letting it fall to the floor.

He took a breast in each hand and lowered his mouth to taste her. Her nipple hardened under his tongue as she sucked in a little gasp of breath. With trembling hands, she unbuttoned her pants and slipped them off. The only thing that stood between him and all the pleasure she had to offer was a thin piece of pale blue satin, and that was about to be removed. But…

"Oh, hell." He released her breasts and slid his hands to her hips.

"What's wrong?"

He pressed his forehead to hers and closed his eyes for a long blink, trying to tame the raging inferno threatening to burn him alive. "I don't have a condom."

"Oh." Her gaze never left his as she roamed her hands over his body, touching him in places he hadn't been touched in years, making him feel things he'd wondered if he'd ever feel again.

"I'm on birth control." She slid a hand down his stomach and rubbed his arousal through his jeans.

A shudder of electricity shot through his core. "Are you sure? We could wait." *Please be sure.*

"I can't wait."

She worked his jeans over his hips, and he kicked off his shoes and stepped out of his pants. Pulling down his underwear, she wrapped her hand around his dick and gave it a stroke. His entire body trembled. He groaned and pulled her to him, roaming his hands over her delicate curves, dipping his head to trail kisses along her neck.

She tightened her grip. "I need you inside me, Sean."

That was all she had to say. He slipped her panties off and laid her on the bed, crawling on top of her and settling his hips between her legs. Every nerve in his body fired on overdrive. His skin tingled with her touch, his heart pounding an erratic rhythm as the significance of the moment sank in. He'd been telling himself he was ready to move on for over a year, and he hadn't done a thing about it. But this was it. Right here. Right now. He put the past completely behind him and looked into the eyes of his future.

Pressing his tip against her opening, he took her mouth in a passionate kiss, tangling his tongue with hers. When a soft whimper escaped her lips, he couldn't hold back any longer.

He pushed inside her, her wet warmth squeezing him, sending an electric current buzzing through his body. He wanted to go slow. To take his time making love to her, but the sense of urgency overwhelmed him. She rocked her hips, gripping at his back and trailing her lips across his shoulders. His speed increased, and when she tightened around him and threw her head back, calling out his name, he lost it.

His orgasm ripped through his body, a raging fire burning him to cinders, Emily raising him from the ashes again. His Emily. Her chest rose and fell beneath him with her heavy breaths as she clung to him and buried her face in his neck.

He lay there for a moment, breathing in her delicious scent, basking in the afterglow of making love to the most beautiful woman he'd ever met. The first woman he'd wanted in years. Her breathing slowed, and she finally released her grip, trailing her fingers up and down his back. He rose onto his elbows and gazed into her sapphire eyes. Her crimson hair fanned out around her like a flame. Like the fire she lit inside him. He kissed her lips, her forehead, her cheek, and he slid off her, pulling her into his arms.

As they lay there on top of the covers with her head nestled against his chest and his arms wrapped around her, he fought to keep his eyes open. She hadn't said a word since they'd made love, and her slow, rhythmic breathing made him think she might have fallen asleep. He kissed the top of her head, and she finally moved to look at him.

"I'm not sure what the protocol is in a situation like this. But if you'd like to stay the night with me, you're welcome to." Long lashes fringed her crystal blue eyes as she blinked, but he couldn't read her expression. She seemed so serious, her eyes tight with concern or regret, he wasn't sure which.

A strand of hair fell across her face, and he tucked it behind her ear. "What do you want me to do?" He held his breath as he awaited her answer.

She pressed her lips together and narrowed her eyes. What he would have given to be able to read her thoughts at that moment. Had they gone too far too fast? Did she regret what they'd done?

Her gaze softened, and a tiny smile curved her pink lips. "I want you to stay."

He hugged her tight. "As you wish."

She let out a giggle and sat up, all the concern draining from her expression as she stroked his chest.

He took her hand and kissed it. "I was afraid you were going to ask me to leave."

"I was afraid you wouldn't want to stay."

"Are you kidding? Spend the night naked with the most beautiful woman in New Orleans? Only an idiot would say no to that opportunity."

She bit her bottom lip and cut her gaze over to her nightstand. "I have to do something though. You might think it's crazy." She picked up a container of white powder and poured some into her hand. "I have night-mares—bad nightmares, but salt keeps them away. I pour it around my bed."

He arched an eyebrow. Salt was known for blocking spirit energy, yet she claimed she didn't believe in ghosts. "What kind of nightmares?"

She visibly shivered. "I'd rather not talk about it. I wasn't even sure if I should ask you to stay because of this, but…what the hell. You'd find out eventually."

"Okay. We don't have to talk about anything you don't want to."

She examined the salt in her hand and chewed her bottom lip. "You don't think I'm weird?"

He sat up and wrapped his arms around her. "Sleep is important. Whatever you need to do to get a good night's rest, do it. I don't think you're weird."

She slid her feet to the floor and poured a ring around the bed. "It keeps the negative energy out so I can sleep."

"I understand." But did *she?* He had a feeling she believed in a lot more than she was letting on, but he wouldn't push her to explain. Not yet. At least now he'd be guaranteed a spirit-free slumber too.

She set the salt container on the nightstand and pulled back the blankets. They slipped beneath them, and she snuggled into his side. She was warm and soft, and she fit so perfectly next to him, like an interlocking puzzle piece, her head resting on his chest, her arm draped across his body.

The soft glow of a streetlight crept in through the window, casting the dark room in a bluish haze. Her hair smelled like flowers with a hint of vanilla, and he couldn't think of anywhere else he'd rather be than lying here, wrapped in her sweet warmth.

He tried to stay present in the moment, but his mind swirled with questions. For someone so adamant about the nonexistence of spirits, Emily was awfully willing to suggest outside energy could affect her dreams. What was she hiding? How bad could the bad experience she'd mentioned have been? Surely he could get her to share something. Any tidbit of information to help him understand her better.

"When you say the salt blocks out negative energy, what kind of energy do you mean?"

Her only response was the soft sound of her breath as she slept on his shoulder. Oh, well. He could ask her another time. If this relationship kept heading in the direction it was going, he'd have plenty of chances to talk to her about her fear of spirits. He couldn't get enough of Emily Rollins, and he planned to do everything in his power to keep her by his side. He'd been intent on teaching Buttercup to learn to live again, but it seemed he was the one who'd needed the lesson.

---

Emily woke to the enticing aroma of freshly baked bread, like she did every day. Living above a bakery ensured every morning was a pleasant one, at least until she got out of bed. Her stomach growled, and she rolled to her side, reaching for Sean.

She found the place where he'd slept cold. Opening her eyes, she let out a sigh and buried her head under a pillow. His scent still lingered on the sheets. But, of course, he was gone. She'd acted like an animal last night. He probably high-tailed it out of there as soon as she fell asleep. What was she thinking coming on to him like that?

She wasn't thinking, and that was the problem. There was no happy medium for her. She either overthought everything, sucking the fun right out of her life, or her brain shut down completely. Last night she'd given in to lust and hormones, and now she'd probably never see him again.

Tossing the pillow aside, she dragged herself out of bed and threw on a pink satin robe. The softness of the fabric gliding across her skin reminded her of Sean's gentle touch and the not-so-gentle way he'd made love to her. She shivered and rubbed her arms to chase the goose bumps away. Well, at least she'd always have the memory.

She took a deep breath and stretched her arms over her head. Wait. Was that coffee she smelled? She inhaled again. Though the aroma of the bakery was overwhelming, the distinct scent of roasted coffee beans danced in the air.

Opening the bedroom door, she stepped into the open living room area and found Sean sitting at the table, sipping from a paper cup and scrolling through something on his phone. When he looked up, he smiled that familiar crooked smile that made her heart stutter.

"Good morning." He put his phone on the table and rose to his feet.

"Hey."

"I hope I didn't wake you." He swept her up in his arms and placed a soft kiss on her lips.

Suddenly very aware of her disheveled appearance and probable morning breath, she pulled away and ran a hand through her tangled hair. "No. It was," she waved her hand in the air to indicate the smell, "bread."

"Does it smell like this every morning?" He offered her a cup of coffee, and she sipped the bitter liquid, thankful for anything to ease the cat litter taste in her mouth.

"Every morning." She sat at the table, and he opened a paper bag.

"The scent is intoxicating. I woke up starving and had to go get something. Their croissants are decadent." He offered her a pastry and took one for himself.

She picked at the croissant, savoring the buttery flavor, but her appetite had disappeared. Sean was still here. Waiting for her to wake up. Not just waiting—he'd left to buy breakfast and come back. The knot that had tied in her chest when she woke up alone loosened.

"Sean, about last night. It was…"

He grinned. "Magical?"

"Well, yes, but I was…"

"Amazing."

She blew out a hard breath. "The way I acted last night? That wasn't me."

"It sure felt like you." He put the croissant down and took her hand.

"I don't know what came over me, but I don't do stuff like that with…other people. I don't want you to think poorly of me." She picked at the flaky layers of her pastry, unable to meet his gaze.

"Emily, look at me." He hooked a finger under her chin and raised her head to meet his gaze. "I will never think poorly of you. Do you want to know what I really think?"

She swallowed the dryness out of her mouth and nodded.

"I think you like me, and I know I like you. And when we're together, amazing things happen. I think we're both doing things we don't normally do because it feels too good to fight it. I don't want to fight it. And every time things get passionate between us, you tell me it's not you. But I really hope it is you, because I like it."

He took her other hand and laced his fingers through hers. "Do you regret what we did last night? Because I don't."

She looked at their entwined fingers and then at the concern in his eyes. He knew exactly the right words to put her fears at ease. She didn't want to fight it either. "No, I don't regret a thing."

"Good." He ran his thumb across her cheek and placed a soft kiss on her lips. "I would love to stay longer and show you just how much I like spending time with you, but I have a breakfast meeting for a fundraiser at eight."

"Breakfast?" She raised her eyebrows and glanced at the croissant on the table.

"There's always room for croissants." He shoved the rest of the pastry into his mouth.

"Are we still on for tonight?"

He swallowed his food and took a sip of coffee. "Absolutely. Still *just* dinner?"

"I think we're beyond that, don't you?"

"Why don't you come to my place, and I'll cook for you?"

"You cook?"

"I dabble in the culinary arts from time to time." He stood and walked behind her chair, massaging her shoulders as he leaned down to kiss her cheek. "Then we can watch a movie and…hang out."

She couldn't fight the grin tugging at her lips. "You mean Netflix and chill?"

He pressed his thumbs deeper into her muscles, and her shoulders drooped in relaxation. "Or you can go home after the movie. Whatever you feel like."

She doubted going home would cross her mind until the next day. Leaning her head against his stomach, she tilted up to look at him. "Well, it will only be our first official date. I'm not sure how far I'll be willing to go. You might not even get to second base."

Sliding his hands down her arms, he pressed his lips against her ear. "Let's just see how it goes, hmm?" His warm breath against her skin raised goose bumps on her arms, and when his teeth grazed her lobe, she shivered.

"Yes. Let's."

He kissed her cheek and stepped away from her chair. "I need to go, but…" His gaze fixed on something behind her, and he ground his teeth together.

"But?"

"That chest." He gestured with his head. "Where did you get it?"

She followed his gaze to her sister's box sitting on the counter. Stepping toward it, she ran a protective hand across the top. "An estate sale. My sister found it."

"Have you opened it?"

"No, I don't have a key."

"Good." He rocked to his toes like he was going to step toward her, but he hesitated. His hands clenched and unclenched by his sides, and he pressed his lips together in a hard line. Finally, he let out his breath in a huff and marched toward her. "That box is… It could contain negative energy."

Oh, not him too. She crossed her arms over her chest. "What? Like a ghost? The woman at the locksmith said evil lived inside it."

He reached out a hand to touch it, but he hesitated. "Locksmith? You said you haven't opened it."

"I haven't. The locksmith was trying to get it open when a woman came running in yelling about it being evil, and she shooed me out the door. I tried to pick the lock myself, but all I managed to do was ruin a ton of hairpins."

"Please don't open it."

"Why not?"

"Do you see these markings carved into the top?" He

pointed to the lid but still didn't touch the box. "Those are ancient symbols for dark…energy. Whoever built this box trapped a lot of negative energy inside it."

"You mean a ghost." And here it started. She'd known his belief in the paranormal would be an issue.

"No, it's not a ghost. I have a feeling it's similar to the type of energy that causes your nightmares. The type you block out of your dreams with salt every night. Only… more concentrated."

She reached for the box and pulled it toward her, a fist of possessiveness clutching her heart. There was nothing wrong with this box. "What are you trying to say, Sean?"

"You need to get rid of it. It's dangerous."

"Dangerous?" She looked at the wooden container. It might break her toe if she dropped it on her foot, but that was the extent of any danger she could imagine.

"How long have you had it?"

"A week or so."

"Have you had any headaches since you got it?"

"No." Aside from the one she had last night, but that was because she fell asleep using the hard surface as a pillow. There was no dark energy making her head hurt.

He sighed and put his hand on her hip, pulling her into an embrace, kissing the side of her head. "I would feel much safer if you didn't have this here. Do you have a storage unit or somewhere…anywhere else you can keep it besides your apartment?"

His strong arms wrapped around her. His warm, firm body pressed to hers. She couldn't help but melt into him. How did he manage to distract her so easily? "If it bothers you that much, I'll get rid of it."

"Really?"

"Consider it gone."

The tension in his muscles relaxed. "Thank you. It could be nothing at all, but you're better safe than sorry when it comes to stuff like this."

"I understand. I'll take it to a dumpster this afternoon."

"Do you want me to take it now?"

"No. I don't want you to be late for your meeting. Go ahead, and I'll take care of it. What time do you want me to come over?"

"How about six?"

"Sounds great." She walked him to the door and watched him go down the stairs and around the corner to his car.

Maybe she should get rid of the box. She had been obsessing over it lately, and it might be better if she didn't have it in her house, reminding her of everything that happened with her sister. She picked up the chest to move it to the table but hesitated. The smooth wood felt nice against her fingers, and if she put a coat of paint on it, it would look perfect with her décor.

And it belonged to Jessica. She couldn't throw it away. There was nothing wrong with this box; Sean was being paranoid. His belief in spirits was already causing problems in their relationship, and they hadn't even been dating a week.

She put the box back on the counter. It was her apartment, and if she wanted to keep the box, she would. She'd just put it in the closet when Sean was over. He'd never know the difference.

# CHAPTER TEN

*S*ean tossed a twenty-pound bag of salt onto his shoulder, and a sharp pain sliced through his arm. "Damn it." Hopefully he didn't rip the wound open. His favorite nurse had done such a good job sewing him up, he usually forgot the stitches were even there.

He dropped the bag and lifted his sleeve to examine the damage. It was a little red from placing twenty pounds of pressure on it, but otherwise, it looked fine. He picked up the bag more carefully this time and carried it to the fence.

He'd never salted his entire house before. He'd never had the need. Learning to control his gift at an early age had allowed him to live a somewhat normal life. Most human spirits weren't dangerous; they only wanted to be seen. Angry ones could drain people's energy if they were trying to manifest, but he could always sense when that was happening, and he knew how to stop it. Spirits couldn't force themselves on him. He had the ability to ignore them.

And real evil had to be invited in.

He scooped out some salt and sprinkled it around the fence line. Emily was sensitive to spirits. She had to be, but she refused to accept it. The only kind of energy salt could keep away was spirit energy, and the only way spirits could be giving her nightmares was if she could sense them. Maybe she never developed her ability. Or maybe she buried it a long time ago when the bad experience happened, but it was there.

And he didn't want any uninvited guests ruining their evening. He scattered the salt around the backyard fence and up the sides of the house. When he reached the front yard, a static electricity formed in the air, pricking at his skin and raising the hairs on the back of his neck. He'd never met a spirit so persistent.

"As soon as I close this circle, you won't be able to cross it for a while. So if you have anything new to say, go ahead and say it." He closed his eyes and inhaled a deep breath, opening himself up to the spirit. When he opened his eyes, the blonde woman stood before him wearing jeans and a Ghostbusters t-shirt. How ironic.

She was still translucent, but less so than the last time he saw her. And, thankfully, she projected herself as she'd looked when she was alive. Looking at a spirit in her death state was creepy, even for someone with his experience.

She lifted a hand toward him and opened her mouth. "Help." Her voice was a strangled whisper, but at least she could make sound now. Not a very helpful word for her to waste her energy on, but it was a start.

"I know you want help. What do you want me to do?"

The image of tears formed in her eyes. He'd always found it strange ghosts could cry. Did they have other bodily functions too? He'd never had a spirit sneeze on him, but the idea of being covered in otherworldly nose goo wasn't the slightest bit appealing.

"Help her."

"Now we're getting somewhere. Help who?"

The spirit tried to speak again, but only a wisp of breath escaped her lips. She was fading, her image flickering as she tried to pull in more energy. The air around him grew so cold he could see his breath, and his skin tingled as her energy attempted to draw from his.

"No, ma'am. I don't play those games with ghosts." He stepped into the salt circle and closed the ring. "You'll have to get your energy from the atmosphere, not from me. Come back in a week or two and try again. I'm taking a break from spirits."

He closed his channel, and the specter disappeared. She was still there, and she'd probably keep following him like she had for the past week, but he was on vacation now. The salt would seep into the earth and keep everything off his property for a solid week or two, so he could focus all of his attention on Emily.

He burned some sage in each room of the house and the back yard to be sure the space was clear and set up for their date. Would Emily let him sage her apartment after she got rid of the box? He closed his eyes and rubbed his forehead. He should've taken it from her right then and there, but he'd been afraid to touch the damn thing.

Someone with experience in black magic had carved that inscription, but the box still could be empty. Lots of people attempted magic and failed. Hopefully that was the case with Emily's box. He hadn't sensed any type of spirit energy in her apartment, but he hadn't exactly been paying attention that night. And the type of energy people liked to trap in boxes like that wasn't usually human. A demon would have no trouble hiding from him if it didn't want him to know it was there.

Emily said she'd get rid of it, and he'd have to take her word for it. Until he could get her to open up about her own experiences with spirits, there wasn't much else he could do. And as long as the box stayed locked, it couldn't hurt anyone.

---

Emily drove her Prius down St. Charles Avenue into the Garden District. As she turned off a side street and went deeper into the residential area, the houses grew grander and more ornate. She'd been to Madeline's mansion, the house where Sean must've grown up, but she assumed he lived in a big apartment somewhere, not in a mansion of his own.

She checked the address on her phone and turned into his driveway. Definitely not what she was expecting. The white two-story house had four columns holding up the gallery and floor-to-ceiling windows with dark green shutters. Four steps led up to a wood and glass front door, and a gas lamp illuminated the porch. It could've been called modest compared to the neighbor's homes, but it was still way bigger than she'd expect a single guy would ever need.

She figured he had money, considering how well-off Madeline was, but his house must've cost several million dollars, definitely not something a simple tour guide could afford. A metal gate slid shut behind her as she rolled to a stop behind his Tesla. She must've been gaping as she climbed out of the car and walked toward the porch because he stepped outside and chuckled.

"You're in the right place."

"Your house is incredible."

He shoved his hands in his pockets and leaned against a column. "Thanks. My dad left me a little money when he died." He wore jeans and a dark green shirt, and an image of what was underneath the shirt flashed in her mind. Heat crept up her neck as she approached and offered him a bottle of wine.

"Merlot. My favorite." He took the bottle and pulled her close, placing a tender kiss on her lips. "You look stunning." His gaze traveled up and down her body, lingering on her feet. "Red looks so good on you."

She smoothed her sweater down and adjusted the hem. "Thank you."

"And you wore the shoes."

"You mentioned you liked them."

"I do. It's going to be hard for me to concentrate on dinner when you look good enough to eat." He glided his fingers down her arm and pressed his lips to hers. Closing his eyes, he inhaled deeply and smiled, his mouth hovering so close to hers, his breath tickled her skin. Her pulse quickened, and she fought the urge to start undressing him right there on the porch.

He opened his eyes and straightened. "Very hard. Let's go inside. Dinner's almost ready."

She stepped into the foyer and set her purse on a table. Her heels clicked on the dark hardwood floor, and it took her a moment to grasp the modern look of the inside contrasting with the antebellum feel the outside projected. The walls were painted a creamy beige with white crown molding, and the modern fixtures and doors gave the illusion she was standing inside a brand-new home.

She followed him through the living room, where a tan sofa sat across from an eighty-inch flat screen television. Surround-sound speakers hung from each corner of the room. The kitchen had slate gray tiles, dark cabinets, and stainless-steel appliances.

"Your house is so…modern on the inside."

He twisted a bottle opener into the wine cork and took two glasses from a cabinet. "I had it renovated before I moved in. It was in bad shape—not much was salvageable. The wood floors are original though."

"There's so much space for a single guy. What do you do with all the bedrooms?"

He took a sip of wine and leveled his gaze on her. "They're empty now, but I hope someday they'll be filled." A timer dinged, and he turned from her to open the oven.

Her stomach did a little flip. Could she be the one to help him fill the empty bedrooms? She'd always wanted children. It was one of the reasons being a nurse practitioner had appealed to her over becoming a doctor. She could have a lighter schedule and have more time to spend with her family—a family she thought she'd have started on by now.

But she'd wasted so much time with Phillip, with someone who only wanted her for better…not for worse. She shook her head to get her cheating ex out of her mind. She'd much rather concentrate on the delicious view of Sean's backside as he bent down to retrieve something from the oven than think about her past. She hadn't known Sean long, but the possibility of having a future with him made her insides flutter. He seemed solid. Stable. The kind of man who didn't give up easily.

"It's ready. Grab your wine. I thought we'd dine *al fresco* tonight." He led her out the door and onto the patio, and her breath caught at the sight.

A small table dressed in white linens stood on the

wooden deck, and strings of lights draped across the awning gave the entire scene a magical glow. Farther into the yard, a white fabric tent with the side curtains tied back revealed their movie theater for the evening. A myriad of colorful pillows lined the ground, and a television sat on a wooden box inside. It must've taken him hours to prepare.

"Did you do all this for tonight? For me?"

He pulled out a chair and motioned for her to sit. "I wanted our first date to be special. Did I go overboard?"

"No. Not at all. It is very special."

He grinned. "Good. I'll go get dinner."

*Wow.* It was the only word her mind would form. No one had ever spent this kind of time and effort on her. He'd paid so much attention to detail. Everything was perfect: the lights, the linens. He probably even put a call in to the weather gods, because the temperature outside was perfect. If she thought spontaneous Sean was amazing, Sean with a plan was spectacular.

"I hope you're hungry." He brought out two plates and kicked the door shut behind him. "And I hope it's good. I've never made this before."

He set the plate in front of her, and her mouth watered. A stack of thick-sliced, breaded eggplant sat in the center, covered with a creamy sauce with six juicy shrimp surrounding it. She sliced into the stack and placed a piece in her mouth. The eggplant seemed to melt on her tongue, the savory flavor melding with the slight sweetness of the sauce to create a perfect combination.

She swallowed and took a sip of wine. "This is delicious. Is there anything you aren't good at?"

"Hmm." He scratched his chin and feigned deep thought. "I'm not very good at staying away from you."

The fluttering feeling returned to her stomach. "That's a good thing."

"I'm glad you think so."

They finished dinner, and Sean rose to his feet. "Movie time."

"Shouldn't we clean this up?"

"I'll take care of it later. Come on." His smile beamed with excitement, and he bounced on his toes like a kid on Christmas waiting to tear into his presents. He took her hand and pulled her into the tent. "Get comfy."

He'd arranged the pillows to form the shape of a small sofa, and she settled into the pile of softness. He grabbed a remote and sidled next to her, wrapping his arm around her shoulders. They fit together with such ease. Something about him made her feel comfortable, safe. He was warm and firm, and his woodsy scent made her head spin. She rested her hand on his stomach while he fiddled with the remote, and she resisted the urge to creep her fingers down lower.

She wanted to touch him again. To feel his bare skin against hers, his lips on her body, his strong arms holding her close. But he'd spent so much time preparing for the evening. She could wait. They had all night.

"Ah. There we go." He tossed the remote aside and linked his fingers with hers on his stomach. "Best movie ever."

She looked at the screen and smiled. "*The Princess Bride?*"

"It seemed fitting."

She snuggled into his side and rested her head on his chest. His heartbeat thudded against her ear, creating a soothing rhythm as she relished the warmth of his embrace. Lying here on the mound of pillows, watching a movie under the stars with the most charming, handsome man she'd ever met…she couldn't think of a more perfect way to spend the evening.

As the movie ended with the famous kiss scene, Sean turned to her and grinned. "Westley and Buttercup's kiss was supposed to be the most passionate kiss of all time?"

"According to the movie, it was."

He glided his fingers across her forehead, tucking a strand of hair behind her ear. "I think our first kiss has them beat."

She scrunched her eyebrows. "Hmm…"

"You disagree?"

"I think I might need a reminder."

"As you wish." With his hand behind her head, he guided her down onto the pillows. His lips grazed her neck, barely brushing her skin, teasing her with promises of things to come. The warmth of his breath seared her skin as it glided along her jawline, melting every solid part of her insides.

When his lips met hers, a flood of heat flushed through her body, and he tangled his hands in her hair, kissing her with a fierceness she'd never felt before. Fireworks would pale in comparison to the explosions rocking through her core.

He walked his fingers up her arm and started drumming them against her elbow. Was he trying to get her attention? She had been so caught up in the passion, her thoughts were a scattered mess. She pulled from the kiss to look at him, and he slid his hands from her hair.

Both his hands.

So what was on her…?

"Ah! Cricket! Cricket!" She leapt to her feet and brushed the insect from her arm. It landed on a pillow and hopped into the grass as she tried to slow her racing heart. With her hand against her chest, she heaved in a deep breath and let it out slowly. "There was a cricket on my arm."

Laughing, Sean got up and pulled her into his arms. "You probably scared it more than it scared you."

"I doubt it."

"I didn't take you for the frightened of bugs type."

She rubbed her arm to smooth away the memory of its tiny legs scratching at her skin. "I'm not. It just startled me."

"Why don't we go inside?"

"I'm really not afraid of bugs."

"I know. But it's getting chilly out here. Come on." He led her up the porch steps and picked up the plates from the table.

"Let me help you clean up."

"I've got it. You go inside and make yourself at home. It'll only take a second."

She wandered through the kitchen into the formal dining room. A large cherry-wood table filled most of the space, but there was just enough room for a row of book-shelves to line one cream-colored wall. Stacks of drawing paper and sketchbooks occupied most of the shelf space, along with jars of what looked like special drawing pencils.

Dishes clanked in the sink, and Sean's footsteps sounded on the wood floor. "Ah, you found my drawing room."

"Why the formal dining room? You could turn one of the empty bedrooms into a studio."

He shrugged. "I like the light in here. I'm going to get the rest of the dishes inside."

"What's in the box?" She pointed to an open cardboard box next to the bookshelf.

"Just some old sketchbooks I'm planning to move to the attic. I've got way too many of them."

"Can I look at them?"

"Be my guest." He sauntered to the back door to finish cleaning up.

She picked up the top sketchbook and flipped through the pages. Her own experience in art began and ended with the required classes she took in elementary school, but she could spot talent when she saw it. This particular book was filled with drawings of Garden District homes. She recognized a few of the sketches from her drive to his house. The amount of detail he put into each one made them so realistic, they could've been mistaken for photographs.

Many of the drawings were black and white, but the ones he'd done in color were saturated in rich, vivid tones that seemed lifelike. His signature adorned the bottom of each drawing, along with a date. He'd sketched most of these over two years ago.

She put the book on the table and pulled another one from the box. The first drawing in this one was of a woman with long brown hair and hazel eyes. She was beautiful, with long lashes and a delicate smile. The next page contained a sketch of the same woman, as did the following page and the one after that.

A burning sensation tightened her chest, and she forced herself to stop grinding her teeth. She had no right to be jealous, but seeing drawing after drawing of the same woman bothered her. Who was she to him? The dates on the sketches ranged from three years prior to just over one year ago.

She chewed her bottom lip. She didn't want to look at these sketches, but her masochistic curiosity forced her to examine every one. The first few drawings were reminiscent of the other work Sean had done—rich in detail, realistic and precise. But the more recent the pictures were, the less detail they contained. Toward the end of the book, the woman was still recognizable, but her features were more generic, almost as if her image had faded from his memory. The last sketch was incomplete, like he got distracted and never came back to finish it.

Sean stepped behind her and wrapped his arms around her waist, resting his chin on her shoulder. "I forgot that one was in there."

"Who is she?"

He tightened his arms around her. "Courtney. She was my wife."

The burn of jealousy in her chest turned to a sharp pain. Why hadn't he told her he'd been married? She swallowed the lump that formed in her throat and stared at the last drawing. "Was?"

"She died three years ago. Car accident."

The stabbing in her heart melted into the liquid heat of shame. "I'm so sorry."

He moved beside her and ran a hand over the incomplete image. "Thank you. It was a long time ago."

"We don't have to talk about it." She started to close the sketchbook, but he took both her hands in his and kissed them.

"I don't mind. And I'm sure you have questions."

"Why didn't you tell me?"

Drawing his shoulders toward his ears, he inhaled a deep breath. "I don't like to dwell on the past. It has no effect on the here and now." He moved his hands to her hips, turning her toward him. "And right here, right now, I'm happy being with you."

"The drawings lose their detail." She brushed her finger across the page. "And you never finished this one."

He glanced at the picture and returned his gaze to hers. His eyes were dark, so full of emotion, she could get lost in their depths. And trust. There was so much trust in his eyes, hers brimmed with tears. She blinked them back.

"Drawing, for me, is a compulsion. When I get an image in my head, I have to put it on paper. When Courtney died…after she…" He sighed. "I dreamed of her a lot after she died. And then the dreams stopped, so I drew. It was how I coped with the loss. But as time passed, so did the pain. The need to draw her just wasn't there anymore, and I realized I was drawing her out of habit rather than compulsion."

He tapped the unfinished drawing and flipped the sketchbook shut. "That was the day I realized I was ready to move on. I didn't need to finish it."

"That was over a year ago."

"Yes, it was. And I have moved on, though my family and friends might tell you otherwise."

"They don't believe you?"

"I've been accused of not trying hard enough. Honestly, they were right. I wasn't really trying at all."

"Oh. You haven't dated?" Surely a man as attractive and charming as Sean had women fawning all over him.

"Until you, I had been on exactly three first dates. I was never interested in a second."

"Why not?"

He grinned and pulled her close, sliding his hands down to cup her butt. "I told you. I won't settle for anything less than fireworks. I hadn't felt them until you."

"I feel them too. Every time you touch me."

"Good. Let me bring in the TV, and then we can do a lot more touching." He stroked the backs of his fingers down her cheek and picked up the sketchbook, tossing it into the box and closing the lid. "My newer stuff is here, if you're interested." He tapped a stack of sketchpads on a shelf and left the room.

She grabbed the top two from the stack and looked through the first one. This book was filled with drawings of animals—mostly dogs and a few cats. Some of them had little jackets on that read "I'm adoptable."

He set the television on the floor and rested his hands on her shoulders. "Those are animals from the shelter we're sponsoring this year. I walk the dogs through the Quarter, trying to help them get adopted."

"That's sweet of you." She flipped the page. "What's the red stuff all over this dog? Is she bleeding?"

He laughed and slid his arms around her waist, pressing his front to her back. "That's Roxy, and she's covered in ketchup. She's been at the shelter a long time." A hint of sadness tinged his voice. He cared about the dog.

"Ketchup? Wait. Is she the reason you got in a fight with Maury's hot dog stand?"

"That's her." He closed the book and slid it onto the shelf. "Now about that touching I promised you." He massaged her shoulders and pressed his lips to her neck.

"Wait. Let me look at one more. I'm in awe of your talent."

"Drawing isn't the only thing I'm good at."

"Just one more." She opened the last book and froze. A woman with long red hair flowing in thick curls over her shoulders stared back at her. The eyes were a perfect shade of blue. The red sequined mask held every bit of detail she remembered. Her lips curved exactly right. Even the tiny freckle beneath her lower lip was in the perfect place. Sean had drawn her.

She flipped to the next page and found another picture of herself in the mask. Her head was turned at a different angle, but she had the same playful smile on her lips. Her hand trembled as she ran a finger over the page and looked at the date.

"You drew me the night we met?"

"I couldn't get you out of my mind." His breath whispered against her ear, sending warm tingles down her spine.

She turned to the next page and found another picture of herself, this time without the mask. Her arms were crossed over her chest, and her lips were pursed in an expression that said "you've got to be kidding me."

"This was the night of the ghost tour. Was I that unpleasant?"

He rubbed his hands up and down her arms. "You weren't unpleasant. Maybe a little stubborn."

She flipped back to a picture with the mask. "Why couldn't you make me look happier, like in one of these?"

"I draw what I see."

Turning to the next picture, she found herself in her white lab coat, a stethoscope draped around her neck and a shy smile on her lips. He'd captured the longing in her eyes perfectly, and the memories of the way she'd felt in that exam room made her shiver.

"You're very good." Page after page was filled with pictures of her, each one more vivid and detailed than the next.

"You don't find it weird?"

She closed the book and put it on the shelf. "I find it

endearing. No one's ever paid that much attention to me before." She turned around to face him, and the smolder in his eyes took her breath away.

"I'd like to pay some attention to you right now, if you don't mind." He pressed his lips to hers, coaxing them apart with his tongue as he slid his hands beneath her sweater. Cupping a breast in each hand, he teased her nipples through the fabric of her bra and trailed his lips down her neck and back up to find her mouth again.

Heat pooled below her navel, and she ran her hands along the ripples of his stomach. Everything about this man was intriguing. His scent, his kiss, the way his strong hands felt against her bare skin. Her knees weakened, and she leaned against the table to steady herself.

"Have I told you how good you look in red?" He clutched the hem of her sweater and pulled it over her head. The sudden coolness of air against her bare skin made her shiver. Or maybe it was the desire in his eyes.

"You've mentioned it."

He ran a finger along the edge of her bra. "Red lace. I like it. Is this a matching set?"

Good lord, his voice was sexy. The deep masculine tone was enough to make her clothes fall off on their own.

"It is."

He arched an eyebrow and unbuttoned her jeans, folding the flaps down so the red lace peeked from beneath. Clutching her hips, he inhaled deeply and slowly dropped to his knees. "Emily, you're killing me." He worked her pants over her hips and slid them down her legs. "You realize you're the first person I've made love to in three years, don't you?"

"I…" She didn't know how to answer. He didn't wait for one.

He slipped off her shoes and helped her step out of her jeans. "It should be against the law for someone to look this good. Put these back on." He held out her heels and helped her step into them.

Sitting back on his feet, he raked his gaze up and down her body. "Beautiful." He stood, still not touching her, though his eyes seemed to caress every inch.

"What are you doing?"

"Memorizing you."

She instinctively wrapped her arms around herself. She needed him to touch her, to bring back the warmth and act on the passion pooling in his eyes. "You're embarrassing me."

He took her arms and wrapped them around his waist. "Don't be embarrassed. You are perfection wrapped in lace. I needed a minute to admire you before I ravage you."

Then he kissed her. Hard. Passionately. Urgently. His hands roamed over her body, trailing up her back to unhook her bra. Sliding her onto the table, he spread her legs to fit his hips between them and laid her down, painting kisses across her stomach and up to her breasts.

He took a nipple in his mouth, teasing it with his tongue until it hardened. Electricity shot from her chest to her womb, and a lustful moan escaped her throat. He continued exploring her, trailing his tongue along her curves, lightly nipping at her bare skin. There was something oddly erotic about being so exposed while he was fully clothed.

"Should we be doing this on your dining room table?"

He glided his lips below her navel and kissed the tender skin along the edge of her panties. "I've never had a meal here. But I wouldn't mind having dessert."

He peeled the lace from her hips and slid it down her legs. When he reached her feet, he slipped off her shoes and let her panties fall to the floor. "You won't be needing these anymore." He stood, leaning over her, letting his hands wander all over her body as he kissed her. "God, you're so beautiful, Emily." His whisper against her stomach made her shiver.

Pulling up a chair, he sat and draped her thigh over his shoulder. He trailed his lips up one leg, across her pubic line and down the other leg, licking, kissing, and grazing every part of her except the one part she desperately needed him to touch. As his lips neared her center, she arched her back to bring him closer, all but begging him to pleasure her.

He let out a chuckle, obviously enjoying her reaction, and flicked out his tongue to finally taste her. She gasped at the warmth and softness of the caress, the feel of his fingers massaging her thighs. He draped her other leg over his shoulder, and a masculine *mmm* resonated from his chest. The vibration of sound against her sensitive middle sent thrilling tingles shooting through her core. And when he slipped a finger inside her, she lost control.

Her orgasm ripped through her body like an electric jolt, and she arched her back, tangling her fingers in his hair. His tongue felt like warm velvet against her skin as wave after wave of pleasure rocketed through her limbs.

When she'd had all she could take, she sat up and slid off the table to straddle his lap, crushing her mouth to his. She pulled his shirt over his head and ran her hands over his body. He was the perfect combination of hard muscles and soft skin, and she needed to feel his hardness inside her.

She unbuttoned his jeans and slid off his lap to pull

them down. His erection sprang out, long and hard, and she wrapped her hand around it. He closed his eyes and sucked in a sharp breath as she stroked him.

"Make love to me, Emily." His voice was raspy, thick with need. His eyes dilated with desire.

She straddled him again, guiding him to her folds, and lowered herself onto him. She shuddered as he filled her completely, as if he were made to be inside her. Rocking her hips, she slid up and down his thick girth and crushed her mouth to his. As another orgasm coiled in her core, she couldn't help but quicken her pace.

He moaned into her mouth, gripping her hips and guiding her faster and faster until release overtook her. She tossed her head back and cried out as he spasmed inside her. He stilled her hips, grinding himself into her until his own release was complete.

Breathless, she rested her head on his shoulder, and he rubbed his hands up and down her back.

"I am never going to look at this dining room the same." He brushed her hair from her shoulder and kissed her.

"You were sensational."

"This was all you, sweetheart. All I did was provide the pole. You did the dance."

Heat spread from the bridge of her nose all the way to her ears. He definitely brought out her wild side.

"And I don't ever want to hear you say you're boring again. A boring woman could not have done what you just did." He kissed her cheek, her neck, her shoulder.

She nodded and ran a finger over his wound, lifting her head to look at it. "These stitches can probably come out now. You're a fast healer."

"You're a good nurse. Do you want to move to the bed?"

"I do, but…" She bit her bottom lip. She wanted to spend the night with him, but was it worth the nightmares she'd have to endure to do it?

He smiled and stroked her cheek. "But…salt?"

He'd read her mind. She nodded and cast her gaze to the floor.

"It's already taken care of. I salted the whole house. The backyard too."

She met his gaze, and her chest gave a squeeze. He was thoughtful. Kind. He could do amazing things with his tongue. She was falling hard and fast for Sean, and there wasn't a thing she could do about it. "The whole house?"

He shrugged. "I didn't want to take any chances. I didn't know where we might fall asleep, and I wanted you to feel safe. So I salted the whole property. Put it directly in the earth, so it'll last a couple of weeks unless it rains."

Pressure built in the back of her eyes, but she would not cry, even if they were tears of happiness. "Thank you."

"You're safe here, Emily."

# CHAPTER ELEVEN

*S*ean scratched his pencil fervidly across the thick cream-colored paper. Golden sunlight poured in through the bedroom window, perfectly illuminating the gorgeous angel sleeping next to him. Her red hair fanned out around her head, and her right hand lay palm up, fingers gently brushing her cheek. The sheets were pulled down around her waist, exposing her flawless breasts, and the sunlight caressed her at just the right angle to brighten her features, giving her an ethereal glow.

A pins and needles feeling shimmied up his leg, and he shifted position to ease the sensation. Emily's eyes fluttered open, a tiny smile lighting her lips.

"Don't move. I've been waiting for you to open your eyes." He moved his pencil faster.

Her smile widened, melting his heart. "Are you drawing me?"

"Mm-hmm."

"You didn't need me to open my eyes. You know what they look like."

"Not when you first wake up in the morning after a night of passionate lovemaking."

A pink blush spread across her cheeks. If only he had his pastels with him, so he could capture the endearing color. He put the finishing touches on the sketch and dated and signed the bottom corner.

"You can move now."

She pushed to a sitting position, not bothering to pull up the sheets to cover herself, and leaned toward him. "Can I see it?"

He put the pencil on the nightstand and handed her the sketchbook. Her eyes widened when she looked at the drawing, a slight hitch in her breath revealing her surprise. Then she pursed her lips and narrowed her eyes.

"What's wrong? Is it that I drew you naked? I promise I won't show it to anyone."

"No, it's not that." She handed the sketchpad to him. "It's just you…" She took a deep breath and lifted one shoulder in a slight shrug. "You draw me prettier than I actually am. I wish I looked like that."

"You do look like this, Emily." He held up the drawing and examined it next to his subject. How could she think the sketch was prettier than she really was? "I draw exactly what I see. Maybe you see yourself differently than I do." He set the sketchbook aside and scooted closer to her, nuzzling into her neck. "All I see is beauty, inside and out."

"And apparently you like what you see." She nodded to the tent he'd made of the sheets.

"Apparently, I do."

A playful grin danced on her lips as she slid her hand beneath the covers and gripped his arousal. "It would be a shame to waste this."

"A terrible shame."

He made love to her again. Slowly. Passionately. And when they finished, he pulled her into his arms and held on to her as if he'd never let her go. Emily belonged here with him. In his bed. In his life.

He'd laughed when his mom told him love at first sight was real. Love was an emotion he doubted he'd ever feel again. But now, lying here with Emily wrapped in his arms, her naked body pressed against him, her rhythmic breaths warming his skin, he couldn't deny it. The flame she'd ignited inside him the night they met had grown into a raging inferno that consumed his very soul.

He knew what love felt like, and this was definitely it. He'd spend every second of every day with this woman for the rest of his life if he could. Lucky for her, he had other responsibilities and couldn't smother her with his presence too much.

"What are you doing today?" He ran his fingers through her silky hair and placed a kiss on her forehead.

"I don't have any plans during the day. Did you have something in mind?"

He ached at the sound of her voice, still raspy from sleep and lovemaking. "I wish I could stay right here in bed with you all afternoon."

"That sounds fantastic."

"Unfortunately, I have a meeting in a few hours."

"Oh." The disappointment in her voice made his chest tighten. He hated to let her down, but the fact that she wanted to spend more time with him thrilled him.

"But I'm free tonight."

She pursed her lips. "I promised Trish a girls' night tonight."

"Damn. Friday then? I have to run a tour that evening, but after…"

"After sounds wonderful." She brushed her fingers along his chest, tracing the contours of his muscles, raising goose bumps on his skin. "What kind of meeting do you have?"

"You know how my mom runs fundraisers all year for a local charity?"

She nodded.

"November's event is a bachelor auction, and I'm on the committee. We're meeting today to finalize the plans."

"Oh. So, women pay money to go on a date with you?"

"Not just me. We have twenty bachelors signed up this year. But it's not as bad as it sounds. It's usually rich, lonely old ladies bidding. The guys take them out to dinner and go dancing. It's all good fun."

Her heart pounded into his side. "How much do you go for?"

"Last year I went for three thousand dollars."

"Do young women ever bid? I mean, ladies you might actually want to date for real?"

He turned on his side to see her face. "Sometimes young women bid. Are you jealous?" He couldn't fight the smile tugging at his lips.

"I might have to take out a loan so I can bid on you."

"I hope you win."

"Me too."

The auction was still a month away, and he'd known Emily less than two weeks. But if her feelings for him were half as strong as his for her, they'd be a couple by then. He had no intention of putting himself up for auction now, but telling her that might not be the best idea. If he got too serious too fast, he might scare her away, and that was the last thing he wanted to do.

"Three thousand dollars?" She let out an astonished whistle.

Was she seriously considering bidding on him? "Yeah. But the committee is pressuring me to offer more than a date this year."

"What?" She gasped and pulled away from him.

He laughed. "No, not that. They want me to offer a portrait session. They think they could double my price if I offered to draw a portrait of whoever wins me."

Her shoulders relaxed. "Oh, well, that's not so bad."

"It is, though. I don't like to draw people."

"Isn't that what you're famous for? All those drawings of the people at the hotels and stuff?"

Interesting how she avoided mentioning the people he drew were ghosts. "I wouldn't say I'm famous for it. But all those people are dead. I don't like to draw the living. It's too intimate."

"But you draw me."

"I like being intimate with you." He pulled her into his arms and kissed her neck.

"Wait." She pushed him away. "Drawing people is sexual for you?"

"What? No." He sighed. He obviously wasn't explaining himself very well. "I draw exactly what I see. I can't bring myself to do otherwise. Facial expressions. The love or hate people hold in their eyes. What they're like on the inside always seeps through to the outside, and most people don't like to see that. Even you weren't happy with the sketch I just did of you."

"It's not that I wasn't happy. It's amazing. You're amazing. I just don't feel like I'm that pretty."

He shrugged. "See. And there's nothing I can do about the way you see yourself, the way anyone sees themselves. And people always want me to make them look better—skinnier, bigger eyes, fewer wrinkles. I don't lie with words, and I don't lie in my drawings either. So I made a decision a long time ago to stick with dead people. They don't complain."

"No, I guess they couldn't."

Oh, they could. But most of them were so happy to be seen, they didn't care. That was a conversation for another day, though. He'd wait until their relationship was a little more solid before he tackled the hard stuff. First, he'd earn her trust. Then she'd open up to him. She'd have to.

---

"How are things with you and lover-boy?" Trish stepped through Emily's front door and dropped her purse on the table. "I want all the juicy details."

"You don't waste any time, do you?" She pulled two Abitas from the fridge and offered one to Trish.

Her friend rolled her eyes and took the beer. "Hi, Emily. How are you?"

"I'm good. Thanks for asking. How are you?"

"Fine. Now spill. What did you do last night? What time did you get home? When are you seeing him again? Did you sleep with him yet?"

Emily sipped her beer, savoring the fizzy sensation as it slid down her throat to warm her from the inside out. "Dinner and a movie. Around noon today. Tomorrow night. Yes."

Trish ticked off the answers on her fingers and

squealed. "So? What's he like? He was so perfect at the ball, you were afraid you'd be disappointed."

"I don't know how to describe it. Everything just clicks, you know?"

"It's going well then? Do you see it getting serious?"

She picked at the label on the beer bottle. She hoped it was getting serious. She'd never felt so much so fast for anyone before. "Well, he had an extra toothbrush he'd gotten from the dentist last week, and he let me use it this morning. When I was done, he put in the holder next to his and said I could keep it there for next time."

Trish raised her eyebrows and grinned. "He's planning a next time. That's a good sign."

"I asked him that—if he was planning a next time—and he said he hoped there'd be lots of next times."

"Emily has a boyfriend," Trish sang like a schoolgirl.

"We haven't made anything official yet."

"Oh, please. You have a toothbrush at his house. I'd call that official."

"I hope—" Her phone buzzed on the table, and her heart did a little flip. Could it be Sean? She picked it up and looked at the screen. "Oh, crap. I'm not answering that."

"Who is it?"

"It's Phillip. He keeps begging me to see him again. Claims he misses me, he made a mistake, yada yada yada."

"You're not going to, are you?"

"Absolutely not. Nothing good would come of seeing him again. I've moved on."

"I'd say you have. You've got Dreamboat now."

"Damn right I do." She clinked the neck of her beer bottle against Trish's and took a drink.

"Speaking of Mr. Perfect, what about the ghost issue? Have you told him about Jessica yet?"

She let out a slow breath. "He was married before. Did I mention that?" Sipping her beer, she said a silent prayer that her deflection would work.

Trish shook her head. "What happened?"

"She died in a car crash a few years ago. We talked about it briefly, but he didn't want to dwell on it."

"Oh, man, that's sad. So, then you told him about Jessica?"

Damn it, she'd only delayed the inevitable. She shrugged. "Jessica didn't come up in the conversation."

"It's going to eventually, and you'll have to tell him why she died. How are you going to handle it?"

"I don't know. He hasn't talked much about his job or seeing dead people, or anything related to it. And I've done my best to avoid the issue. I guess I've been enjoying him so much, I've let myself forget about his fatal flaw."

"You don't know if it will be fatal for him."

"It was for Jessica." She downed the rest of her beer.

"He still thinks you don't believe in ghosts, doesn't he?"

"I *don't* believe in them. Not anymore." As long as she kept telling herself that, she would stay convinced. "I don't want to think about this right now. Let me bask in the excitement of Sean for a while, okay?"

The doorbell chimed, and she jumped from her seat, saved by the bell. Peering through the peephole, she saw the back of a man's head receding down the steps. As she opened the door, she found a small package lying on the mat. The mail carrier gave her a wave before climbing into his truck and driving away.

She carried the box to the table. "It's from Robert. He said he found a key that might fit the box."

Grabbing a knife from the kitchen, she slit open the tape and pulled a wad of tissue paper out. "At least it's not those stupid packing peanuts this time."

"Is there a note or anything?" Trish reached into the box and pulled out a slip of paper. "'This is all I could find. I hope it's what you're looking for. Robert.' He's a man of few words."

"I think he's just ready to move on. I can't say I blame him." Emily unwrapped the tissue paper and found a copper key and a small ceramic statue of a butterfly sitting on a daisy. Holding her tattooed wrist next to the statue, she admired the artist's work. He'd done a beautiful job recreating the butterfly to mimic the one on the figurine.

"Is that the statue that started your sister's butterfly collection?"

"This is the one. I was ten years old when I gave it to her." A fresh pang of guilt shot through her chest, and she set the statue on the table. "I have a bad habit of starting her obsessions, don't I?"

Trish rubbed her hand across Emily's back. "Her death wasn't your fault."

"So my therapist says." She shook her head to chase away the intruding thoughts. "Let's go see what's inside this box."

Taking the key to the kitchen countertop, she pulled the box away from the wall and ran her hand across the top. The etched inscription felt rough against her fingers, and a tingling sensation spiraled up her arm, turning into a sharp pain at her shoulder. She yanked her hand away. Had that ever happened before?

"Are you okay?" Trish stepped behind her.

"Yeah. It shocked me a little."

"It's wood. How could it shock you?"

"I don't know. Maybe I touched the metal hinges. It's fine." She ran her thumb across the key in her palm. "Here goes."

A *thud* drew her attention away from the box. She snapped her head around and found the butterfly statue lying on its side on the table. "Did you knock it over?"

Trish raised her hands. "I was standing right here. I didn't touch it."

She stepped to the table and picked up the trinket. "I bet I set it down on the edge of the tissue paper, and it fell over." That had to be what happened. There was no other explanation…none that she would entertain, anyway. She moved the statue to the small table by the door and set it in the place her sister's picture once stood.

She made it halfway to the kitchen when something thudded on the carpet. Turning around, she found the figurine lying on the floor. She snatched it up and examined it. Luckily it wasn't broken. She nestled it behind some books on a shelf, hoping that would keep it in place.

Trish eyed her warily. "That's weird, Em."

"What's weird?"

"Your sister's butterfly keeps flying around."

She let out an exasperated sigh. Her thoughts could not go in the direction Trish was leading them. "It didn't *fly*; it fell."

"Twice."

"So?"

"Maybe it's Jessica telling you not to open the box."

She crossed her arms. "There's no such thing as ghosts."

"You're only fooling yourself. I was there, remember? I

may not have seen what you and Jessica saw, but I sure felt the effects."

*No, no, no.* She would not think about it. As long as she believed ghosts didn't exist, nothing could hurt her. "We were teenagers; it was our overactive imaginations. Besides, even if it was Jessica's ghost, she died a year ago. Why would she come back now?"

"Maybe she's attached to the box. Didn't Robert say she loved it?"

"She used to stare at it a lot, and she didn't want anyone else to touch it." Jessica had practically wrestled it from the estate planner's clutches when she bought it. She'd seen something in the antique hunk of wood for sure.

"See? Maybe she's attached to it."

"All the more reason to open it, then." Emily slid the key into the lock and waited, holding her breath and half-expecting everything to fly off the bookshelf. It was stupid. This whole ordeal was idiotic. It was just a box. The butterfly was only a trinket. There were no spirits attached to anything because spirits didn't exist, and she would keep telling herself that for as long as she lived.

Still, she hesitated to turn the key. A nagging voice in the back of her mind screamed at her to stop, but she silenced it. Just like she'd silenced every inkling of thought that had anything to do with spirits for the last ten years.

Trish gripped her shoulder. She turned the key. A small click sounded as the lock disengaged.

"Don't open it." Trish put her hand on Emily's. "What if the lady at the antique store is right? What if it's not your sister's ghost attached to it? What if it's evil?"

"It's not evil."

"Maybe it has some negative energy attached to it."

"Now you sound like Sean." She lifted the lid and peered inside. Her heart sank. "A feather." She'd spent the past week obsessing over what treasures could have been inside her sister's box, and all she found was a stupid feather. "Well, that's disappointing. Why would she have a feather?"

"I don't know." Trish picked up the plume. The slick, iridescent feather was so black, it seemed to turn blue in the sunlight. "It looks like a crow feather. Crows are bad omens."

Emily arched an eyebrow at her friend. "Seriously?"

"When you see a crow, it's supposed to mean someone you love is going to die."

"That's ridiculous." She snatched the feather from Trish's hand and dropped it into the box.

"You should get rid of it. Just in case."

"It was Jessica's. I don't want to get rid of it."

"I know, Em. But it gives me the creeps. And you said Sean doesn't like it either. Is it worth causing problems with Mr. Perfect?"

She closed the lid and sighed. "I did already tell him I'd get rid of it. He didn't even want me to open it."

"Whatever Jessica kept in this box, it's gone now. And it doesn't sound like Robert wants to talk about it anymore. It's time to let it go."

"You're right. It's only a box, and I have her butterfly. That's more sentimental than a rotten piece of wood." She scooped the box into her arms, fully prepared to walk out the door and head straight to the dumpster. But she couldn't bring herself to do it. It was almost as if the box *wanted* her to keep it, which was ridiculous because it was just wood and metal. But still…

She set it on the counter and pushed it against the

wall. "I'm not even going to worry about it now. Let's go have some fun, and I'll toss it in the dumpster when I take out the trash tomorrow.

Trish eyed her skeptically. "Are you sure?"

"Absolutely." She was absolutely sure the box was going on a shelf in the back of her closet where no one else would find it.

CHAPTER TWELVE

Sean sat at his dining room table and ran his hand across the smooth wood surface. Images of Emily in her red lace lingerie danced behind his eyes, and he couldn't help but smile. It was true he'd never had a meal at this table, but the way he'd feasted on the delectable Emily last night would forever be seared in his mind.

He reached for his sketchbook, tempted to immortalize his luscious vixen with pencil and paper, but he refrained. With any luck, he'd be the only person to ever see her in that state of undress again. And he already had one intimate sketch of her. No need to press his luck with another.

Putting the sketchpad away, he pulled out his notes from the afternoon meeting. The committee protested when he withdrew from the auction. He'd still be there to run the logistics, but he wasn't about to put himself up for bidding when his heart belonged to Emily. Unfortunately, they'd already run the press releases promising twenty available bachelors. He'd have to find a replacement, but that shouldn't be too hard. His newest employee, Eric, had all the women swooning on his tours. He was young, but that could play in his favor. Now all he had to do was convince him to cooperate.

He tapped his pencil on the table and chewed his bottom lip. The house was quiet. Too quiet. He almost wished a ghost would pop in to say hello, but he'd poured enough salt around his property to keep it spirit-free for two weeks. He'd blocked out all forms of spirit energy from his consciousness so he could focus on building Emily's trust. But since he wasn't seeing her tonight, it wouldn't hurt to go for a walk and see if any of his old friends were hanging around.

He slipped on his jacket and left through the front door. Taking a right when he reached the sidewalk, he strolled under the canopy of live oaks, admiring the play of light and shadow on the colorful façades. The grand houses of the Garden District always seemed more magnificent at night all lit up from the inside, gas lamps burning on their front porches.

Closing his eyes, he inhaled deeply and relaxed the block he'd created in his channel. His head felt lighter, but not in a dizzying way. It was almost as if he'd been relieved of a headache he didn't realize he had. If any spirits wanted to be seen tonight, he was open to seeing them.

As soon as he rounded a corner, the blonde woman appeared in front of him. Of course, the first spirit to show itself would be her. He'd sensed her following him ever since he blocked her out. Shoving his hands in his pockets, he stopped walking and nodded.

"Good evening, ma'am."

She had definitely gotten stronger. Her appearance was almost solid, not a trace of death remaining in her features. The sadness in her eyes tugged at his heart. She lifted a hand and mouthed the word *please.*

"You're still having trouble with your voice. I wish I could coach you on what to do, but I don't know what to tell you."

"Help her." The strangled sound was barely audible.

"Can you tell me who I need to help?"

She opened her mouth to speak again, but no sound emitted. Her image wavered as panic flashed in her eyes.

"Okay. Stop trying to talk. I think that's draining your energy. Maybe you can find some other ghosts around. Talk to them, and maybe they can help you figure out how to use your voice."

She clasped her hands in front of her chest, pleading with her eyes.

"Tell you what: I'll ask you some questions, and you shake your head yes or no. Okay?"

The ghost nodded as a couple walked by, the woman eyeing him suspiciously.

He smiled and nodded a greeting. "Good evening. I'm just talking to a spirit friend."

The woman gripped her partner's arm and picked up her pace to get away from him. Sean grinned. He'd gotten used to people thinking he was crazy for talking to ghosts from time to time. Of course, they only thought he was crazy until he talked to a ghost they'd known. Then he was suddenly amazing. A blessing, they would call him.

He focused his attention on the blonde ghost. "I'm guessing by the trouble you're having, you're not recently deceased. Have you been dead a while?"

She nodded.

"And the person you want me to help isn't you?"

She shook her head. "Help her." Her image faded as

she said the words. She reached for him, and then she dissipated.

She'd be back. A spirit that determined wouldn't quit until she got what she was after. Hopefully he could figure out a way to help whoever needed helping before it was too late.

---

Bass thumped so hard Emily thought her heartbeat might lose its rhythm. She scanned the mass of writhing bodies, bumping and gyrating to the blasting music, certain she felt a pair of eyes boring into her. Other than the same drunk guy she'd been fending off all night, no one paid her any mind.

But the sickening suspicion she was being watched followed her to every bar and dance floor she and Trish had visited. She downed her fifth gin and tonic, hoping to dull the sensation, but the alcohol only made her more suspicious.

She was being stupid. She'd let all the talk of spirits and evil and negative energy go to her head. Now she was certain there was a monster lurking somewhere in the shadows, waiting to scare the daylights out of her as soon as she let her guard down.

She clutched Trish's arm and pulled her off the dance floor. "Can we go somewhere quieter? This place is giving me a headache."

"Oh, poo. You're not having any fun." She stamped her foot and lost her balance, falling into Emily's arms.

"Hey, now. That's my thing, remember?" She laughed and stood her friend upright. "And I am having fun, but it's too loud here. Let's go back to the piano bar."

"All right. But Josh is coming with us." She grabbed the guy she'd been grinding against and pulled him toward the door. Unfortunately, his drunk friend came with them.

They walked down Bourbon Street, Trish hanging on to Josh's arm, and Emily trying her best to stay away from Josh's friend. She'd already forgotten his name, and she didn't care to remember it. He smelled like cheap beer and ashtray.

She walked a few feet in front of the guy, but he still managed to reach out and lay a clammy hand on her shoulder.

"Hey!" She spun around. "Hands off. I'm not interested."

He looked at her like she was crazy. "I didn't touch you."

"You grabbed my shoulder."

"Em, he didn't." Trish put a hand on her elbow. "Are you okay?"

Was she okay? Her head was still pounding. She still felt like someone was watching her from the shadows, and now she was imagining people touching her. Was it the alcohol or was she going crazy?

"I'm fine. My head just hurts. I think I'm ready to go home."

"Okay. Do you mind if I stay out with Josh?" She raised her eyebrows, emphasizing exactly what she meant.

Emily pulled her friend out of Josh's earshot. "Are you sure? You've had a lot to drink."

"No more than you. Anyway, I know Josh. We've hooked up before. It's nothing serious." She winked.

Emily had to laugh at that. "You haven't changed. Okay. Be safe."

"I will. I'll call you tomorrow."

She managed to make it home, though she stumbled over her own feet more times than she was proud of and looked over her shoulder more times than that. She was being paranoid, and the alcohol had intensified the feeling rather than dull it. Standing at the bottom of the stairs, she peered up at her door. Climbing seemed like such a daunting task.

She sat on the bottom step and held her head in her hands. Staying outside all night wasn't an option. She needed to haul her butt up to the top and faceplant into her bed. With a heavy sigh, she heaved herself to her feet and trudged up the stairs.

She counted six steps before her head started spinning, and she had to sit down again. Only nine more to go. Or was it ten? Or Twenty? Hell, she couldn't even remember the walk home, much less how many stairs led up to her apartment. Grabbing the rail, she pulled to her feet and placed one foot above the other until she reached the landing.

The lock seemed to have shrunk. She turned the key in every direction, trying to fit it in the hole, but it wouldn't go in. Leaning against the frame, she gave the key a final shove into the lock, yanked on the knob, and flung the door open.

As she stepped inside and flipped on the light, the heaviness in her head flushed out with the adrenaline that flooded through her veins. Tables lay on their sides; chairs were upended, and the contents of her bookshelves lay scattered about the floor. Instinct drew her to her sister's box first, but it sat unscathed on the counter where she'd left it. Lifting the lid, she found the feather still nestled in the bottom, but the key was missing.

A quick scan of the living room revealed the key lying

in the middle of the mess. She scooped it up and shoved it into her pocket. Someone had broken in. That was the only logical explanation. But wasn't the front door locked when she got home? She searched her mind for a memory of unlocking it, but her thoughts scattered like billiard balls every time she tried to grab on to something.

Police. She needed to call the police.

"911. What's your emergency?"

"I need to report a break-in at my apartment." She gave the operator her address and checked her bedroom. Everything here seemed to be in place.

Was anything stolen? That would be the first question the police would ask. She went back to the mess in the living room. She didn't have anything of much value. The TV was still there. Her iPad lay on the floor amidst the mess with the screen cracked. Lovely.

Nothing seemed to be missing. And if no one broke in, then it must have been…

No. She would not let her thoughts go there.

The police arrived and examined her apartment. No sign of a break-in. Her front door must have been unlocked when she left with Trish that evening. She tried her best to keep her head straight while she gave her statement, hoping the officer would take her seriously. Was she slurring her words? She couldn't tell.

Since she couldn't report anything missing, they wrote it up as vandalism and reminded her to keep her doors locked.

Vandalism. That's what it was. Just some punk kids having their fun. She could wrap her mind around that explanation, and she would hold on to it until the *other* idea in her head drowned with the hangover she was sure to have tomorrow.

The officers left, and she shuffled toward her bedroom, ready to curl up under the blanket and hibernate her buzz away. She glanced at the floor to avoid tripping and found Jessica's butterfly statue lying on the carpet, one wing snapped off and lying next to it.

She bent down to retrieve it and choked on a sob. Tears streamed down her cheeks as she scooped up the broken figurine and carried it into the kitchen. Stupid alcohol was making her emotional. It was only a statue. It wasn't like her actual sister was broken, though the rush of emotions made it feel that way. But Jessica was dead, and she wasn't coming back. Not even as a ghost.

What was wrong with her? She needed to go to sleep, but she didn't want to be alone. She dialed Sean's number before she realized what she was doing.

"Emily?" His raspy voice, thick with sleep, calmed her racing thoughts.

"I'm so sorry. Did I wake you?"

"It's okay, baby. What's wrong?"

She sucked in a shaky breath. "Someone broke into my apartment and vandalized it."

The sheets rustled as he got out of bed. "Are you there now?"

"Yes."

"I'm on my way."

She put the phone down and ran a hand across the box. *Oh no.* She'd told him she'd get rid of it. Snatching it off the counter, she hurried to her bedroom and put it on a shelf in the back of her closet. She set the key beside it and closed the closet door.

Sean found Emily sitting on the top step outside her apartment door. Tear stains streaked her face, and as she raised her gaze to meet his, his heart gave a squeeze.

"Are you okay?" He knelt on a step in front of her and clutched her shoulders.

She held a butterfly statue in one hand and a piece of the wing in the other. "It's broken."

"We can fix it. Come on." He pulled her to her feet and wrapped his arms around her. "What did the police say?"

"I must've forgotten to lock my door when I left this evening." She sobbed into his shoulder.

"Let's go inside." He pulled her through the door and stopped in the entryway. The entire living room looked like a war zone. Everything she owned was scattered about the floor, lying in pieces everywhere. Even the sofa was flipped onto its back.

She sobbed harder. He held her tighter.

"I'm sorry, Sean. You were the first person I thought to call. Trish went home with Josh, and I don't have any family here."

"Hey." He ran his fingers through her hair and gazed into her sad eyes. "Don't apologize. I *want* to be the first person you think to call in a situation like this."

Though this situation didn't appear to be vandalism. The way her things were tossed about and the furniture flipped over, this looked more like a poltergeist than the work of vandals. He closed his eyes and opened his senses, sifting through the air for spirit energy. He felt a slight tingle, the leftovers of whatever had turned her apartment upside down, but nothing fresh. The spirit had zapped all its energy doing this, and that was a sign it wasn't very powerful. She should be able to banish it, if he could get her to say the words.

"Whoever did this isn't allowed to do it again." His own words wouldn't work against the spirit, though. Emily needed to say it herself. "Say that out loud for me. Maybe it'll help you feel empowered."

She giggled and wiped her eyes. "You think so?"

"I know so. Say it for me. Please?"

She pulled from his embrace and stumbled. He caught her by the arm, and she giggled again.

"How much have you had to drink?"

"Too much." She rubbed her temples.

"Say it for me."

"Whoever did this isn't allowed to do it again."

"Louder. Say it like you mean it."

She laughed and shouted, "Whoever did this isn't allowed to do it again."

"There. Don't you feel better now?"

"Sure. I think I should go to bed now. Wanna come?" She linked her hands behind his neck and trailed kisses up to his ear.

"As tempting as that sounds, sweetheart, I'd rather have you when you'll remember it."

She poked her bottom lip out. "Okay. Suit yourself." She turned and headed for the bedroom.

"Hold on." He caught her by the hand. "You're coming home with me tonight."

"But my bed is right here."

"I'll feel safer with you at my place. Just for tonight." Her words probably worked to stop the poltergeist from doing this again, but just in case it was vandals, he preferred to keep her close.

Sunlight painted the back of Emily's eyelids red, and an aching in her temples spread all the way to her forehead. She squeezed her eyes shut harder, hoping when she opened them, the events of last night would have only been a dream.

She opened one eye. Then the other. As the room came into focus, her heart sank. It wasn't a dream. She lay there alone in Sean's soft bed, the sheets cold where he should have lain. Oh, god. What had she done last night? She scooted to a sitting position and rubbed her head. She needed to think, to gather all the scattered thoughts and put the pieces of last night back together in her mind.

She'd gone out with Trish, had too much to drink, gone home, and… Her apartment. The mess. *Oh, no.* And she'd called Sean, and he'd seen her in her drunken stupor and brought her home with him. What did he think of her now?

Her overnight bag lay on the floor beside the bed, so she rummaged through it. At least she'd been coherent enough to pack a decent change of clothes. Her shirt smelled like sweat and alcohol, and she could only imagine her breath was ten times worse. She tiptoed to the bathroom for a shower before she faced Sean.

She avoided looking in the mirror as she ran the hot water, but she couldn't help but smile at the toothbrush— her toothbrush—sitting in the holder next to his. Hopefully he'd still want her to keep it there.

With her hair washed and teeth brushed, she pulled on her jeans and long-sleeve t-shirt and padded into the kitchen. Sean sat at the breakfast table, sipping a cup of coffee and looking at something on his phone. He'd combed his hair, and he wore jeans and a light blue button-up shirt. He'd obviously been up for a while.

She cringed as he raised his gaze to meet hers, expecting to see anger or disgust in his eyes. Instead, they held sympathy, and the corner of his mouth quirked into an adorable grin.

"Good morning, sunshine. How's your head?" He reached for the coffee pot and poured her a mug.

"It's been better."

"Here." He put a muffin on a plate along with two white tablets and set it on the table. "Food, coffee, and Tylenol: the trifecta of hangover remedies."

"Thanks." She lowered herself into the chair and nibbled on the muffin. "I'm sorry about last night."

"Nothing to apologize for."

"Thanks for taking care of me."

"Thanks for thinking to call me." He reached across the table and tucked her damp hair behind her ear. "I'm glad you're okay."

She forced a smile and swallowed the pills. "I woke up without any pants on. Did we…?"

He chuckled. "No. Although you did try several times, and you can be very persuasive."

She let out a slow breath. "Thank god."

He raised an eyebrow.

"I mean…not that I'm glad we didn't. I just…don't remember doing it, so I'd feel bad if we did."

"Well, we didn't. You passed out as soon as your head hit the pillow. Nothing to worry about."

"Good."

"I did hold you for a while, though." He traced his fingers down her arm and held her hand. Warmth spread through her body at the idea of him still wanting to be close, even in her condition.

"Until you elbowed me in the nose and muttered something about a boxing kangaroo. I left you alone after that." He released her hand and carried his coffee mug to the sink.

The blood drained from her face. "Oh, god. I'm so sorry. Did I hurt you?"

He pressed a hand to his nose. "I'll survive."

"I understand if you don't want to see me again. I was a wreck last night."

"Whoa now. Where'd that come from?" He furrowed his brow and crossed to the table in two long strides. "You needed someone, and I was happy to be there for you. I will always be there for you." He pulled her into his arms and pressed his lips to her forehead.

"Really?"

"Really. But be honest with me. Do you think it was vandals last night?"

She stiffened. "It had to be." She couldn't let a thought about the alternative slip into her mind.

"Okay. I've got to work this afternoon, so let's get you home and get your place cleaned up. Are you okay to go back?"

"Oh, yeah. I'm fine."

---

Sean set the last photo frame on the table by Emily's front door. She seemed convinced by the police report that vandals had ransacked her apartment. He didn't see any reason to upset her with his own theory. He'd tried several times to reach out to any spirits that might be lurking in the corners of her apartment, but he'd found nothing. If anything was there, it was either really good at hiding, or Emily telling it not to bother her anymore last night had the desired effect.

Either way, the salt she kept around her bed would keep her safe from spirits at night. The locks on her door should keep her safe from anything else. "You've got two deadbolts and a chain. Make sure they're all engaged when you're home."

She smiled and gave him a mock salute. "Yes, sir."

"I'm serious. Are you sure you'll feel safe here alone?"

She picked up the broken butterfly statue. "I'm sure. Will you look in that drawer? I think I have a tube of superglue."

He rummaged through the drawer, gave her the container, and turned her hand over to see her tattoo. "It's an exact match."

She slid from his grasp and glued the figurine together. "Yes, it is."

"You must really like this particular butterfly."

"I do."

"Why?"

She took a deep breath and let go of the wing. The glue held it in place. "I'm not ready to talk about it, Sean."

"You can trust me, you know?"

"I know. But it's not a happy story, and I don't talk about it much. Give me a little time, okay?"

"Take all the time you need, sweetheart. I'm not going anywhere."

# CHAPTER THIRTEEN

*S*ean stood on the steps of the St. Louis Cathedral, shaking hands and saying goodbye to his customers. He'd given the ghost tour so many times, he seemed to run on autopilot, and now he focused his attention on the crowd, looking for Emily. Two weeks had passed since their first "official" date. They'd had ten dates more since then, and he'd lost count of how many romps between the sheets, but he still couldn't get enough of her. She was starting to spend more time at his house than in her own apartment, and that was fine with him. He liked having her around. His house actually felt like a home when she was there.

He spotted her shiny red hair in the mass of tourists and bounded down the steps to meet her. Sweeping her into his arms, he spun in a circle and planted a possessive kiss on her lips. The curves of her body conformed to every angle of his like they were built as two parts of the same whole.

She slid her hands down his back and slipped her fingers into his pockets. "I missed you too." The soft moonlight glinting her eyes gave them a mischievous sparkle.

"You sure you're up for this tonight? My crew takes laser tag very seriously."

She nipped his earlobe between her teeth, sending shivers running down his limbs. "I think I can handle it." Her lips brushed against his ear as she spoke, and she gave his ass a squeeze, pressing her hips into his.

"Good god, woman, you drive me crazy. Why don't we go home and play tag between the sheets instead?"

She laughed and pulled away. "We'll have time for that after. Besides, I want to get to know your friends."

"Okay. But don't say I didn't warn you."

They met Sydney, Eric, and Jason in front of Polly's Funhouse and Arcade just in time for their half-hour reservation. He made the introductions, and Syd gave him that knowing smile that meant she knew something he didn't want to know. She'd made good on her promise of keeping her premonitions to herself for years now, but ever since he started dating Emily, he knew she'd seen something. And by the huge grin on her face, he could only assume it was something good. Still, he wasn't about to ask. She only saw glimpses of what *could* happen. Things could change. Or they couldn't. He'd learned that the hard way.

Jason greeted Emily with a handshake, but Eric took her hand and pressed his lips to her fingers. "It's nice to see you again, Emily."

She blushed and cut her gaze to Sean before looking at Eric. "Hi. I'm sorry I ditched your tour. It was nothing personal."

"No worries." He flashed a grin and hung on to her hand way longer than necessary. Eric was a flirt by nature, and he seemed to have a way with the ladies. But not this lady.

Sean pulled her to his side, out of Eric's grasp, and cleared his throat. "Let's get this game started."

"Since we've got an uneven number, are we going every man for himself?" Jason asked.

"Or how about girls against boys?" Sydney suggested.

Jason laughed and stood between Eric and Sean. "Three against two? You won't stand a chance."

"What do you say, Emily?" She linked her arm through hers. "Want to show these boys how to fight like girls?"

Emily grinned and caught Sean's gaze. "Let's do it."

He straightened his spine and grinned back. She already fit in with his friends, and she was up for a challenge. He loved this woman more every day. "You better muscle up, Buttercup. We don't take prisoners."

"Bring it."

By the time they finished the game, Sean was panting with exhaustion. The guys had their asses handed to them by a couple of girls. He knew Sydney was good at laser tag, but he'd have sworn Emily had some kind of commando training the way she dodged his shots and landed her own with precision.

They headed to the bar next door and ordered a round of beers. He slid into the seat next to her and draped his arm around her shoulders. The ease with which they fit together never ceased to amaze him.

"She's a keeper," Syd whispered in his ear.

He clenched his teeth and lowered his voice. "I don't want to know what you saw."

She smiled and shrugged. "I'm just saying I like her.

That's all." She sauntered around the table and slid into the chair on the other side of Emily.

"What's your secret?" he said to Emily. "How'd you get so good at laser tag?"

She lifted a shoulder and wiped the condensation off her beer. "I used to play paintball with my sister in high school."

"I'd like to meet your sister sometime."

She flashed a half-smile and clinked her bottle against Sydney's, turning her back to him. "We make a good team, don't we?"

Sydney smiled. "We sure do."

What an odd reaction. Did she have a strained relationship with her sister? Add another item to the list of mysteries he needed to investigate about Emily. She had secrets, but he had a feeling he was close to figuring them out. She'd become so much more open and relaxed with him over the last few weeks. It was a slow row, but he was earning her trust.

"Who's up for a game of pool?" Eric held two cue sticks in his hand.

"Count me in." Sean kissed Emily on the cheek and followed Eric to the table. As Eric racked the balls, Sean leaned on his cue and watched Emily talk with Sydney. The way she smiled and laughed reminded him of the night they met at the masquerade. It was that same playful smile and musical laugh that had attracted him to her in the first place. And his feelings for her grew stronger and stronger with each passing day.

---

The view of Sean's backside as he bent over the pool table

sent Emily's heart racing. Who'd have thought after nearly a month of knowing him, she'd still get this worked up just looking at him? She sipped her beer and smiled as he caught her eye.

"I'm glad he found you." Sydney's voice pulled her from her thoughts. "We were worried about him for a while." She absently rubbed her tattooed arm, and Emily couldn't help but notice the intricate sleeve extending from beneath her shirt down to her wrist. A beautifully detailed pocket watch adorned the underside of her forearm, with a chain wrapping around her elbow and leading up to what appeared to be the bottom half of the White Rabbit from *Alice in Wonderland.*

She was tempted to ask about the tattoo but refrained for fear of Sydney asking about hers in return. Instead, she focused on her comment about Sean. "Who's we?"

"His friends. His mom, especially. I don't know how much he's told you, but he hasn't dated much."

"Since Courtney."

"Yeah."

"He said he's been on three dates."

Sydney laughed. "And those were just to appease his mom and her incessant nagging. Madeline wants grandchildren so bad she can taste it. It's nice he finally found someone."

"Oh." She picked at the label on her beer bottle.

"Not someone to have babies with. I mean...someone who makes him happy. I'm sorry. That didn't come out right."

"It's okay. I like children." The thought had crossed her mind more than once about filling all those empty rooms in his house.

Sydney tightened her lips as if fighting off a smile. "Of course you do."

What a strange thing to say. Emily was about to ask her what she meant when a tall red-headed woman stumbled toward Sean. Her brunette friend tried to grab her hand, but she flung herself toward him, and he caught her around the waist before she face-planted into the pool table.

"It's my birthday, Sean. I want a kiss." She grabbed him around the neck and planted her hot pink lips on his.

Emily was on her feet and marching toward them before she realized she was moving. Heat burned from her chest down to her stomach, and her hands instinctively clenched into fists. Sean's eyes widened as he gripped the woman's shoulders and pried her lips away from his face.

"That wasn't so bad, was it?" The woman stumbled in her stilettos, and her friend caught her by the arm.

He wiped his mouth with the back of his hand, leaving a hot pink trail of lipstick marring his skin. Emily clutched his bicep and put a possessive hand on his chest.

"He's taken." She didn't recognize the venom in her own voice, but the jealousy burning inside was definitely hers.

Sean wrapped an arm around her shoulder. "Paisley, this is my girlfriend, Emily."

Paisley curled her lip. She ran a disapproving gaze up and down the length of her before sticking her nose in the air. "Girlfriend? We'll see how long that lasts. I saw your name on the auction list, and Daddy's giving me extra money to bid on you this year."

"Come on, girl. Let's get you home." Her friend flashed an apologetic smile and led the stumbling woman away.

Sean grabbed a napkin and wiped the lipstick off his hand and his mouth. "That wasn't what it looked like."

She hooked a finger in his belt loop and pulled him close. "It looked like a drunk woman making unwanted advances on my boyfriend."

"Okay. It was what it looked like, then."

"Who is she?"

He sighed and shook his head. "She's an…old friend of the family. I swear there's nothing going on."

She narrowed her gaze at him. "I believe you. But I seriously might have to take out a loan to bid against her at the auction. There's no way she's winning a date with you."

He slid his fingers into her hair and pressed his lips to her forehead. "No one's going to win a date with me, sweetheart. I backed out of the auction."

"But she said your name was on the list."

"The committee sent out the press release before I told them."

She hugged him tighter, the tension in her chest melting away. "I bet they weren't very happy with you."

He lifted one shoulder in a dismissive shrug. "Bachelor auctions are for single guys. I'm taken, remember?"

She bit her bottom lip and cast her gaze to the floor. "I'm sorry. I don't know what came over me. When I saw her kissing you, I just acted. I didn't even think about it."

"I think it's called jealousy."

She cringed. "I'm not usually like that."

"It's nice to know you'll fight for me." He slid his hands down to cup her butt and pressed his hips into hers. "It's kind of a turn on." His breath against her ear made her shiver. "If you'll let me finish kicking Eric's ass at pool,

I'll take you home and show you how much of a turn on it is."

"Mmm. That sounds like an excellent idea." She leaned in for a quick kiss, but his enticing scent and strong arms made her linger. His tongue slipped between her lips to brush with hers, and her knees turned to pudding.

"All right, you two. Break it up." Eric clapped Sean on the shoulder. "Are we going to finish this game, or are you forfeiting?"

He pulled away to look at her. "What do you think?"

She grinned. "Finish him."

"As you wish."

Sydney smiled as Emily made her way back to the table. "That was exciting. I probably would've clawed her eyes out."

She laughed. "I thought about it. I guess Sean has a thing for redheads."

"Oh, he's never had a thing for Paisley."

"He called her an old friend of the family. Isn't that guy code for they used to date?"

Sydney shook her head. "Trust me. I've known Sean since we were kids. His mom would disown him if he even thought about dating her."

"Why?"

"Paisley's mom tried to steal Sean's dad away from Madeline when they were young. She's hated her ever since, but they run in the same circles. I guess that makes them frenemies."

"Scandalous."

"Right? Anyway, you don't have anything to worry about. Sean is crazy about you. I've never seen him so happy." She traced her finger on the wood pattern of the table as if contemplating her next words. "I've got a feeling you two are going to be very happy together for a long time."

"Funny." She caught his gaze as he approached the table. "I have the same feeling."

"The ass-kicking is complete." Sean squeezed her shoulders. "Ready to go, babe?"

"Yeah. It was nice talking with you, Sydney."

As soon as they stepped onto the sidewalk in front of the bar, Sean swept her into his arms. "I'm glad your couch is comfortable, because we may not make it all the way to your bedroom."

He nuzzled into her neck, but she pulled away. "I'd rather go to your house if you don't mind."

He looked hard into her eyes, his brows furrowed with concern. "I love that you like coming to my place, but it seems like you never want to go home anymore. Is something wrong? Are you having problems with the...vandals?"

"No, it's just..." She pinched the bridge of her nose and squeezed her eyes shut. Sean didn't believe vandals had broken into her apartment, no matter how hard he tried to act like he did, so she hesitated to tell him what was going on now. He was sure to insist something supernatural was at play, though there was a scientific explanation for the way she'd been feeling.

She sighed. She should tell him. He hadn't pressured her to spill her other secrets, so why would he start now? "Whenever I'm at home, I start feeling sick. I get nauseated; my head hurts, and my chest feels heavy. I think I might have mold."

He searched her eyes, and she braced herself for his otherworldly explanation. "Why haven't you mentioned this before? We need to have it checked out; that stuff can make you sick."

"I'll call someone tomorrow."

"All right. And you can stay with me until it's taken care of. I don't want you breathing in all those toxins."

"Oh, I don't want to impose." Though the thought of living with Sean—even temporarily—kicked her heart into overdrive. "I'm sure I can crash on Trish's couch if I need to."

"I'm sure you could." He cupped her cheek in his hand and ran a thumb across her lips. "But you could also sleep in my bed. With me."

And she turned to putty again. Just like that. Trish's couch versus Sean's bed, especially with him in it—it was a no-brainer. She leaned into his touch and gave in to the melting sensation turning her insides to mush. "That sounds nice."

---

Sean considered taking Emily by her apartment to pack a bag, but he didn't want to give her time to change her mind. They could deal with the mold—whether or not that's really what it was—tomorrow. Right now, he needed to be with her.

She clung to his arm as they walked up the front steps to his house. "I had fun tonight. I like your friends."

He opened the door and led her inside. "They liked you too. Although the guys were a little miffed about being beaten by a couple of girls."

She grinned. "I'm glad I could even the playing field for Sydney."

"Speaking of playing fields." He wrapped his arms

around her waist. "Want to go play a game of tag between the sheets?" Sliding his hands beneath her shirt, he unhooked her bra. If he didn't get her out of these clothes soon, he might spontaneously combust.

"Actually," she wiggled from his arms, "I got a little sweaty playing laser tag. I think a shower might be in order before we go to bed."

He let out a defeated sigh. "I suppose I can wait…"

She flicked out her tongue to moisten her lips and flashed a seductive smile.

Blood rushed to his groin as the realization hit. "Oh, you mean *we* should take a shower?"

She slipped a finger into the waistband of his jeans. "It would be a lot more fun if you were there." She popped the button and slid her hand into his pants. "Care to join me?"

"Oh, god yes." He followed her to the bathroom and turned on the water. She undressed slowly, obviously aware of the effect she had on him. His gaze never left her body as each article of clothing dropped to the floor. She stood there naked, her silky hair spilling around her shoulders, porcelain skin begging to be touched.

That playful smile curved her lips, and she rested a hand on her hip. "Well?"

"Well what?"

She opened the shower door and stepped inside. "Are you going to take your clothes off and join me, or are you just going to stand there?"

Water ran in ribbons around her breasts, flowing down her stomach to caress her tender parts before cascading to the drain. She tipped her head back to dampen her hair, and he marveled at the rise and fall of her gloriously wet nipples as she breathed. Good lord, she was beautiful. And he needed to touch, to kiss, to taste every inch of her supple body before he made love to her.

He undressed quickly, but he took his time washing her, running his soapy hands over her soft curves, trailing his lips over her freshly rinsed skin. He massaged her scalp with shampoo and shivered at the soft moans resonating from her throat.

She leaned her head back to rinse her hair, and white suds cascaded down her body. "I thought you were in a hurry to get me to bed."

He ran his hands over her slick skin, cupping her breasts in his hands, teasing her nipples with his thumbs. "I was. But I realized this is the first time we've showered together, so I decided to savor it."

She picked up the soap and made a lather in her hands. "Well, then. Would you like me to wash you?"

"Yes, please."

Her soft hands sliding over his wet skin sent another wave of blood rushing to his groin. If his cock got any harder, there wouldn't be any blood left for his brain. Not that he minded. She ran her hands down his stomach and out to his hips, carefully avoiding the one place he wanted her to touch most. When his front side was thoroughly soapy, she slid her hands around to his back and pressed her body to his. She was warm and wet, and he couldn't help but grab her ass and press his hips harder into hers.

"Not yet. You're not rinsed." She pulled him under the stream and wrapped her hand around his length. His entire body shuddered as she slipped her tongue into his mouth and stroked him.

"God, Emily. What did I do to deserve you?" He wanted to take her right there in the shower, but he refrained. He'd taken it slow so far and had relished every second of it. He intended to draw this out and make love to her slowly to show her just how special she was to him.

He put his hand on hers to slow her stroking and shut off the water. "I'm not done with you." He grabbed a fluffy blue towel from a shelf and patted her dry.

"Be careful spoiling me like this, Sean. A girl could get used to this kind of treatment."

He wrapped the towel around her hair and squeezed out the water. "I hope you do." Pulling a brush from the drawer, he ran it through her hair from scalp to ends, gently loosening the tangles until it flowed like damp silk.

He watched her watching him in the mirror. The way her eyes fluttered every time the brush touched her scalp. The sweet smile curving her perfect pink lips. God, he loved this woman. It took all his strength not to tell her right then and there. It was too soon. She was still holding back, and when he said the words, he wanted to be sure she'd be ready to say them too.

He kissed her cheek and rested his chin on her shoulder, sliding his hands over her stomach. "You are sincerely the most beautiful woman I have ever seen."

She twisted in his embrace to face him. "Take me to bed, Sean."

"Yes, ma'am."

She lay in the center of the mattress and spread her legs to allow his hips to settle between them. As he pushed inside her, she closed her eyes and let out a soft *mmm.* He made love to her slowly. Filling her completely. Losing himself in her essence as two separate beings became one. A tangle of limbs, their bodies moved together in fluid motion, her lips gliding over his shoulders and neck, her teeth lightly grazing his skin. No sensation in the world existed but the feel of her body wrapped around him, the excruciating intimacy of lying with her. Vulnerable.

As her hands glided across his back, she held more than his body in her arms. She held his heart. He gave himself to her completely. There would never be another woman for him. She gripped his shoulders, arching her back to take him deeper, writhing beneath him as he pleasured her. Wrapping her legs around his waist, she cried out, her body shuddering as she found her release. The feel of her center contracting around him, her moans of satisfaction and the scent of her sweat-slickened skin sent him over the edge. He buried his face in her hair as his own orgasm overtook him, and he collapsed on top of her. Their pounding hearts beating as one, he lay there motionless, unable to break their intimate union just yet, and she hugged him tighter.

"That was amazing, Sean."

"It keeps getting better." He rose onto his elbows and gazed into the deep blue of her eyes. He belonged to her. He was completely and utterly devoted, yet she was holding back. He needed her trust more than he'd needed anything in his life, and he would find a way to earn it.

She ran her fingers through his damp hair. "You seem lost in thought."

He rolled onto his back and pulled her to his side. "I'm just thinking about how wonderful you are and how I want to know everything about you."

"I think you know every inch of me."

"On the outside, maybe. But you haven't told me everything."

She rose onto her arm and rested her hand on his face. "I know. And I will tell you. Just…not tonight. Can we just enjoy being together for a while?"

"We absolutely can."

"Is the salt still working?"

Funny that her mind immediately went to the salt at the mention of her keeping things from him. What could have possibly happened to her to make her so afraid of spirit energy?

"Probably not, but I have a dreamcatcher." He pointed to the round, feathered web hanging above his bed. "It works like the salt to trap negative energy."

She eyed him skeptically.

"Salt blocks out all energy, good and bad. The dreamcatcher only traps the bad, but I promise it will keep the nightmares away."

She chewed her bottom lip and stared intently into his eyes as if deciding whether or not to trust him. "Are you sure?"

His chest ached at her hesitation. What would it take for her to trust him? "I'm positive. But if you don't believe me, you're welcome to grab some salt from the kitchen and pour it around the bed."

"No. I believe you." She settled next to him and rested her head on his chest.

Finally, he'd managed to chip away a little of this wall she'd built in her mind. He didn't care how long it took, she would learn to trust him—and hopefully open her heart to love him.

# CHAPTER FOURTEEN

*E*mily shot up in bed, clutching her chest, her heart threatening to beat a hole through her ribs. She gasped for breath and wiped the tears from her cheeks as she tried to banish the images of the dream from her mind.

Sean sat up and wrapped his arms around her. "What's wrong, sweetheart?" The deep, sleepy sound of his voice and the warmth of his embrace helped to slow her breathing.

"I thought you said that thing would keep me from having nightmares." She flung her hand toward the dream-catcher hanging on the wall above the headboard.

He brushed her sweat-dampened hair from her face. "It traps negative energy. If you had a bad dream, it must've come from your mind. What happened?"

She inhaled a shaky breath and shook her head. It had come from her mind. It had to have. "It doesn't matter."

He guided her head to the pillow and took her hands in his. "It might help to talk about it."

She opened her mouth to say no, but she hesitated. It

was just a dream. What harm could talking about a dream bring? "It was my sister. She was trying to tell me something, but her voice sounded strangled. Something about locking. Keep it locked, I think. Is the door locked?"

"Yes. I set the alarm as soon as we got home."

"It's probably just my overactive imagination. After the vandalism at my apartment, I'm paranoid about locking doors."

"Do you want to call her? Maybe it'll put your mind at ease to hear her voice."

A lump formed in her throat as she swallowed the dryness from her mouth. She toyed with the corner of the pillowcase, unable to meet his gaze. "I can't call her. She died a year ago."

"I'm so sorry. I didn't know." He pressed his lips to her forehead. "What happened?"

Oh, no. She'd been avoiding this conversation for a month now. Did she really want to open this can of worms at six o'clock in the morning? She didn't want to open it ever, but looking at Sean's furrowed brow, the concern in his dark brown eyes… He deserved the truth—at least a slice of it.

"She killed herself." There. She'd said it. That wasn't so bad. He didn't need to know all the details leading up to her death. The fact that she'd died was enough. He pulled her close, and she snuggled into the comfort of his strong arms.

"I'm sorry. That must have been so hard for you."

"I'd rather not talk about it."

He pressed his nose against her head and inhaled deeply. "Sometimes talking—"

"Sean, please. I can't." She wouldn't. That was not her

sister's spirit trying to make contact; it was a dream. Nothing more.

"Okay."

They lay together in silence, Sean's rhythmic breathing lulling her senses, calming her frazzled nerves. Her lids fluttered; she couldn't fight the heaviness in her eyes, and she let them close. Content to be nestled in the safety of Sean's embrace, she allowed sleep to pull her under again. His sudden intake of breath roused her from her short slumber.

"Did your sister look like you?"

Not this again. Why wouldn't he let it go? "No, she looked like my dad. I look more like my mom."

He rose onto his elbow, and a strange urgency lit in his eyes. "What did she look like?"

"Blonde. Brown eyes. A few inches shorter than me. Why?"

"And her voice sounded strangled in your dream?" Excitement danced in his eyes, but his brow still creased in concern.

"Yes, but can we not talk about it?"

"Hold on." He dove to the other side of the bed and grabbed his sketchbook. Flipping through the pages, he settled on one and clutched it to his chest. "I saw a blonde woman in my dreams too."

She narrowed her eyes. What was he getting at?

"I've been dreaming about her." He turned the book around to show her the picture, and her stomach tied in a knot.

He'd perfectly captured the sad look Jessica's eyes always held when Emily refused to talk about ghosts. Her bobbed haircut. The mole above her lip. There was no mistaking this for anyone else. Sean had drawn her sister.

Her hand shook as she reached for the sketchpad. It wasn't possible. "How did you? Did you see a picture of her in my apartment?"

He pressed his lips together and shook his head.

"How did you know what she looked like?" Embers of thought warmed at the back of her mind. If she allowed them to spark, she'd know exactly how he knew what she looked like, but she squelched the ideas before they could form.

"I think you know, and I think it's time to talk about it."

"No." She gave her head an adamant shake. "No, you saw a picture of her. It's the only explanation." It had to be. But the embers ignited. The thoughts began to swirl.

*No.*

She wouldn't allow her mind to go there. She couldn't.

"Emily, I didn't see a picture. I saw her spirit."

"No." Her hands trembled as she flipped to the next page of the sketchpad. Blank. She turned back a page, and he reached for the book.

"Don't look at that one."

She yanked it away and peered at the sickening image. The bulging eyes. The rope burn on her neck. Tears pooled in Emily's eyes, cascading down her cheeks. "This is what she looked like when I found her." Her voice was barely a whisper forced over the lump of hot coal wedged in her throat. "Is this some kind of joke?" She wanted to look away, but she couldn't tear her gaze from the page.

"No. I would never joke like that, Emily. I hope you know that."

She chanced a glance at Sean, but the hurt in his eyes was too much to bear. She focused on the drawing. Emily had been the one to cut the rope while Robert held on to

Jessica's lifeless body and lowered it to the ground. A sickening feeling churned in her stomach, and the page tore under her clenched grip.

Sean pried the book from her hands and set it on the nightstand. "Sometimes spirits have a hard time crossing back over. When they first try, the only way they can show themselves is in their death state. The first few times she appeared to me, this is what she looked like. As she gained strength, she was able to appear as she looked in life."

"No, Sean. Just…no." She rolled out of bed, kicking the tangled sheets from around her legs and stumbling to the bathroom.

Leave. She needed to leave.

"Emily."

"No." She shoved her legs into her pants and pulled her shirt over her head. Clutching her shoes and underwear in her hands, she stomped to the door. She couldn't stay here. Couldn't think about this. Ghosts weren't real. Her sister hadn't visited her in her dream.

"Emily, wait."

She was vaguely aware of Sean following as she threw open the door, and the alarm beeped a countdown.

"Damn it, Emily. Stop." He punched in the code and followed her out the door.

The damp grass on her bare feet sent a chill running up her spine to the top of her neck. She fumbled to put her shoes on and dropped her bra in the grass.

Away. She focused on the only safe thought. She had to get away.

"Where are you going to go? We came here in my car." Sean leaned against the door frame and crossed his arms. Barefoot and bare-chested, his hair tousled from sleep, he was the epitome of sexy. She instinctively stepped toward him.

A pang shot through her heart. She couldn't do this. As much as she cared for him, she couldn't continue to live in denial when he made his living on the one thing she wanted to avoid. Sean could see ghosts; therefore, they had to be real. Her knees nearly buckled as she finally allowed the thought to take hold in her mind.

Ghosts were real.

She shook her head. She couldn't deal with this now. "I want to go home."

"I want you to stay." He walked down the steps and held out his arms. "Please, Emily. You can trust me."

She stood in the yard, the morning fog dampening her skin, and looked at the road. She couldn't walk all the way to the French Quarter with her underwear in her hand, so she shoved them into her purse and looked at Sean. If she were to trust anyone with this secret, it was him. But could she trust her own mind? She took a tentative step toward the sidewalk.

He didn't make a move to stop her, but his pleading gaze pinned her to the spot. "Please come inside."

Taking one last look at the street that could lead her away from the explosion of worms opening this can would cause, she nodded and shuffled back inside. He didn't reach for her as she passed, allowing her to come in willingly.

She could do this. It was only a conversation. She settled onto the sofa as he closed and locked the front door. She took a deep breath in and let it out slowly, clutching her trembling hands in her lap. "How long has she been talking to you?"

Sean sat next to her and rested his hand on her knee. "It started shortly after I met you."

That made sense. If Jessica was trying to contact her, she'd find someone who was open to spirits. But why on earth would her sister need to talk to her now, after a year? "Why do you—"

Her phone rang from her purse, and she shoved her hand inside to grab it. Thankful for the interruption, she answered it even though the number was blocked.

Sean sighed and leaned back into the sofa, his irritation obvious. But she needed a distraction. Anything to postpone swimming her way out of this sea of denial.

"Hey, Emily. How are you this morning?"

A flush of ice washed through her veins at the sound of Phillip's voice. "What do you want?"

"To talk to you. I miss you, and you haven't been returning my calls."

She tightened her grip on the phone and lowered her voice. "Is that why you blocked your number?"

"Well, you wouldn't have answered if I didn't."

Her eyes rolled involuntarily. "It's six-thirty in the morning, Phillip. Why are you calling?"

Sean arched an eyebrow, and she gave him an apologetic smile. The tension in the room was already palpable. But now with her boyfriend sitting next to her and her ex-boyfriend on the phone, she could've sliced through the pressure with a butter knife.

"Why are you in the Garden District this early in the morning? I thought you lived in the French Quarter."

"How do you know where I live? Wait…how do you know where I am?"

Phillip laughed. The sound used to be music to her ears, but now it sounded slimy and cruel. "You never turned off location sharing on your phone. C'mon, Em, you know deep down you wanted me to find you."

"No. That's creepy." She glanced at Sean, who sat silently watching her, an expectant look on his face.

"You've been spending a lot of time at this address. Are you seeing someone?"

"What does it matter if I am? We broke up seven months ago."

"Are you screwing him? You must be if you're spending so many nights with him."

A spark of anger ignited in her chest and spread through her body like flames. How dare he have the audacity to speak to her this way? "Yes, okay? I'm screwing him. I screw him almost every night, not that it's any of your business. And I'm going to keep screwing him, and there's nothing you can do about. Don't call me again, Phillip." She pressed end and opened the phone settings menu. Her fingers trembled, but she managed to shut off the location sharing feature.

"We're screwing?" Sean sat rigid, his hands fisted on his knees. "Is that all this is to you?"

"What?" She dropped her phone into her purse. "No. Those were his words. I threw them back at him."

"So we're screwing." He shot to his feet and paced around the sofa.

"No, we're not screwing. He asked if we were, so I told him. What did you want me to say?"

"Oh, I don't know. Maybe that you have a boyfriend. That you're in a relationship. Not that you're screwing someone." The pain in his eyes broke her heart. Could she make this situation any worse?

"He caught me off-guard. He knew where I was. He knows where I live. I just…I'm sorry."

He stood there, his arms by his sides, looking so help-less. "Are you still in love with him?"

"No. God, no. I'm not in love with anyone…except… I mean…"

"Me? Don't try to say you're in love with me. I know you're not."

"Sean…" She reached for him but let her hand fall into her lap.

"It's okay, Emily. I know you don't love me. You're still holding back, and I get that you don't trust me yet. But here's the deal: you have *all* of me. One hundred percent. I feel like I've only got about half of you."

"You have more than half." And she did love him, didn't she? Why couldn't she bring herself to say it? "But my feelings for you are complicated."

"Why?" He sat next to her. "Why are they compli-cated? My feelings for you are simple. So simple it's not even funny."

He stood again and paced in front of her. "I love you, Emily. Completely. Unconditionally. With every fiber of my being, I love you." He let out a cynical laugh. "This isn't the way I imagined telling you. I was hoping for moonlight and flowers, but you need to know. I would do anything for you."

He held her gaze with the sincerest eyes she'd ever looked into, and despite everything…despite the ghosts, the trouble Phillip caused, the way he just told her…in spite of it all, she smiled. Sean loved her. And she loved him too. If she could only make herself say the words.

"Sean, I—"

"Don't, Emily. Don't say you love me just because I said it to you. I wouldn't believe you anyway. Not as long as you're keeping secrets from me. I know you believe in ghosts. I know you've had some kind of experience that left you scared to death, but you can trust me. I would never ever hurt you. I might even be able to help you."

Tears pooled in her eyes, and she reached for him. She needed the safety and warmth of his embrace to give her courage. She hadn't talked about it in more than ten years. "Please come sit with me."

He lowered himself onto the sofa a few feet away, so she crawled into his lap and buried her face in his neck. Her tears dampened his skin as he wrapped his arms around her, and she molded her body to his. She needed this man like she'd never needed anyone, but could she handle what opening herself up to him would bring?

"I'm so scared, Sean."

He stroked her hair and pressed his lips to her head. "I know you are, but we need to talk about this. I've been so careful not to mention my ability around you, and that's hard. It's part of me. It's who I am, and I've been avoiding that part of myself a lot since we met."

She sobbed. It wasn't fair to him. He deserved better. "I'm sorry."

"It's okay. Honestly, I haven't minded too much— aside from the headaches I get from blocking things out. It's been worth it to get to know you. To fall in love with you. But I can't avoid it forever. I see dead people. All the time. And I hope that's something you can learn to live with because I would be devastated if you left me."

She closed her eyes and inhaled his masculine, woodsy scent. She'd never felt safer than when his arms were wrapped around her. If she was ever going to deal with her past, right here with Sean was the time to do it.

Lifting her head from his shoulder, she gazed into his deep, dark eyes. "Okay. I'll tell you."

Sean wiped a tear from Emily's cheek and gave her his full attention. He didn't know how much she'd be willing to share, but he didn't want to miss a single syllable. Leaving her legs draped across his lap, she slid back and leaned against the arm of the sofa.

She sucked in a shaky breath and stared at her clasped hands. "I know ghosts are real because I've seen them before."

He held his breath, waiting for her to continue. When she didn't speak, he rested a hand atop hers. "Take your time, sweetheart. I've got all day."

She nodded and pressed her lips together hard like she was trying to hold back tears. "I have vague memories of seeing them as a child. My sister and I both saw them, I think, but our mom would always tell us to ignore them. Pretend they weren't there. It must've worked because, like I said, the memories I have are vague and from when I was very little. I guess I blocked them out?"

She looked at him now, and he nodded, encouraging her to continue.

"Anyway," she cast her gaze to their hands, "I stopped seeing them when I was awake, but they always came to me in my dreams." She traced the tendons in his hand with her finger. "I don't know why I couldn't block them from my dreams. I tried, but they kept coming." She let out a long sigh and laced her fingers through his, never lifting her gaze.

"That's normal, you know? Not being able to block them from your dreams. Even I can't do that. You're much more open when you're sleeping. You can't block the channel."

She glanced at him, the corners of her mouth turning up into a sad smile. "Well, my mom did some research and discovered the salt trick. They never bothered me again after that."

"Dreamcatchers do work, by the way. I wasn't lying about that. They only trap negative energy." He clamped his mouth shut. This wasn't about him. He needed to stay quiet and let her say what she needed to say.

"I know. I didn't think you were lying. I do trust you, despite how I may come across."

"So you've been blocking out the spirits since you were a kid?" He needed to get her back on track. There had to be more to the story.

"Sort of. When I was sixteen, Jessica was eighteen. Her boyfriend, Ricky, was murdered, his body dumped in the bay. It was gang-related; he wasn't the nicest guy." She let out a cynical laugh. "I hate to admit it, but at the time I was relieved. It's not the kind of lifestyle you want for your sister, you know?"

"I can see why you'd feel that way."

She turned his hand over and traced patterns on his palm. "Jessica was devastated, of course. She sat in her room and cried all the time. No one knew who killed him, and that killed her. So we tried to contact him. Jessica and I took Trish to the cemetery to Ricky's grave. He hadn't been buried a week. The upturned earth was still fresh."

She wiped a tear and shook her head. "God, I can still smell the damp dirt. The piles of decaying flowers. The grave was new; the dirt hadn't settled, so we set the Ouija board on the mound of mud over his coffin, Jessica and I on one side and Trish on the other. We sat with our knees in the dirt, our fingers on the planchette, and we called to Ricky."

She rubbed her hands over her face and tipped her head back. "I can't believe I'm talking about this."

"You're doing great, sweetheart." He rested his hands on her thighs and gave a light squeeze. "Please keep going. You called Ricky…"

"We called to him, and nothing happened. It was June, and the air was sticky-wet like it usually is in Houston in the summer. I let go of the planchette and sat on my heels. I said, 'This isn't working. Maybe we just imagined seeing ghosts when we were kids.' Boy, was I wrong.

"A frigid gust of wind flipped the Ouija board off the grave, and the plastic planchette shattered against a tombstone. It felt like my blood turned to ice, and my goose bumps grew so hard it felt like needles piercing my skin all over."

She shivered and wrapped her arms around herself. "I was so scared."

"Hey." He reached for her, pulling her back onto his lap. "It's okay. You're here with me now, and I will keep you safe. Do you need to stop?" *Please don't stop.* He needed to hear how the story ended.

"No. I'm okay. I just haven't thought about this in a long time. Ricky was there, along with what seemed like every other corpse in the graveyard. Looking back, there were maybe five other spirits, but to a panicked sixteen-year-old it felt like more."

"I can imagine."

"And they all looked…well, like that first picture you drew of Jessica. They were mangled and messy, bloated and bloodied. Ricky had a bullet hole in the center of his forehead, and a single stream of blood oozed down to his right eye. I know Jessica saw them too, because she went whiter than a sheet and her mouth hung open. She was frozen to the spot.

"I screamed, and as soon as I did, Trish jumped up and ran. I grabbed Jessica by the arm and dragged her away, all the while yelling at the spirits to go away and not follow us. I've never been so scared in my life."

"Wow. That must've been awful. Did Trish see them too?"

"No. She didn't see a thing. She felt the wind and saw the board fly, but she only ran because I screamed. I started having nightmares—obviously from my imagination because I poured the salt extra heavy after that. So…I convinced myself it wasn't real. That ghosts didn't exist. Jessica went the opposite way. She was obsessed. She tried again and again to contact Ricky, but I guess he didn't want to talk to her. She found others to talk to, or she told me she did, anyway. Of course, I didn't believe her. It started to affect our relationship. I didn't want to be around her anymore, because all she wanted to talk about was ghosts. She was upset with me for 'ignoring my gift,' even though I didn't believe in it.

"Finally, she stopped talking about it, but our relationship was never the same after that. There was always a heavy weight between us that we couldn't get rid of."

"I'm so sorry. That must have been hard." Thank goodness she was telling him this. Opening up to him. He couldn't imagine having that same heavy weight between the two of them.

"I was always worried about her. She really was obsessed. Always trying to find ways to communicate with the dead. And not the way your ghost hunting team does with investigative equipment and stuff. I mean séances, and spells and rituals. Magic. She'd do anything to communicate with spirits.

"It finally broke her. I think she went crazy. She got so moody—sad one minute, furious the next. Robert—that's her husband—he didn't know what to do. We would trade off taking care of her, but she didn't want to talk to us. Then one day, he called me. He said she'd locked herself in an upstairs bedroom for two hours and wouldn't come out. He wanted me to come talk to her."

She stared straight ahead, her eyes not seeming to focus on anything, and a tear rolled down her cheek. "I talked to her through the door for fifteen minutes, but she didn't respond. Finally, we broke the damn thing down and found her. The bedroom had attic access. She'd tied a rope…" A choked sob escaped her throat, and she covered her mouth with her hand.

"Oh, sweetheart, you don't have to say any more."

"No. No, I need to finish." She inhaled deeply and set her jaw. "She'd tied a rope to a rafter and wrapped it around her neck. Robert held on to her while I cut her down. She looked exactly like that picture you drew."

"I'm so, so sorry. I can't even begin to imagine what you must've felt. And then to see the picture. I should've been more careful."

She shook her head. "It's okay."

"No, it's not okay. I'm sorry I made you relive that horrible memory."

She brushed her tear-salted lips to his and pressed her forehead against his. "Don't be sorry. I'm glad you know."

"You think your sister went crazy from her gift, and you're afraid the same thing will happen to you?"

"I'm fine as long as I ignore it. I haven't had a problem

since I convinced myself ghosts weren't real, and if I continue this way, I'm not worried. But…"

"But you are worried about me."

"Yes."

"I can assure you there's nothing to worry about. I've been this way my entire life, and I'm one of the sanest people you'll ever meet. I never let spirits use my own energy, and I definitely do not practice any kind of magic—black, white, or any other color. Have I ever done anything to make you question my sanity?"

"No." She bit her bottom lip.

"We can make this work, Emily. Please give me a chance. You might see me talking to invisible people from time to time, but I promise that's as crazy as it gets. And if you want to learn to use your gift, I can help."

She shook her head adamantly. "No. I haven't seen a ghost since I was sixteen, and I don't want to ever see one again."

"Okay. Then keep that channel blocked. You can believe in ghosts without actually letting them in. But will you be okay with me seeing them?"

The muscles in her throat worked as she swallowed. "Are you sure you won't go crazy?"

"Positive."

She finally offered a small smile. "Okay. We'll give it a try."

Relief unfurled in his chest, the tension releasing with his breath. "Thank you."

She furrowed her brow, opening her mouth to speak but hesitating. "Do you…do you think you can find out what my sister wants?"

"I've been trying to for the past month." And Emily must be whom she wanted him to help. Now the question was, what did she need help with? "Since I know her name now, it should be easier to communicate with her."

Her gaze darted about the room. "Could she be here now?"

"I don't allow spirits to enter my home."

"Only your dreams?"

"That I can't help. Can we talk about your apartment now? Do you really think it was vandals?"

She inhaled deeply and slid off his lap, sitting cross-legged on the couch. "I guess it could have been Jessica. Maybe it was her way of warning me to be sure my door is locked?"

"Why do you think it was her?" He tried to hide the doubt in his voice. A benevolent spirit wouldn't cause that much damage, even if she were trying to make a point.

She turned her hand and gazed at the tattoo on the inside of her wrist. "That butterfly statue was Jessica's."

He traced his finger across the delicate design. "The reason you like butterflies."

A dry laugh slipped from her lips. "I hate butterflies."

"Then why the tattoo?"

She shook her head and clenched her hands in her lap. "I gave her that statue when I was ten years old. She didn't have anything with butterflies on it; I just thought it was pretty. After that, she started collecting them. She became obsessed with butterflies. Her curtains, her bedspread, her notebooks for school…everything had butterflies on it. I started her obsession."

"What's wrong with that? Lots of people like butterflies."

"That's not the only obsession I started for her. It was my idea to take the Ouija board to the cemetery to contact Ricky. I started her obsession with spirits. If I hadn't taken her to the cemetery that night, she'd still be alive today."

"Oh, Emily. Jessica made her own choices. You are not responsible for your sister's death." He wrapped his arms around her and pulled her to his side. No wonder she'd been holding back; she'd been carrying so much fear and guilt for so long. His heart ached at the years of torture she must've endured. No more. He was going to help her heal.

Her laugh turned cynical. "That's what everyone tells me. But you're right; it's time to move on. I came to New Orleans for a fresh start, and that includes letting go of my fear of spirits."

He straightened and turned toward her. "I know the perfect way for you to do that."

"Oh?" She eyed him skeptically.

"Tomorrow is Halloween. My team's investigating the ballroom at the Maison Des Fleurs, and I know the friendly spirits there."

"The children in the portrait?"

"That's a couple of them. Do you want to come investigate with us?" He tried to catch her gaze, but she wouldn't look at him.

She unfolded her legs to rest her feet on the floor and stared at her hands in her lap. "I told you I don't want to see spirits."

Kneeling in front of her, he placed his hands on her thighs and peered through the curtain of hair framing her face. He needed to see her, to gauge her reaction so he didn't push her too hard. "You don't have to see them. Just see the effects. Interact with them on a physical level, and you'll see they aren't scary. They're just people without bodies."

"I don't know." Her brows knit together as if she were considering his offer.

She needed this. If he could get her to go and experience the children, watch his crew communicate, she'd see there was nothing to be afraid of. He took her hands in his. "I'll talk to them before we go in. They won't try to show themselves to you. Sydney can't see ghosts either, and she'll be there. Please? Give it a try for me? If it's too scary, we can leave, but I promise you will be safe."

She chewed her bottom lip and stared at their entwined hands for what felt like an eternity. Finally, she met his gaze with a look of sheer determination. "All right. If I'm going to admit ghosts exist, I might as well be all in. I'll go with you."

Cool relief flushed through his body, loosening the knots in his stomach. He pulled her close and placed a soft kiss on her lips. "This 'us' thing…we're going to be okay."

She took a deep breath. "I hope so."

# CHAPTER FIFTEEN

*S*ean, Emily, and his crew gathered outside the double doors leading into the Maison Des Fleurs ballroom. He took off his Dread Pirate mask, shoved it into a gear bag, and ran a hand through his hair. He might as well have called it a Zorro mask for all the people who still mistook his character's identity. But it was worth it to see the smile on Emily's face when she showed up at the ghost tour earlier in the evening.

When she saw him, she squealed "Westley!" and ran to him. And in typical Emily fashion, she tripped over her own feet and ended up throwing herself into his arms. A perfect way to start the night. She even tagged along on his tour and actually watched the evidence this time.

She wore her usual work attire—slacks and a sweater —but a pair of cat ears sat atop her head, and she'd pinned a tail to her pants in honor of Halloween. She'd also painted a little nose and whiskers on her face. They were smudged now, but no less adorable.

He glanced at Sydney and tapped his own mouth.

"Might want to take out the fangs. We don't want to scare the kids."

"Ghosts can get scared?" Emily set the gear bag she carried on the ground and stretched her arms over her head. Her midriff peeked from beneath her shirt, a quick flash of pale, creamy skin that sent his heart racing. It was going to be hard to focus his mind on the spirits when all his body wanted was to be on Emily.

"They're just people without bodies, remember?"

She nodded.

"And the main ones we're trying to talk to tonight are the kids, so we need to be sure we're approachable. I'm going to go in first. Give me ten minutes to try and make contact, and then you guys can come in and set up the equipment."

Emily reached across her middle to rub her arm. He stepped close and lowered his voice so only she could hear.

"You'll be okay for ten minutes?"

She nodded.

"Sydney and the guys are here. And the ghosts are generally only active in the ballroom, so you won't experience anything until you come inside." He pressed his lips to her cheek and gave her hand a squeeze.

The door clicked shut behind him, and he walked to the center of the dark, quiet ballroom. Soft moonlight trickled in through the high windows, casting a silvery glow across the empty space. His footsteps echoed on the wooden dance floor as he made his way toward the stage. He turned in a circle, taking a deep breath and opening his channel to the spirits.

"My team is investigating tonight. Alice, Jonathan, if you're here, we'd love for you to come out and play."

The little girl giggled and appeared in front of him.

"Where's your brother?"

She pointed to the stairway leading up to a balcony. Jonathan lifted his hand in a tiny wave and disappeared.

He looked at Alice. "I have someone special here with me tonight. Her name is Emily, and she's afraid of spirits."

She put her hand on her chest and furrowed her brow.

"She's afraid because she doesn't know you. I need your help proving to her that ghosts aren't scary, okay? Will you help me?"

She grinned and nodded.

"Fantastic." He stood straight and addressed the room. "No tricks tonight if anyone else is here. You are not allowed to scare the redhead. And, Eli, you're not allowed to show yourself at all. Stay away."

He'd already informed his team there'd be no pranking Emily tonight. Hopefully the ghosts would cooperate. Since he didn't own this property, he didn't have as much power over the spirits. But they usually did as he said.

The door opened, and his team entered the room. Emily set her bag on a table and hurried toward him. She was trying to be brave, but her eyes were tight with worry. Hopefully by the end of the night, he could dispel her fears.

"What do you want me to do?" She splayed her fingers and squeezed them into fists over and over.

He needed to calm her nerves, so he pulled her close and slid a hand down her ass. "I can think of a few things."

"I'm serious." She swatted his chest and pulled away, a playful grin dancing on her lips. Mission accomplished.

"There are some toys in that bag over there. Set them up on the dance floor. I'm going to position the camera so we can catch any movement if the kids decide to play."

She took the bag to the middle of the floor and pulled out a red ball, some trucks, and a doll. As she turned to reach into the bag again, her foot bumped the ball, and it rolled across the floor.

She squealed and jumped to her feet. "It's moving already." She ran toward him. "The ball moved."

He clamped his mouth shut, trying desperately not to laugh. Eric snickered, and he cast him a warning look. The last thing he needed was for Emily to leave now, before they even got started.

"You kicked it, sweetheart."

She stopped and dropped her arms to her sides. "I did?"

He nodded, still trying to fight a smile. "Were we rolling, Syd?"

"Yep," Sydney said. "Everything's running."

"I can show you the footage. Your shoe bumped the ball when you were reaching for the bag. Do you want to see?"

Her cheeks flushed pink. "No. I believe you. I'll be more careful."

He shrugged, trying to play it off. "No worries. It happens to everyone. And now it's been what we call debunked. Most of the activity we pick up ends up being debunked as wind, machinery, human error."

He nodded toward the toys where Alice tiptoed toward the baby doll. "Look now, though. If the doll moves, that will be supernatural."

Alice reached for the toy, but her hand passed right through it. She furrowed her little brow and held her tongue between her teeth as she tried again. This time, she was able to focus her energy, and the doll's arm lifted when she grabbed it. The ghost giggled and clapped her hands.

Emily clutched his arm, digging her nails into his shirt. "Was that a ghost?" Her voice was strained, higher-pitched than normal.

He patted her hand. "Yes, but she's a little girl, maybe eight or nine years old. Look at the portrait." He pointed to the framed sketch adorning the wall. "Does she look scary to you?"

"No."

"Do you want to talk to her?"

"I don't. I can't." She tightened her grip on his arm.

"You can talk. She can listen. We have ways for her to respond to people without the gift. Sydney's talked to her before."

Sydney approached and put a hand on Emily's shoulder. "She likes to use the dowsing rods." She held out a pair of metal L-shaped rods. "You hold them like this, and the spirits can move them to answer your questions." She demonstrated holding the short end of a rod in each hand, pointing the long ends away from her body.

Emily looked at him, and he nodded.

"This is an EMF detector. It measures the electromagnetic field. When a spirit gets close to it, it makes a noise like this." He walked toward Alice and held out the device. The little girl rolled her eyes and touched it, making a high-pitched beep sound from the machine as a red light blinked.

"She doesn't care much for our technology, but she'll usually respond to the rods." He looked at the spirit, and she nodded. "What do you say, Emily? Want to give it a try?"

Emily took a deep breath and tried to calm her sprinting heart. Eric sat on the stairs holding a small gray device while Jason fiddled with a black cylinder. She pointed to the guys. "What are they doing? That looks a lot less…interactive."

"EVP session," Sydney said. "And that's a REM Pod. It also measures fluctuations in EMF."

She shook her head and looked at Sean. "I don't understand all your acronyms."

"EMF is electromagnetic field. A REM Pod radiates its own electromagnetic field and can detect changes in it. EVP is electronic voice phenomenon. Sometimes we can catch a spirit's voice on a recorder, even when you can't hear it with your ears."

"Can we do that instead?" The idea of holding something while a ghost moved it had her trembling.

"We will," Sean said. "I'll have a recorder running the whole time. But Alice really likes the rods."

Sydney offered the metal sticks to her, and she took them. She needed to get over this fear, and Sean seemed to think it was safe. Surely he wouldn't ask her to do anything that could get her hurt. "Okay. What do I do?"

"Sit here." He guided her to the steps leading up to the stage. "She'll move the left rod for yes and the right one for no. Are you ready, Alice?"

Emily nodded. "Oh, you weren't talking to me."

He sat next to her and bumped her shoulder with his. "Are you ready, Emily?"

"Ready as I'll ever be."

"Ask her a yes or no question."

"Okay. Umm…hi, Alice. I'm Emily. How old are you?" Nothing happened. She glanced at Sean.

"She can only answer questions with a yes or no answer."

"Oh, right. Sorry." She squeezed her eyes shut and berated herself for asking such a stupid question. "Do you like the ballroom?" The rod in her left hand slowly turned ninety degrees. Her heart rate kicked up, and her stomach twisted. "Oh, god. Is that a yes? Did she just answer me?"

Sean chuckled and rubbed her back. "She did. You're doing great. Ask her something else."

"What do you like about the ballroom? Oh, shoot. She can't answer that." She glanced at Sean, and his eyes grew wide.

"She said she likes the dancing. I've asked her that question many times, and she just giggles. Ask another question."

"Did you die here in the hotel?" The right rod twisted in her hand, and excitement bubbled in her chest. "Where did you die?"

Sean sat silently, staring at the empty space in front of her. "She said it wasn't a hotel when she died." He turned to Emily and lowered his voice. "Don't ask her anything else about her death. She doesn't like to talk about it, and I want her to stick around tonight."

"Okay." She swallowed the thickness from her throat. She was actually communicating with a ghost. "I saw the portrait Sean drew of you and the little boy. Is that your brother?" The left rod moved. "This is so cool."

Sean grinned. "You like Emily, don't you?" The left rod moved, and he held out the recorder. "Can you say that really loud so maybe she can hear you?" He paused. "And say again what you want her to do. I don't think she'll believe me unless she hears it from you." He laughed.

"Thank you, Alice. You go rest now." He took the rods and set them on the stage.

"She's gone?"

"It takes a lot of energy for spirits to communicate like that. She needs to recharge. But listen, let's see if we caught her voice." He pressed a button on the recorder and held it up to her ear. Sean's voice came through first, asking her if she liked Emily. Then a tiny, muffled sound.

"I heard something. What was it?"

"Let me turn up the volume." He pressed a button and the audio repeated more loudly. The voice was quiet, but she was just able to make out the words *she's pretty.*

She covered her mouth with her hand. "Is that for real? Did she say that?"

His mouth quirked into a crooked grin. "Are you still accusing me of faking evidence when you're sitting right here?"

"No, I…"

"She said it. And listen to this." First his voice asking Alice what she wanted Emily to do. Then *dance with you* in the quiet, feminine tone.

"She wants me to dance with you?"

"She probably saw us at the masquerade." He stood and offered her his hand. "How can you say no to such a cute little thing?"

"I suppose we can't." She took his hand and let him lead her to the dance floor. "Although it won't have the same effect without music."

"Got it covered." He pressed his phone screen a few times and "Just the Way You Are" played through the speaker. The same song they first danced to at the ball. He winked and set the phone on a nearby table, then swept her into his arms and twirled her around.

"You planned this, didn't you?"

"That feels like an accusation." He turned her in another circle and pulled her body closer to his.

"Don't tell me you just happened to have this song cued up and ready to play."

He pressed his lips to her ear. "Truth?" The warmth of his breath sent shivers running down her legs.

"Always."

"I was hoping to do this after everyone left. Just me and you. Alone in the ballroom. Doesn't that sound romantic?"

Her heart stuttered. "Yes, it does."

"But when Alice asked, I couldn't tell her no. This is still romantic, isn't it? Even with an audience?"

As he turned her, she caught a glimpse of the others watching them. Heat flushed her cheeks, and she buried her face in his neck. "It was until I saw them staring at us."

"Ignore them, sweetheart. The song's almost over." He gave her a final spin and dipped her so low, her head nearly brushed the floor. When he pulled her upright, he caught her in his arms before she had a chance to stumble and captured her lips in a kiss.

As she stood there in the center of the dance floor with Sean's strong, warm arms wrapped around her, she felt another pair of ice-cold arms slide around her leg. She sucked in a sharp breath and looked down, but nothing in her field of vision matched the sensation she felt. She looked at Sean. "Is she…?"

"She's hugging you."

Tears stung her eyes, so she rested her head on his shoulder to hide them. She'd been lying to herself her entire life, convinced she'd be in danger if she believed in spirits. That they somehow possessed the power to control her mind, to hurt her. Maybe her sister's obsession and eventual demise weren't caused by spirits at all. Maybe it was a personality flaw. Jessica did have a tendency to fixate on things. And standing here in the middle of the haunted ballroom with Sean and his friends, she didn't feel threatened or even frightened. Ghosts were just people without bodies, after all.

The cold embrace on her leg dissipated, and Sean hugged her tighter. "How you doing, Buttercup? Not too freaked out?"

"Not at all." She blinked back her tears and pulled away to look at him. "This has been amazing. I'm so glad I came."

"You and me both." Something over her shoulder caught his gaze, and he froze. At the same time, one of the REM pods sounded a high-pitched squeal, and lights flashed all over it. With one arm wrapped tightly around her waist, he rushed her off the dance floor, away from the culpable machine.

"Who is it?" Jason bounded down the stairs to join them, and Emily's sense of calm eroded into confusion.

"What's going on?" She looked to Sean and each of his friends as they gathered around her, but none of them answered. "Sean?"

"Is it Eli?" Sydney asked.

"He's not showing himself to me, but if I had to wager a guess…" Before he could finish his sentence, the table shook, knocking his phone to the floor. It bounced off the carpet and landed face-down on the wood. "That better not be broken," he muttered.

The next table closer to them shook, and a chair turned on its side as if someone knocked it over. Emily gripped Sean's arm and swallowed the bile that crept up her throat. The air filled with tingling energy, making every hair on her body stand on end.

Ghosts could be dangerous, just like she'd thought.

"Eli, I told you you aren't welcome here today." He patted her hand as if trying to comfort her. "Remember he's just a person. He can't hurt you without a body."

"If he can flip the chair over, I'm sure he can." Panic tipped in her voice.

"Leave, Eli."

"Leave, Eli," Sydney repeated his words.

Jason stepped forward. "Eli, go away."

"You aren't welcome here, Eli," Eric said. But the table didn't stop shaking.

"Emily, tell him to leave."

"Like that will help. He didn't listen to any of you." She stepped back, but her legs hit the edge of the stage.

"We don't own this space, so he doesn't have to listen to us. But if everyone in the room orders him to go, he will. Tell him to leave."

"Go away." Her voice came out as a tiny squeak.

Sean squeezed her hand. "Use his name, and say it like you mean it."

"Go away, Eli." As soon as the words left her mouth, the shaking stopped. The static charge in the air dissolved, and the heaviness in her chest lifted. Everyone around her relaxed, but she trembled as she tried to catch her breath.

Sean rubbed her back and shook his head. "Sorry about that. We haven't heard from Eli in nearly a year. I thought he'd moved on."

"Who?" She sucked in a shaky breath. "Who is Eli?"

"Our best guess is he was some sort of criminal in the late 1800s. He likes to mess with people. Move stuff around. But it's okay. We got rid of him."

"How did we get rid of him?"

"Spirits have to obey the living. Once we all told him to go, he had no choice. If we owned this space, we could banish him for good. As it is, he can come back after we all leave, but he usually doesn't cause any problems."

"Usually?" She wrapped her arms around herself and rocked back and forth. "He could have killed us."

"No, he…" Sean sighed. "Let's pack it up, guys." He picked up a recorder, but Sydney took it from his hands.

"We'll get the equipment. Go talk to her."

"Yeah." He pried Emily's hand away from her body and laced his fingers through hers. "Let's get out of here, sweetheart. We need to talk."

---

She was silent on the drive to Sean's house, hardly sparing a glance for him as they entered the front door and went to his bedroom. He picked up a container of salt from the kitchen and poured a ring around the bed as Emily climbed onto the mattress. He sat next to her, but she still just stared at her hands clasped in her lap. She didn't move when he tucked a strand of hair behind her ear and glided his fingers across her cheek.

How could he have been so stupid? He should've at least prepared her for Eli. Told her there might be one that liked to move stuff around. Then maybe she wouldn't have freaked. Or maybe she would have, but at least she would have been expecting it.

"Sweetheart, talk to me. Tell me what you're thinking."

She raised her gaze to his, her eyes full of distrust and confusion. "You had me going there for a while. I believed you."

"What do you mean?"

"The whole 'ghosts can't hurt you' thing. I fell for it hook, line, and sinker. I wanted to believe you, so I turned off the nagging little voice in my mind, the one that's kept me safe all these years."

"You are safe, and ghosts can't hurt you."

"He turned over a chair, Sean. And my sister might've been the one who tore my apartment up. If they're strong enough to do that, they can hurt you."

He inhaled deeply and rubbed his forehead. How could he explain this so she'd understand? "This is our world. Spirit energy can't touch us; it passes right through. If a ghost tried to hit you, his fist would fly through your body."

She shook her head. "I felt that little girl hug me."

"You felt her energy. Believe me, if she had hugged you any tighter, her arms would've passed through your leg. Alice has been a ghost for more than a hundred years. She knows how to touch people so they'll feel it, but she can't apply any type of pressure. None of them can."

"Then why can they move objects?"

"I don't know. That's just how it is. I've done a lot of research, talked to a lot of people, and everyone has the same consensus. Spirits can focus their energy to move inanimate objects, but not living flesh."

"How?"

"I don't know how. I'm sure there's a scientific explanation, but it doesn't matter. It is what it is, and that's always been good enough for me."

"It's not good enough for me."

"Well, sweetheart, it's going to have to be. I don't have another way to explain it. And what happened tonight with Eli…with the chair…that can happen in front of anyone, whether you have the gift or not."

She pulled her knees up to her chin and wrapped her arms around her legs. "What if he channeled his angry energy into you or one of the guys? You could have hurt one of us."

"Eli is just a person without a body. He can't do much more than what you saw. Ghosts can't affect your mood or your mind." Demons certainly could, but he wasn't about to bring up nonhuman entities when she still wouldn't accept human ones.

"So my sister…" She rested the side of her face on her knees and gazed up at him.

"A ghost didn't make her go crazy."

She closed her eyes for a long blink and unfolded her body. Scooting closer, she snuggled into his side, and the knot in his chest untied. He hadn't lost her just yet.

"I'm scared, Sean."

"I know. But I'm still the same guy. The only difference is now maybe I can talk about my work with you. Share more of myself, because I want to give you everything I have. Can you handle all of me?"

"I'm going to try."

He hugged her tighter and kissed the top of her head. "That's all I ask."

# CHAPTER SIXTEEN

"Thank goodness for slow days." Emily sat behind the reception desk with Trish and caught up on her paperwork. She had an office in the back of the clinic, but she preferred the company of her friend over the stuffy matchbox room.

Trish minimized her browser and spun around in her chair. "How have things been going with…you know?"

She shrugged and signed the last document before closing the folder and setting it aside. "Fine, actually." She could hear the surprise in her own voice. "It's been two weeks since the ghost hunt, and nothing really has changed."

"Is that a good thing or a bad thing?"

"I suppose it's good. Sean seems even happier, if that's possible. He talks about ghosts every now and then, but not constantly like I'd expected. He doesn't seem obsessed like Jessica was."

"And you don't feel like anything's messing with your mind?"

"He assured me ghosts can't do that."

Trish furrowed her brow and bit her bottom lip. "So back when we were kids…what you saw in the cemetery? And the wind and stuff?"

She took a deep breath and nodded. "It was real. It's always been real; I've been in denial." She'd been using logic as an excuse to convince herself ghosts didn't exist, but her reasoning hadn't been logical at all. She'd seen the spirits with her own eyes, and she'd been lying to herself ever since. "But that's over. I'm moving on, and I'm happy now." She relaxed the muscles in her clenched jaw.

Her friend beamed a smile. "And I'm happy for you. Of course, I'm sure staying with Dreamboat for the past two weeks has helped with the happiness factor too. You aren't sick of him yet?"

"Not in the slightest. But they're done with the mold repair. We'll be staying at my house tonight."

"That was fast. I thought mold problems took forever to solve."

Emily shrugged. "It was such a small amount and only in the kitchen. I must be super sensitive to it because they said most people wouldn't have noticed it until it got out of control."

"Huh. Lucky you."

The door chimed, signaling the entrance of a customer, so Emily rose to her feet to greet him. As soon as her gaze met those pale blue eyes, she froze. Her stomach dipped, and a flush of irritation warmed her veins. "What are you doing here, Phillip?"

Trish stood next to Emily and crossed her arms over her chest. "You've got some nerve, buddy."

Phillip spread his hands. "Em, baby, come on. You know you're happy to see me."

She crossed her arms to mirror Trish's posture and

clamped her mouth shut. It'd been nearly eight months since she caught the lying snake cheating on her, and she wasn't the least bit happy to see him now.

"Not even a little bit?" He held his thumb and index finger close together to indicate a small size.

"Please tell me you didn't come all the way out here to talk to me?"

"Oh." He forced out a chuckle. "Nah, I'm here with Bobby for the Saints game. You being here too is a bonus."

Her lip curled as she stared at the man in disgust. His slicked-back blond hair and narrow eyes. The cocky smile that used to melt her heart. All those things now screamed "cheater." How could she have ever been attracted to such a slimy snake?

"Well," she picked up a patient file and clutched it to her chest, "I don't want to keep you from your game."

He moved closer to the reception desk. "It's not till tomorrow night. You get off at seven, right? We can have dinner."

"I don't want to have dinner with you."

"Coffee?"

"Goodbye, Phillip."

He let out a dramatic sigh and shoved his hands into his pockets. "I miss you."

She tightened her grip on the folder, crumpling the edges. *"Goodbye,* Phillip."

"Bye, Emily." He shuffled out the door, and Emily plopped into a chair.

"Did you know he was in town?" Trish rubbed her shoulder and pulled out a chair next to her.

"I had no idea. He stopped texting me after I talked to him on the phone. But I had location sharing turned on all that time. He knows about everywhere I've been."

"Hopefully he'll take the hint and leave you alone."

She drummed her fingers on the desk. "You warned me not to date him. Remember?"

Trish laughed. "But you didn't listen. You were in love with being in love."

She squeezed her eyes shut and rubbed her forehead. "Am I doing the same thing with Sean? I mean, he's the first guy I've dated since Phillip. Am I being blind again?"

"Oh, hell no. Sean's different. And you didn't latch on to him the first time you saw him."

"I wanted to."

"But you didn't. You let it simmer. You thought about it. Trust me, I'd tell you if I saw any red flags, and I don't. Sean is perfect for you."

The tension in her shoulders loosened, and she sat up straighter. "He is, isn't he?"

"So perfect, in fact, if you weren't my best friend, I'd try to steal him for myself."

She arched an eyebrow at her friend.

"I'm kidding. But seriously, Mr. Perfect actually is perfect in this case. Don't let your past sway your thoughts on your future."

"Wise words from a single woman."

Trish flipped her hair off her shoulder. "Hey, I'm single by choice."

"I know."

―――――

Sean followed Emily into her apartment and set her suitcase by the door. A little pang shot through his heart at the thought of having to spend his nights alone now that she had her own place back. He'd gotten used to spending every evening with her, waking up with her by his side. But he couldn't keep playing house with her. She needed her own space. While she seemed to be adjusting to him talking about his ability, her jaw still tensed every time he mentioned ghosts.

He watched her walk the space, running her hand along the new sheetrock in the kitchen, trailing her gaze over the living room. A sad smile curved her lips, and her eyes didn't hold the excitement or relief he'd expected to see.

"Home sweet home." She shrugged and stepped toward him, pulling him into a hug. "Thanks for letting me stay with you."

"Sweetheart, the pleasure has been all mine, believe me." He closed his eyes and inhaled the sweet floral scent of her hair. He'd miss that scent lingering on the sheets after she crawled out of bed each morning. "It'll be nice to have your own place again. To not have to deal with me every night, right?"

"I guess."

He pulled back to look at her. "You guess?"

She slid her hands into his back pockets. "Maybe I like dealing with you."

The temperature around them plummeted, and Emily shivered. "It's cold in here. Let me turn the heater on."

Her sister's ghost appeared near the door, but Emily didn't seem to notice as she shuffled toward the thermostat. He cut his gaze between the spirit and Emily as thoughts tumbled through his head. He hadn't seen nor heard from Jessica since Emily started staying at his house. How odd for her to suddenly appear when they came back to the apartment. Could be attached to something here?

"Help her." Jessica's voice no longer sounded strangled, but she still wasn't giving him any new information.

He glanced at the door and turned to Emily. "Lock it."

Emily furrowed her brow. "What?"

"Didn't you say your sister told you to lock it when she came to you in a dream?"

The ghost nodded, her lips curving into an encouraging smile.

Emily adjusted the setting on the thermostat. "Yeah. Why?"

"The door's unlocked."

"Oh, right." She reached for the deadbolt and turned the knob.

The spirit's posture deflated. That must not have been what she meant. Maybe she just wanted to be seen. For Emily to know she was there, watching over her.

"How would you feel about your sister's ghost being here, inside your apartment? Would you want her here?"

"No! Sean, I'm trying really hard to deal with this whole spirit thing, but I definitely don't want them in my house. Why? Is she here?" Her gaze darted about the room.

He hesitated. Should he tell her the truth? "Do you want her to be?"

She ran a hand through her hair and paced the room. "Oh, god. She's here. I don't… No, I don't want any ghosts in here. No offense, Jessica, if you can hear me. I need a safe place, Sean. You blocked them out of your house. Can't you block them out of mine?"

"This is your space. Only you can do that."

"How?"

"State your intent and mean it. Human spirits have to obey the living when they're in our realm."

She took a deep breath and blew it out in a huff. "I'm sorry, Jessica. But ghosts aren't allowed in my apartment. Please leave."

The spirit shot him an angry glance and disappeared. If he knew what the hell the ghost wanted him to help Emily with, he'd have done it already. "She's gone."

"Good. What did she say?"

"Same. She wanted me to help you, but she doesn't tell me what I need to do."

She rolled her head from side to side and circled her shoulders. "Maybe she was the one making me sick. I've got a headache now."

"Come sit down. I'll rub your shoulders." He'd never heard of a human spirit making living people sick. Emily sat between his legs on the sofa, and he massaged the tight muscles at the base of her neck. "Why do you think your sister would make you sick?"

"Maybe she knew about the mold. She knew I'd eventually get really sick from it, so she made me feel like I was getting sick, so I'd have it checked out."

It was a nice theory. Impossible, but nice. If an entity was making her feel this way, it wasn't a human spirit. But he didn't sense anything negative lurking in the shadows. Of course, if the entity were powerful enough, it could easily hide itself from his perception.

The hairs on the back of his neck stood on end. Could there be something else in the apartment? Could that be what Jessica wanted him to help Emily with?

"Other than the headaches, have you experienced anything else weird here? Any feelings of anger or strange temperature fluctuations?"

"Just the nausea that goes with the headaches and the

time everything got thrown around. Why? You don't think it was her?"

He kneaded his thumbs into her muscles, and they relaxed under his touch. "She won't be coming inside again, so if it was her causing the headaches, they should stop now." And he'd have to pay extra close attention to the atmosphere. Just because he didn't sense anything now, it didn't mean there was nothing here. "How's that?"

She rolled her head from side to side. "Better. Thank you."

He kissed her cheek and wrapped his arms around her as she leaned into him. It was possible something evil had resided here before Emily moved in. But if that were the case, she should have been feeling the effects from the beginning. He cut his gaze to the kitchen counter where she had that box the first time he came here. The space sat empty, and she'd told him she was getting rid of it. But if something had been attached to it, could it have stayed behind when she threw out the box?

"Emily, do you remember—" The chime of the doorbell stopped him midsentence. "Are you expecting someone?"

"No." She padded to the door and peered through the peephole. "Oh, for crying out loud." She turned the lock and paused with her hand on the doorknob. "I'm sorry, Sean. I'll get rid of him."

She swung open the door and crossed her arms over her chest. "What are you doing here, Phillip. I told you I'm not having dinner with you."

Phillip? Her cheating ex? Heat flushed through his body, and he shot to his feet. Wait. Why was he angry? Emily certainly didn't look happy to see the guy. He sat on the arm of the sofa closest to the door and relaxed his clenched fists.

"Can we please talk, baby? I miss you like crazy." His words sounded slightly slurred like he was balancing between tipsy and completely buzzed.

"Well, I don't miss you, and I've asked you nicely to leave me alone."

"Hey." His fingers grasped the door jamb, but his face still wasn't in view. "Whose Tesla is that in the alley? Those cars are fine."

"It's mine." A wave of possessiveness washed over Sean, and he stepped behind Emily and wrapped his arm around her waist. "And *she's* mine."

Phillip let out a nervous laugh and took a step back. His dirty-blond hair was slicked to his scalp, and his eyes were such a pale blue, they were almost transparent. Anger rolled through Sean's body like a freight train, and he tightened his grip on his woman's waist.

Phillip straightened his posture. "This is the guy you've been screwing?"

Emily stepped out of Sean's grip and rested a hand on his shoulder. "This is my boyfriend, Sean. Sean, this is Phillip, and he was just leaving." She stepped farther into the living room and tried to pull Sean with her. But Phillip didn't budge, so neither did he.

"I'm staying right here until you talk to me, Emily." Phillip crossed his arms and widened his stance.

Another rush of anger flashed through Sean's body, tinting his vision red. The next thing he knew, Phillip lay sprawled at the bottom of the stairs. Emily crouched over him shouting something, but he couldn't make out her words. He stood there in the doorway, staring at the scene as the memory of the past few moments slowly came into focus.

Oh, god. What had he done?

---

Emily glanced over the chart on the end of the hospital bed while Phillip lay there moaning and rubbing his head. Nothing like a fall down the stairs to sober a guy up. "They'll be releasing you soon. Nothing's broken. Bobby's on his way to pick you up."

"I'd rather you take me to my hotel."

She sighed and sat on the edge of the bed, resting her hand on the sheet. "That's not going to happen. *We* are never going to happen."

"Cheating on you was a huge mistake, and I'm sorry. What do I have to do to convince you?"

"I'm convinced you're sorry, and I forgive you. But I will never go back with you, Phillip."

He placed his hand on top of hers. "I love you, Emily."

"I don't love you. Not anymore."

He cut his gaze toward the open door. "Do you love *him?*"

"Sean?" She slid her hand from his grasp. "Yes, I do."

"He tried to kill me."

"He didn't try to kill you." Though she'd never seen so much anger in Sean's eyes. The way his face contorted with rage, she almost didn't recognize him.

Phillip crossed his arms and stuck out his bottom lip like a pouting child. "He pushed me down the stairs."

"He punched you, and you fell down the stairs."

"And then he just stood there like a zombie. Something's wrong with that guy, Em. He's crazy."

"Sean is not crazy." He was in shock. Surely he didn't expect Phillip to tumble down the stairs. She had rushed after him because she was trained to react in emergency situations. Sean wasn't; that's why he just stood there. "Don't tell me you've never been jealous before."

"There's something wrong with him."

"Hey, Buddy." Bobby stepped into the room. "You okay? I hear Emily's new boyfriend laid you out." He didn't even try to hide the humor in his voice.

"I'm fine."

Emily stood and made her way to the door. "I'm glad you're okay, Phillip, but we are over. Do you understand?"

"Yeah." He stared at his hands in his lap. She lingered in the doorway for a moment to see if he would say goodbye, but he wouldn't meet her gaze. Letting the door fall shut behind her, she padded toward the waiting room. Now she had to deal with Sean.

He'd been silent on the drive to the hospital. Once she'd examined Phillip and determined his injuries weren't life-threatening, she'd opted for them to drive him there themselves. She could tell Sean was still rattled, because he'd let her drive his Tesla. And he didn't even react when she nearly rear-ended a pickup truck that slammed on its brakes at a red light.

She found him in the waiting area, sitting with his elbows on his knees, his head in his hands. Tentatively, she approached him. Would she find that same scary-wild look in his eyes? The violent way he'd reacted to Phillip had been so out of character for Sean she was almost afraid to speak to him.

"Sean?" She sat on the edge of the chair next to him

and rested her hand on his back. "Bobby's here now. We can go."

"You're not going to take him home?" He didn't raise his head.

"Why would I?"

"I saw you holding his hand in there. I was going to come in and apologize again, but then I saw you…"

"Oh, Sean." She slid her arm across his back and laid her head on his shoulder. "He was hurting. I was comforting him. Nothing more."

He took three breaths before he spoke again. "Do you still have feelings for him?"

"Not at all."

He lifted his head and let his hands fall between his legs. "I'm sorry I hit him. You have to understand that wasn't me."

"I know. It was jealousy."

He sat up straight. "No, it wasn't even that. It wasn't *me*. I don't fully remember what happened, but I would never throw a first punch. Ever." He held her gaze with piercing sincerity. "I'm not a violent man."

"I know you aren't. Things got out of control. Tempers flared."

He shook his head. "I don't have a temper like that. Something made me act that way."

"You were standing up for me."

"No." He shot to his feet. "I mean, yes. I was standing up for you, but not like that. I think there's an entity in your apartment."

"But I told the spirits they weren't welcome." She lowered her voice and stepped toward him to avoid drawing any more attention. "You said that was all I had to do."

"That works for human spirits, but I don't think that's what we're dealing with."

"There's another kind of spirit?" Her stomach turned. "You had me convinced spirits weren't scary, Sean, but you didn't tell me everything, did you?"

He clenched his fists at his sides and drew in a deep breath. "I think it's something evil."

Her mouth fell open. "That's for real?"

"Evil is very real."

"And you didn't tell me about it because…?"

"Because you're having a hard enough time dealing with the existence of human ghosts. And evil doesn't just show up in your house. It has to be invited in. All I can figure is it was there before you moved in, or you brought it in with that box. You did get rid of it, didn't you?"

Her sister's box. She'd been so wrapped in Sean lately; she'd forgotten about the stupid thing. It was still sitting on a shelf in her closet, but she wasn't about to tell him that. The only thing inside it was a freaking crow feather. Nothing sinister flew out of it when she opened the lid, so that obviously wasn't the cause of Sean's tantrum. He just needed to deal with the fact that he was jealous, and he acted like a stupid man. Even Mr. Perfect was allowed to make mistakes sometimes.

She straightened her spine, but she couldn't meet his eyes. "I told you I would throw it out." It wasn't a lie. She did tell him that. And she still planned to get rid of it the first chance she got. A stupid chunk of wood was the last thing they needed standing between them. It would go in the dumpster as soon as she got some time alone, and she'd be done with it. No need to argue about it now. She glanced across the waiting room where a mother sat clutching her little girl and staring at them.

She took his hand. "Let's get out of here. We're making a scene."

He followed her into the parking lot and stopped. "We need to cleanse your apartment. Salt the perimeter and keep it fresh. We can pick up the supplies from my place and do it tonight."

She fought the urge to roll her eyes. He was as serious as could be about cleansing her apartment, and if it made him feel better about punching a drunk guy, she'd go along with it.

He shoved his hands in his pockets. "And once that's done, I think you need to stay at your place for a while."

"Why do we need to stay at my place? To make sure the bad guy doesn't come back?" She smiled, trying to lighten the mood.

He leveled his gaze on her. "Not we. You. To give you some space from me."

Her chest pinched. "What? Why?"

He sighed and ran a hand through his hair. "Because I've been smothering you. You've been a good sport about the ghosts and all, but I can tell even now you're having a hard time believing me. Maybe if you took some time on your own to process things, sort through your feelings…" He dropped his arms at his sides. "I love you, Emily, but I can't keep pretending you feel the same. Some time apart will do us both good." He shuffled toward his car.

"Sean, wait."

He stopped, but he didn't turn around.

"Please don't do this. I don't want to spend time apart. I want to be with you." Tears welled in hers, and she didn't try to stop them. This couldn't be the end. She couldn't let him leave her.

Shoving his hands in his pockets, he slowly turned to face her. "Emily…"

She stepped toward him, determined to keep this amazing man in her life, but she tripped over a parking block and fell face first toward the ground. He caught her before her face smacked the concrete and pulled her upright.

"Damn it, Sean. How many times do I have to throw myself into your arms to convince you I love you?"

His dark eyes searched hers with uncertainty.

"I don't want time away from you. I want to be with you always. Forever and ever. I love you, Sean. I've loved you all along, I just—"

He took her mouth with his, slipping his tongue between her lips to tangle with hers, and she lost herself in his familiar embrace. The firmness of his chest. The warmth of his body pressed to hers. The minty taste of his kiss, and the soft tickle of his tongue as it traced the bow of her lips. She needed this. She needed *him.*

Placing her hands on either side of his face, she peered into his soulful eyes. "Life without you would be…"

"Inconceivable."

"Unbearable."

"I love you, Emily."

"I love you too." She laced her fingers through his. "It's late. I've been working all day, and I'm exhausted. I think we should spend one more night at your house, and we can battle evil tomorrow. What do you say?" She leaned in and nibbled on his ear lobe.

He shivered. "It'll be easier to banish the bad guy in the daylight anyway. Let's go home."

# CHAPTER SEVENTEEN

*B*y the time Emily finished showering, Sean had already packed a bag full of evil-vanquishing gear, along with a stack of DVDs, two bottles of wine, snacks, and an overnight bag. He seemed to think once they performed their banishing rituals—or whatever they were going to do—they should stay inside all day to exert their control over the property. She was happy to play along if it meant spending the entire day snuggled up on the couch with the man of her dreams. Hopefully, once he was satisfied there was no evil living in her apartment, they could put the whole ordeal behind them.

As soon as they walked through her front door, Sean dropped his gear on the table and stood in the center of the room with his eyes closed. Aside from the rise and fall of his chest with each deep breath, he went utterly still. As the moment stretched on, anxiety tightened her chest. Could something already be affecting him?

"Is everything okay?" She rested a hand on his shoulder and gave it a little squeeze.

His eyelids fluttered open, and he exhaled a hard

breath. "There's a low vibration in the air I'd never have noticed if I wasn't looking for it. Let's work fast, so it doesn't have a chance to get to us."

He opened the bag and pulled out a giant bundle of herbs and a half-empty bag of salt. Handing her the salt, he pulled a lighter out of his bag. "This is sage. I'm going to do something called smudging. The smoke from the burning herbs will cleanse the area, and I want you to pour the salt around the entire perimeter of your apartment. Keep it along the walls, under the shelves and cabinets. Make sure the entire area is enclosed in salt to keep away whatever I'm about to force out."

"Okay." She smiled and opened the bag.

"Emily." He stopped her with a heavy stare.

"Sean?"

"This is serious. I know you still don't fully believe in this, but—"

"I understand. And I do believe you. I have experience with salt, remember?" She kissed him on the cheek and made her way to the bedroom, where she vacuumed the remnants of her old ring around her bed. She wouldn't need that if the whole apartment was protected.

She applied the salt around the entire room, even going to the back edge of the bathtub to be sure nothing evil could lurk behind the shower curtain. Her knees ached by the time she reached the closet, and she was tempted to apply the barrier across the front of the door and be done with it.

Sighing, she stepped inside and dropped to her knees again. She ran the salt along the baseboards, under her clothes and around the corner. When she reached the section of built-in shelving, her heart kicked up in a little sprint. That stupid box sat at eye level, taunting her.

Things were going so well with Sean right now, she couldn't risk him knowing she hadn't chunked it yet.

As soon as he left tomorrow, she'd toss it in a dumpster and be done with it. For now, it would have to be covered. She ran her hand across the top of the box.

Or she could keep it. Who was he to tell her what she could or couldn't have? It was her apartment. Her box.

She yanked her hand away and tossed a t-shirt over it. It was going in the trash tomorrow. End of story. She lowered herself to the floor and spread the salt in front of the shelves.

Rising to her feet, she moved to step through the door but ran smack into Sean's chest. She squealed, and he laughed.

"How's it going in here?"

"Oh, fine. It's all done. Time to move on." She grabbed his hand and tried to pull him away from the closet. "Come help me with the living room."

"Hold on. I need to smudge every room." He stepped into the closet, and she held her breath as he turned in a circle, releasing smoke into the air. "This space is for the living. All entities are now banished. You are not welcome here." He turned to her. "Repeat what I just said. You'll need to say it in every room."

Her palms went slick with sweat as she recited the words, and Sean stepped toward the shelves and peered at the floor underneath.

"I promise I was thorough." Hopefully he didn't hear the hint of panic in her voice. She did not want to get into an argument over a stupid chunk of wood.

He pointed to the ground. "You've got the salt running in front of the shelves. Make it go all the way to the baseboard in back. If something resides in the walls, we don't want to give it any wiggle room." He stepped out of the closet, and she let out her breath.

"Right. I did that in the bathroom. I'm not sure why I didn't here."

"It's okay." He grinned and kissed her cheek. "We're almost done."

She vacuumed the salt from in front of the shelves and poured a trail along the baseboards beneath them. Then she followed him through the house, reciting the words to banish the evil spirits, and he helped her finish salting the living room and kitchen. By the time they were done, her knees were bruised, and her back ached from crawling on the floor.

She plopped onto the couch as Sean opened a bottle of wine. "Vanquishing evil is hard work."

He laughed. "It is. But it's done now. I don't sense that low vibration I felt earlier."

"So we're evil-free?"

"It seems that way." He gave her a glass of wine and snuggled up next to her on the couch. "How's your head?"

"It's fine."

"And I don't feel like punching anyone, so I think we're good." He clinked his glass to hers and took a sip. "Movie time?"

"Sounds great."

―――――

They spent the entire day in her apartment, and Sean couldn't think of anywhere else he'd rather be than wrapped in Emily's soft embrace. As the last movie in their marathon ended, she sighed and rested her head on his shoulder.

"Everything okay, sweetheart?"

She slid her hand up his inner thigh, and his stomach tightened at the intimacy of her touch. "Everything's perfect." She lifted her head and placed her other hand on the back of his neck. "I love you."

His heart raced at her words. The sexiest, smartest, most amazing woman alive was in love with him. How did he get so lucky? "I love you too."

She flashed her seductive smile and flicked out her tongue to moisten her lips as she trailed her fingers from his leg up to his stomach. His jeans grew tighter across his hardening groin, and when she slipped her fingers beneath his waistband to brush his tip, he shuddered. "I think it's time for bed."

"I agree."

Taking his hand, she led him into the bedroom and slowly undressed for him. Never moving her gaze from his, she let each article of clothing drop to the floor until she stood before him, gloriously naked, and ran her hands down her own soft curves.

His fingers twitched with the urge to touch her. To take her in his arms and caress every inch of her luscious body. But the look in her eyes told him she wanted to take the lead this time, and he was happy to oblige.

"Take your clothes off."

She didn't need to ask him twice. He grabbed the hem of his shirt and yanked it up, but she stopped him with a hand on his stomach.

"Slowly. I want to watch you."

*Oh, holy hell.* The sultry sound of her voice turned his insides soft and his outsides rock hard. He slowly peeled his shirt over his head and dropped it on the floor. She raked an approving gaze over his chest and nodded.

"That's better. Now your pants."

He popped the button and slowly slid down the zipper, trying to give her the same sexy show she'd given him. She smiled appreciatively as his jeans dropped to the floor, but his shoes kept him from stepping out of them as easily as she had. Toe to heel, he kicked them off and nearly fell on his ass as he stumbled out of his jeans. "Sorry. I'm not normally this clumsy." He winked as he mimicked her classic line.

"Aren't you though?" She covered her mouth and suppressed a giggle. "Continue."

He dropped his boxer briefs to the floor, and her pupils dilated as her gaze locked on his dick. Her breasts rose as she took in a deep breath and licked her lips.

"Lie down."

"As you wish." He moved to the center of the bed and lay on his back. Every nerve in his body tingled in anticipation as she crawled onto the mattress and straddled his legs. She didn't touch him, but her gaze caressed his body as she looked him up and down.

She walked her hands up the bed and rose into a push-up position, hovering over him. Her long hair cascaded over her shoulders and onto his chest, the only sensation of touch she allowed him to feel. His entire body tensed in need as she leaned down to linger her lips a scant centimeter from his. If it were possible to die of anticipation, his sweet demise would be torturously slow. Her breath warmed his mouth, her soft hair tickling his skin as she parted her lips.

"Where do you want me to touch you?"

"God, Emily, anywhere. Everywhere. You're killing me."

She grinned, lowering her knees to the bed and running a single finger down his chest. "Anywhere?"

His stomach tightened.

"What about…here?" She wrapped her hand around his length, and electricity shot from his groin to his toes.

"Oh, god yes." Reaching his fingers into her hair, he pulled her mouth to his. Never breaking the kiss, she guided him to her folds and took him in, and he shuddered as her wet warmth enveloped him. He couldn't hold back anymore.

With one hand supporting her, he rolled her onto her back and made love to her. Her nails dug into his back as he pumped his hips, pushing harder and faster until he lost control. The intense release made his head spin, and when she screamed as her own climax overtook her, he collapsed on top of her, panting with elated exhaustion.

He pressed his lips to her ear. "Do you have any idea how sexy you are? That was incredible."

She glided her hands down his sweat-slicked back and squeezed his ass. "The pleasure was all mine."

---

"Emmy. Emily, wake up." The panicked voice sounded so much like her sister, Emily knew she was dreaming. She fought to keep her eyes closed and go back to sleep.

"He needs you."

She rolled to her side and reached for Sean, determined to ignore the dream voice. But the bed was empty, the sheets still warm where he had lain. She pried her heavy eyelids open and waited for her pupils to adjust to the darkness.

"Emmy, help him."

The temperature around her dropped as if a freezer door opened in her bed, and she whipped her head around in the direction of the voice. Her heart jackhammered in her chest as she focused on an image of her sister. Jessica wore the same clothes she'd died in, but her face appeared normal, almost living.

"Jessica?" This had to be a dream. She couldn't see spirits. She squeezed her eyes shut. When she opened them again, her sister wouldn't be there. She couldn't be.

She was.

"Save Sean." She pointed to the double doors that led onto the gallery. One door hung open, the salt ring broken where it swept across the floor.

Sean stood on the gallery, one hand clutching the railing and the other holding the wrought iron pole that led up to the roof. As he moved to hoist himself onto the rail, she sprang from the bed and ran to him.

"Sean! What are you doing?"

He stopped but didn't turn around. "Go inside, Emily." His voice was deep and gravelly like he hadn't spoken in a long time.

"You can't be out here naked. Come inside with me." She reached for his hand, but he yanked from her grasp.

"Go inside, or I will make you go inside."

"You'll *make* me? Come on, Sean. This isn't funny. What are you doing out here?"

"I'm going to jump." He pulled himself onto the banister and swung one leg over the edge.

"Like hell you are!" She grabbed him around the waist and pulled. As his body weight shifted from the railing to her arms, she lost her balance and fell on her butt. Sean tumbled on top of her but shot to his feet as soon as he hit the ground.

"I said get inside." His eyes were dark. Too dark. The pupils dilated until his irises were no longer visible.

She scrambled backward, crab-walking through the door and into her bedroom as he loomed over her, his face contorted with rage. "Sean, please. What are you doing?"

"I'm not Sean." He raised a fist to strike her when the air in the room turned frigid. Jessica rushed him, her spirit form passing through his solid body and making him stumble back. He curled his lip in a snarl and whipped his head around as if looking for the ghost.

Jessica appeared next to her. "He's the evil from the box. Get the box."

Sean grunted and stormed toward the gallery doors.

"I won't let you kill yourself, Sean!" She shot to her feet and grabbed him around the waist, but her strength was no match for his. He dragged her to the threshold, pried her arms from around him, and shoved her to the ground.

"I *will* kill him, just like I killed Jessica. Like I intend to kill you." The voice wasn't Sean's, but hearing those words from his lips was like a sledgehammer to her heart.

With an icy hand, Jessica clutched her shoulder. "Put him back in the box, Emmy."

"The box." That's what she'd wanted her to lock. She clambered to her feet and darted to the closet. Yanking the t-shirt off the chest, she scooped it into her arms, grabbed the key, and ran to the bedroom.

"Order him back inside." Jessica's form wavered, her spirit image becoming transparent.

"Help me, Jessica. I don't know how." She choked on a sob and set the box on the floor.

"I don't have the strength, but you have the power.

Order it into the box and lock it." As her image faded, so did the chill, like the freezer door closed.

"Get back in the box." Her voice came out in a squeaky whisper.

Sean looked at her and growled. With his hands clenched into fists, his veins protruding, he prowled toward her. Oh, god, what could she do? What would Sean say if he were himself? "Say it like you mean it," she mumbled. That's what he'd tell her.

She straightened her spine and looked the evil square in Sean's eyes. "I command you to get back in the box."

"No."

"Get out of Sean and get in the box. Now." She opened the lid, and Sean's face fell slack. A black shadow poured from his eyes and swirled toward the open chest. Another growl filled the room, but it didn't come from her boyfriend. It seemed to resonate from every corner of the world, grating in her mind like a freight train squealing down the tracks. As the shadow disappeared into the box, the horrid sound ceased, and the lid slammed closed.

Sean swayed on his feet, his face expressionless. She turned the copper key in the lock and raced to catch him before he fell. Guiding him to the bed, she lowered him onto the mattress.

Kneeling over him as he lay on his back, her panic turned to resolve as she went into nurse mode. His pupils shrank to a normal size, and his pulse felt strong and only slightly quickened. She ran a hand across his clammy forehead and rose to her feet.

"I'm going to call an ambulance. I'll be right back."

"No. No hospitals." His voice was thick and hoarse, but the venom she'd heard in his words earlier was gone.

"Yes. I don't know what happened to you, but you might need medical attention."

"No. Please." He rose onto his elbows and squeezed his eyes shut before pushing himself into a sitting position. "What would you say if a guy came into your clinic claiming he'd been possessed?"

She opened her mouth to insist he see a doctor, but she stopped. He had a point. "I'd check his vitals and suggest he see a psychiatrist."

"And how are my vitals?"

She sat on the edge of the bed next to him. "You'll live."

He stared straight ahead at the chest on the floor. "You said you got rid of it."

"I know. I meant to."

"Is it locked now?" He pulled on the lid. When it didn't open, he took the key from the lock and set it on the nightstand. "Where did you hide it?"

She took in a quick breath, prepared to insist she didn't hide the stupid thing, but she did. She'd shoved it in the closet and covered it with a t-shirt. The very definition of hiding. "It was on a shelf." Lifting an arm, she gestured toward the closet.

He clenched his hands into fists. "And you ran the salt line behind the shelf, so the damn thing was inside the circle of protection the whole time."

"You told me to put the salt against the wall!" She'd done exactly what he'd said. How was she supposed to know the box really held an evil spirit? For most of her life, she'd convinced herself ghosts didn't exist at all.

"I didn't know you had a conjure box."

"What the hell is a conjure box?"

He grabbed his clothes from the floor and curled his

lip at the culpable object. "The markings on the top? Black magic. Someone summoned a demon and trapped it inside that box. I should have told you exactly what it was from the beginning. If I'd known you still had it, I…" He shoved his legs into his jeans and fought to turn his shirt right side out.

"You'd what, Sean? What would you have done?"

He yanked his shirt over his head and looked her hard in the eyes. "I never would have stayed here. And I wouldn't have let you, either."

She threw on a robe and cinched the belt at her waist. "You wouldn't have *let* me? You think you can tell me what to do?" How dare he assume he had that kind of control over her? She was an independent woman; no one told her what she could or couldn't keep inside her own apartment.

His jaw clenched. "Why did you lie about it? Why did you hide it?"

"I planned to get rid of it, but every time I picked it up to take it to the dumpster, I…changed my mind." And changing her mind was her right.

"Because it was affecting you. You started getting headaches after you opened it, didn't you?"

She forced herself to hold his gaze. "Yes."

"And you didn't stop to think *that* could be the reason why?" He jabbed a finger at the box.

Her teeth clenched, and she crossed her arms. "No, I didn't. Until just now, the idea that an evil spirit could be living inside a box was ludicrous."

"Well, it's not so ludicrous now, is it?" He picked up the box, shoved the key in his pocket, and marched into the living room.

Panic surged through her chest. "Where are you going?"

"I'm going to get rid of this."

"No!"

He set it on the table and whirled around to face her. "No? The demon inside this thing has possessed me twice. I almost killed your ex-boyfriend, and I could have killed you."

Her jaw trembled, tears pooling in her eyes. "You tried to kill yourself. You only came after me because I stopped you."

"How did you stop me?"

"Jessica. I saw her." *Oh, no.* The evil thing said it killed Jessica. Her sister committed suicide. Sean was trying to throw himself over the gallery rail. All the pieces started clicking into place.

"She told you what do to because she's dealt with this demon before, hasn't she? All this time she's been begging me to help you, and it was because you wouldn't get rid of this goddamn box."

Anger seethed in his words, and he had every right to be mad at her. She lied to him. She'd had plenty of chances to come clean. To throw out the stupid chest. But she kept it, and she lied about it because she didn't see the danger. She was closed off to spirits, so it couldn't affect her the way it had affected Jessica. It couldn't get inside her mind so easily because her mind wasn't open to the supernatural.

Jessica's was, and the evil entity had preyed on her weakness. Her sister hadn't gone crazy. She was possessed. And the demon had possessed Sean too, because he was open to it. And as long as he kept himself open to spirits, he was open to demons. To danger and death.

She couldn't live like that. She'd spend every second of the day worried for his life. Every bad mood he took on, she'd wonder if a spirit was messing with his head. This was exactly why she'd closed her mind to spirits, and from now on, it would stay that way.

"I can't do this, Sean."

"You can't get rid of the box?"

"No, I can't do *this.* Us."

He froze, the anger in his eyes making room for confusion. "What are you saying?"

"I thought I could handle you and your ability, but I can't. The whole ghost thing? It's not…" She let out a frustrated sigh. She couldn't seem to force the words out. "I don't want anything to do with spirits. I love you, Sean, but unless you're willing to close yourself off to it all…to stop talking to ghosts…I don't think I can be with you." She tucked her hands beneath her arms to stop them from trembling.

His eyes softened as he knit his brow. "You're breaking up with me?"

"I don't want to. But are you willing to close your channel? Will you stop communicating with spirits?"

"That's like asking me to stop breathing. It's who I am. And if you're going to love me, you have to love all of me." He took her hand and clasped it between both of his. "This is silly, Emily. The only danger I've ever been in was because of that box. Just get rid of it, and we can put this all behind us."

She rested her free hand on the chest and stroked her fingers across the inscription. It wasn't dangerous as long as it was locked. She didn't need to throw it away.

He dropped her hand. "It's still affecting you. Don't you see? It's not just me. You have the ability too, and stuff like this *can* get to you. Maybe not as easily, but it can."

He snatched the box from the table and flung open the door.

"Wait!" Her heart sprinted in her chest, but her feet felt glued to the spot. The chest needed to go. She knew it did, but she didn't want to lose it.

"I'm getting rid of this thing before it hurts you." He stopped abruptly in the threshold and inhaled a deep breath, blowing it out hard through his nose.

Her lip quivered. "What are you doing? If you're going to leave, leave."

He turned around, a heavy scowl furrowing his brow. "I can't."

"Why not?"

"I physically can't get it out the door. It's stopping me." He shoved it onto the table, pulled out his phone, and tapped on the screen.

"What are you doing?"

"I'm sending you the contact information for a Voodoo priestess. If you won't get rid of the box, at least get her to exorcize it."

She scoffed. "Voodoo, Sean? Really?"

"Either call her or a Catholic priest."

"I think you should go." As soon as the words left her lips, she wanted to take them back. She didn't want him to leave. She wanted to be with him always, but she couldn't deal with the spirits. She couldn't watch another person she loved lose his life for the love of ghosts.

He looked at her hand resting on the chest and let out a cynical laugh. "Since you seem to care more about that damn box than me, I guess I should." His jaw set stubbornly, and he pinned her with a heated gaze as if daring her to contradict him.

She crossed her arms over her chest. He didn't understand. It wasn't about the stupid box; it was about him being susceptible to who-knew-what other kinds of evil things lurking in the shadows. It was about her keeping her sanity and not being in a constant state of worry.

"Please call the priestess."

She held his gaze, refusing to respond. She didn't trust her own voice. If she tried to speak now, she'd only ask him to stay.

He inhaled a deep breath. "Fine. But I'm keeping the key." He patted his pocket, turned on his heel, and marched out the door.

She watched through the window as he walked down the steps, stopping at the bottom to look up at the door. He kicked a beer can someone had left on the sidewalk and raked his hands through his hair.

A sob bubbled up from her chest, and she let the curtain fall, blocking her view. She'd just broken up with the most wonderful man she'd ever met. She didn't need ghosts to make her go crazy. She was already insane.

No, she wasn't. She was completely sane, and she wanted to stay that way. Being with Sean would only make her crazy. Breaking up with him was the smart thing to do. The right thing. She told herself that over and over as she sobbed into a pillow, trying to ignore the gaping hole his departure had left in her chest.

CHAPTER EIGHTEEN

"You're doing the right thing." Trish put a hand on Emily's shoulder. "I'm proud of you."

Emily sighed as she stared out the window at the woman approaching the apartment. The priestess wore a long, brown crepe skirt and a tunic in shades of orange and yellow. A burnt orange scarf encircled her head, and her dark hair poked out the top in tufts like an aloe vera plant.

"Even after everything that happened, it still took me two days to call her, though."

"You've always been stubborn." Trish gave her a comforting smile and moved toward the door. "Are you ready for this?"

A knock sounded, and Emily straightened her spine. Even now, with the Voodoo priestess right outside her door, she hesitated to part with her sister's box. The thing inside it was powerful enough to exert some influence, even through the locked lid. Still, she was drawn to it, which was all the more reason why she needed to get rid of it.

"Let's do it." She opened the door. "Hi. You must be Natasha." She shook the woman's hand and motioned for her to come inside.

Natasha's focus went straight to the box on the kitchen table. She glided toward it and set a pair of orange reading glasses on her nose. Her lip curled as she examined the inscription on the lid, and she shook her head. "Sean wasn't kidding. This one's bad."

"You talked to Sean?" Her heart fluttered at the mention of his name. He'd given her Natasha's number before he left, but he didn't say anything about calling her himself.

"Mmmhmm. The boy's been worried sick about you keeping this thing. Tried to get me to come take it by force, but that's not possible. You invited the evil in; you have to be the one to send it away."

She crossed her arms. "I didn't invite it in. It was sent to me."

The priestess arched an eyebrow. "And who carried it through the door?"

Her chest deflated, and she dropped her arms by her sides. "I did. How do I get rid of it?"

"You carry it out the door. Then I'll come back in and do a cleanse. Make sure nothing else evil is hanging around in here."

"Sounds easy enough."

Natasha grinned. "We'll see. Why don't you bring it out to my car?"

"Sure." She scooped the box into her arms and stepped toward the door, but a sickening feeling formed in her stomach. If she put it back in her closet and poured a salt ring around it, it couldn't hurt her. Getting rid of it really wasn't necessary, was it? As long as it stayed locked, it couldn't bother anyone. "You know what? This is silly." She put the box on the table. "I'm sorry to waste your time, Natasha. I'm going to keep it."

"Emily…" Trish touched her elbow. "Let her take it. You don't need it."

She rubbed her forehead, her thoughts scattering like billiard balls every time she tried to grab one. She'd called the priestess for a reason. The box had to go. "You're right. I'm getting rid of it."

Picking up the box again, she took two steps toward the door, but she couldn't force herself to go any farther. "I can't. It wants to stay here. You carry it, Trish." She shoved the chest into her friend's arms. As soon as she broke contact with the wood, her resolve to be rid of the damn thing returned. She marched to the front door and flung it open. "I want it out."

Trish started to shuffle outside, but Natasha stopped her. "Hold on a minute. This isn't going to work. Emily invited that evil inside, and she has to be the one to take it out."

Emily inhaled deeply and took the box from Trish. "She's right. Sean tried to take it, and he said he couldn't get it out the door."

Her body felt like lead; her feet melted to the floor. The thing in that box wanted to stay so badly, she couldn't tell her own thoughts from the demon's. With Trish and Natasha behind her, she forced herself to take three more steps. As she passed through the door, it felt like she was swimming through a wall of gelatin. She moved in slow motion, forcing one foot in front of the other through a thick sludge of anger and hatred.

As she crossed the threshold, her body felt lighter, the intense desire to hang on to the hunk of wood lessening with each step down the stairs. By the time she reached the bottom, she ran to the priestess's Toyota, threw the damn thing into the trunk and slammed the lid.

Her head spun as the elephant that had been sitting on her chest for the past month finally got up and walked away. A hysterical giggle bubbled from her throat, and she pranced back to her apartment. She vacuumed the salt from the baseboards while Natasha did her cleansing ritual, and when they were done, her entire apartment felt brighter, her heart lighter. The constant nagging pain in the base of her skull was gone. She was free.

"Thank you, Natasha. I can't tell you how much I appreciate your help. How much do I owe for your services?"

She waved a hand dismissively. "Sean already paid for it."

Emily looked at Trish. "How did he know I'd go through with it?"

Her friend grinned. "I don't think he's done with you, Em."

"You ladies have a nice day." Natasha stepped through the door and stopped on the porch. Emily started to close the door, but the priestess spoke again.

"Oh, no. That's none of my business."

"Excuse me?" Emily swung the door open, but Natasha didn't appear to be speaking to her.

"If you want a love potion, go see a witch. I don't get involved in other people's relationships."

Trish stepped next to her. "Who's she talking to?"

"I don't know."

"That's not part of my services. I was paid to rid her of a demon, not teach her to see spirits."

Her heart thudded in her chest, and she gripped the doorknob tighter.

"I don't…" Natasha let out a dramatic sigh and turned to Emily. "You got a dead sister?"

She swallowed. "Yes." Why was Jessica still trying to talk to her? She'd gotten rid of the stupid box. What more did she want?

"She's very persuasive." The priestess narrowed her eyes and marched back into the apartment. "And she says you should be able to see her, but you refuse."

"I can't. I…can't see ghosts."

"You saw her before."

"I was asleep. She came to me in a dream."

"You still saw her when you woke up."

Emily fisted her hands at her sides. "That was different. She caught me off guard."

Natasha sat in a chair and rested an elbow on the table. "She has a message for you. It would make my life a whole lot easier if you'd open up and see her so she can tell you."

Emily's mouth went dry. She wouldn't know how to open up if her life depended on it. She still had no idea how she'd seen her sister the night she helped her save Sean. "I don't know how."

"Well, I ain't got the time to teach you. What about your friend?" She nodded to Trish.

"I've never been able to see spirits." Trish lowered herself into a chair and folded her hands on the table. "Em, you need to hear what she has to say."

Natasha sighed. "I can't believe I'm about to do this." She pointed a finger at Emily. "This is only because Sean is such a great guy, and it involves him. Don't you tell nobody I did this for you, or there'll be a line out my door."

"Okay." She sat across from her. "What are you going to do?"

"Channel her. Let your sister's spirit talk through me." She threw a hand into the air. "But only for a few minutes. And first you're gonna have to prove you are who you say you are."

"Do you want to see my driver's license?"

"Not you. The spirit. Tell me something only you would know about Emily." She looked off to the left and nodded her head. "She says you had a crush on Tim Johnson in the tenth grade. Cried yourself to sleep every night when Trish started dating him."

Emily's mouth dropped open. Of all the secrets Jessica could have shared, she picked that one?

"You liked Tim?" Trish gaped at her. "Why didn't you tell me that, Em? I wouldn't have gone out with him if I'd known."

"Thanks a lot, Jess." She looked at Natasha. "It's her." She turned to her friend. "It's no big deal. You were so happy when he asked you out, I didn't want to spoil it for you."

"Emmy made me swear never to tell you."

They both looked at Natasha in stunned silence. Her entire demeanor had changed. She sat up straight, her hands folded in her lap, a huge smile on her face. And though her voice had the same tone, the cadence and inflections she put on the words sounded just like Jessica.

"Well, don't just sit there. She's giving me five minutes to talk to you, and I don't want to waste it in a staring contest."

"Jessica?" Her mouth still hung open, so she snapped it shut.

"In the flesh. Well…someone else's flesh, but you get the point. I need to talk to you about Sean, and since you refuse to see me in spirit form, this is the best I can do."

"But you… I just…" She had so many questions. So many things she wanted to say, but she couldn't form sentences.

"Hey, Jess. How you been?" Trish seemed to find her voice just fine.

"I'm good now. You have no idea how hard it is to cross over after you've been dead for a year. It took forever to figure out how to communicate. I've got the hang of it now though. How are you?"

"I'm great."

Emily looked back and forth between Trish and her sister in Natasha's body, having a normal conversation like Jessica was still alive. Why wasn't Trish freaking out like she was?

"Tick tock, Emmy. Are you ready to listen?" Jessica curved Natasha's lips into a smile.

"Yes. Wait. First I need to tell you I'm sorry. I shouldn't have shut you out like I did. Maybe if I'd listened to you, if I'd shared your curiosity for the spirit world…" Her heart wrenched, and a tear rolled down her cheek. "You'd still be alive if I'd listened to you."

"Come on. You saw for yourself the hold that box can have on you. Do you really think you could have saved me?"

"I could have tried."

She waved a hand in the air dismissively. "There's no way I would have given that box up. Anyway, it's water under the bridge now. There's nothing you could have done, so don't beat yourself up over it."

"But—"

"I'm here to talk to you about that hunk of a man you dumped for no good reason. Are you insane? He was perfect for you."

Emily crossed her arms and straightened her spine. "You know why I broke up with him. You were there."

"Because you're afraid he's going to die like I did?"

"That's exactly why. You don't know how hard I took it when you died. I can't go through that again. I won't." No matter how much she missed Sean, she couldn't be with someone who willingly put himself in danger like that.

"You won't have to go through it again. Sean isn't like me. He knows what he's doing. He's careful."

"You were careful."

"No, Emmy. No, I wasn't. Not at all. You were right when you said I was obsessed. I knew exactly what was in that box when I bought it at the estate sale. I willingly brought a demon into my house because I thought I could control it. I'd learned a little black magic and thought I was invincible. I was stupid, and I'm the one who should have listened to *you*. You were the smart one. Sean is a smart one."

She shook her head. She didn't want to hear this. "What he does is dangerous. It could get him killed."

"Driving a car can get you killed. I've been watching Sean since you met him. What he does isn't dangerous. He doesn't mess with demons or magic. He tried to convince you to get rid of that stupid box the moment he saw it, didn't he? He knew what could happen, and I guarantee you, he'd have done something about it if he'd known you still had it. And honestly, Emmy, the demon would have gotten to you eventually. Evil is dangerous for anyone, even those who don't recognize it."

Emily dropped her head into her hands and squeezed her eyes shut. "What are you trying to say, Jess?"

She folded her hands in her lap and sighed. "It's your fault the demon possessed him. Both times, but especially the second. Own it. Apologize. Stop being an idiot and get that boy back. Ghosts aren't the problem. Sean's not the problem. *You* are the problem. Get over yourself and get on with your life."

"I…"

"Oh, and I'm sorry about messing up your apartment. I was hoping you'd think the demon did it, and you'd get rid of the box. But you can be so stubborn."

Something between a sob and a laugh rolled up from her throat. "I love you too, sis."

"Seriously, though. She's kicking me out. I've got to move on too. Take care of yourself, little sister. I love you."

She closed her eyes, and when she opened them again, Natasha slumped in her chair. "Woo. That was more than five minutes, wasn't it?"

Trish brought her a glass of water. "Just a little. Are you okay?"

Natasha took a sip from the glass and waved her away. "I'm fine. I'm fine. And before you freak out any more, spirits can't enter your body like that unless you invite them in. Sean would kill me if I put any more crazy ideas into your head." She rose from the chair and swayed on her feet.

"Maybe you should stay a while." Emily tried to help her back into the chair, but she refused.

"I'm going home to sleep it off. Like I said, don't you dare tell anyone I did that. I've got enough people trying to take advantage of my gifts. Nobody wants to pay these days…" She continued muttering to herself as she shuffled down the stairs.

"Do you think she'll be okay?" Emily closed the door and plopped on the sofa.

"Probably. Seems like she knows what she's doing." Trish sat next to her. "Jessica's right, you know? It wasn't Sean's fault."

She sighed and dropped her head back on the sofa. "I know. But it was a lot easier for me to think it was. What do I do now?"

"Do you love him?"

"Yes. God, yes. More than anything, but I'm scared to death. I'll always be worried about him."

Trish shrugged. "That's normal. If he were a cop or a firefighter, you'd be worried about him. But you'd get over it, wouldn't you? Or would you dump him the first time he was in danger?"

"I suppose I'd get used to it."

"So, this is the same thing. Don't you think it's worth the risk?"

Trish was right. So were Jessica and Natasha. They were all right. She was throwing away her one chance at happiness because she was afraid of ghosts. Jessica didn't go crazy; she wasn't careful. Sean took every precaution he could. She'd seen him work; she knew it was true. So why was she still acting scared? She came to New Orleans for a fresh start and to add some excitement to her life. Sean had been both those things, and she'd dumped him.

"I'm an idiot."

"You have your moments."

"I need to apologize. I have to get him back." She

peeled herself off the sofa and grabbed her phone. When the screen lit up, the date stared her in the face. "Crap."

"What?"

"Today's Saturday. He's running that bachelor auction. He'll be busy all day." She dropped her phone in her purse and flopped onto the couch. "I'll have to call him tonight."

Trish sat up straight. "Or you could go there and surprise him."

"He'll be too busy to talk."

"Look, you go on and on about all the romantic things he does for you. Now's your chance to do something romantic in return."

She crossed her arms. "I don't see how showing up at a fundraiser he's supervising is romantic. He'll probably be annoyed."

Trish grabbed her hand and pulled her to her feet. "Just imagine it. He's up there on the stage, calling out the next bachelor when he looks into the audience. And there, standing in the aisle is the woman of his dreams who only two days ago broke his heart to pieces."

"Trish…"

"But now, here she is. Looking up at him with bright blue eyes. He drops the microphone and jumps off the stage. He runs toward you smiling, arms outstretched, and sweeps you into a passionate embrace. Before you ever get the chance to speak, his lips meet yours, sealing your future with a kiss."

Emily laughed. "Okay. I think you've been reading too many romance novels."

She shrugged and stuck her nose in the air. "It could happen."

"I suppose I could go up there. Maybe talk to him at intermission. Do they have intermission at auctions?"

Trish grinned. "Let's go find out."

———

Sean stood backstage in the Saenger Theatre and went over his list of bachelors again. Of the twenty men signed up for the auction, only two hadn't shown up yet. Eric was one of them. Sean grumbled under his breath and dialed his number. No answer. The kid better not flake out on him. The auction started in twenty minutes.

He dropped his clipboard on a table and ran a hand through his hair. This event happening so soon after his break up with Emily had been a blessing. He'd been so busy preparing for it, he only had time to miss her every *other* minute of the day. An image of her beautiful face flashed in his mind, and his heart gave a squeeze.

At least her sister was satisfied with the outcome. She'd finally found her voice—too little, too late—and thanked him for saving Emily from the demon. Though he hadn't done a single thing to save her. She was the one who'd rescued him. After she lied and put him in danger in the first place.

That's right. She lied, and he was angry with her for putting his life on the line. He needed to remember that, because being mad was so much easier than missing her. Still, he couldn't help but wonder how it would have played out if he'd paid more attention to Jessica's spirit. Maybe he could have found a way to help her communicate. If she'd have been able to tell him what help she needed from the beginning…

But he couldn't dwell on the what-ifs. He had an

auction to run and a life to live. With or without Emily in it.

Sydney rounded the corner and fixed a steely gaze on him. She'd been acting funny all afternoon, but she got that way sometimes, especially when one of her visions was bothering her. And he wanted nothing to do with her glimpses of the future. Been there. Done that. And there was nothing he could do to change the outcome.

"Everything ready to go, tech goddess?" He flashed a grin, hoping to ease the tension charging between them as she approached.

"Of course it is. But you and I need to talk." She jerked her head toward a dressing room and ducked inside.

"Hey, Sean. Sorry I'm late." Missing bachelor number one signed in on the clipboard. "Traffic was hell."

"No problem. Grab a drink. We'll be starting soon." *And Eric better get his ass here soon too.* He slipped into the dressing room and let the door fall shut behind him.

Sydney sat on the makeup counter, the ring of bright lights shining around her like a halo. She gripped the edge of the desk so hard, her knuckles turned white. "Why haven't you made up with Emily yet?"

He sighed and shoved his hands in his pockets. "She broke up with *me*, remember?"

Her feet dangled from the ledge, and she crossed them at the ankles. "I had a vision."

"And that's my cue to leave." He turned for the door.

"Wait, Sean. You need to hear it."

Gripping the knob, he rested his head against the door frame. The cool metal sent a chill running down his back. "Why, when there's nothing I can do to change the outcome?"

"You can change this. I know you can because you've already changed it once."

He let his hand fall by his side, and he turned around. "You think so? Because I sure as hell couldn't do anything about Courtney. You told me two weeks before she was going to die, and she *still* got in that car and wrecked it."

Sydney fisted her hands on her lap and swung her legs. "Because she had free will. Only she had the power to stop the car crash from happening. How many times do I have to tell you that? You did everything you could."

"And it still wasn't enough, so what's the point? I don't want to know what you saw. It doesn't matter anyway."

She hopped off the counter and crossed her arms. "You know who you sound like right now?"

He raised his eyebrows, waiting for her to continue.

"You sound like Emily. Pretending something isn't true doesn't make it any less real."

He opened his mouth to spout off a witty comeback, but the words didn't make it past his throat. She had a point. Wait. No, this was different. "I know your visions are real, Syd. I just don't want to hear them."

"Same thing." She let out a growl of frustration. "I've had two visions about your future lately. I won't tell you what the first one was, but it was a good one. You were happy. But something changed. Last night, I had a different one."

"Don't, Syd. I don't want to—"

"I saw you out with Paisley. On a date. Your mother was furious with you."

He laughed. "That'll never happen."

"It will if you don't do something to change it."

He put a hand on her shoulder to calm her down. "There is no way in hell I would ever go out with Paisley

Monroe. Even without the sordid family history, the woman's got a voice like a pterodactyl."

"I saw it, Sean."

He raised his arms and dropped them by his sides. "What do you want me to do, then?"

"Make up with Emily. Believe me, you *want* my first vision."

"How do you know what I want?"

"Because I know you. And I know you love her."

Wasn't that the truth? He leaned against the wall and ran a hand through his hair. "I do love her, but she lied. She almost got me killed."

"Did she apologize?"

"No."

"Did she at least have good reason to lie?"

He sighed. "A demon."

She crossed her arms and tapped her foot impatiently. "You're not mad at her, so stop pretending to be."

"She doesn't want me. She wants me to change who I am, and you know I can't do that. Sure, I could sell my company. I could stop doing investigations. But I'd still see ghosts. Always have, always will."

"She'll get used to it."

"She made it very clear that she wouldn't." He reached for the doorknob, but Sydney threw out her arm to block him.

"Fight for her. Make her understand."

"I tried. I—" His phone buzzed in his pocket. "Hold on, that might be Eric." He pressed the device to his ear. "Where the hell are you, man? The auction starts in five minutes."

"I'm so sorry. I've been puking all morning. I thought

I'd be okay by now, but…Well, I tried to drive out there, but I ended up vomiting in my car."

He tried to temper the frustration in his voice. "Are you hungover?"

"No. I wouldn't do that to you. It's a virus or something." He let out a hacking cough.

"All right. No problem. Get some rest." He pressed end and shoved the phone in his pocket.

Sydney chewed her lip and glanced at her watch. "I need to go cue the music. Think about what I said, okay?"

"I will." But right now, he had a more immediate problem. They'd promised twenty bachelors, and he only had nineteen.

# CHAPTER NINETEEN

"Wow. This place is packed." Emily scanned the auditorium for two empty seats together, but couldn't find any.

Trish giggled. "Who knew so many women were desperate enough to pay for dates?"

"It's for charity, so I think that makes it okay." She spotted Madeline standing behind the registration table. "There's Sean's mom. Let's go talk to her."

They wove their way through the crowd and made it to the table as bachelor number one entered the stage.

Madeline fanned herself with an auction paddle. "I hope you're here because you've come to your senses and realized my son is the best thing that's ever happened to you."

"That's exactly why I'm here."

"Good, because that boy has done nothing but mope since you broke up with him." She dropped the paddle on the table and crossed her arms. "What were you thinking?"

"I wasn't. But I'm here to make amends. When will this be over?"

"Oh, don't wait till it's over, honey. Go on backstage. He'll be thrilled to see you."

A roar of applause filled the auditorium as the bachelor left the stage.

Madeline nodded her approval. "Two grand. Not bad."

"Bachelor number two is Eric Landry," the auctioneer announced. "Oh, hold on. Maybe not."

Sean walked onto the stage and whispered something in the woman's ear. She grinned and adjusted her microphone. "Well, folks, we've got a special treat for you. Eric called in sick, so his replacement is Mr. Sean LeBlanc himself."

Emily's stomach dropped to her knees as a murmur fell across the audience. Well, what did she expect? She'd dumped him. He had every right to date whomever he chose. Still, the thought of him going ahead with the auction had never occurred to her.

"Uh-oh." Trish put a hand on her shoulder. "What are you going to do?"

Madeline rushed around the table. "I'll put a stop to this."

"No, wait." This was her fault. All of it was, and it was her mistake to fix. Trish wanted her to give him romance. A grand gesture. Now was her chance. "I'll bid for him."

The auctioneer started the bidding at three hundred dollars. "We've got three hundred from Miss Paisley Monroe in the front row. Can I get four hundred?"

Another paddle went up in the air. "Four hundred from Miss Erin Smith. Can I get five?"

The two women went back and forth until the price reached a thousand dollars. "One thousand going once."

Madeline tossed Emily a paddle. "You better win him."

Emily threw her arm into the air, waving the paddle like a madwoman. She was stuck behind a standing-room-only crowd. Would the auctioneer see her in time?

"Looks like we have another bidder in the back. I can't see your face, dear, are you bidding fifteen hundred?"

"Yes!" She waved the paddle around again.

"You've got some competition, Ms. Monroe. Can I get two thousand from you?"

Sean stood on the stage, his hand shielding his eyes from the lights, but Emily doubted he could see her. The auctioneer couldn't even see her. Paisley agreed to the two thousand, and Sean grimaced. Hopefully Paisley would tap out soon. Emily only had a few thousand in savings she could spare.

"We're up to three thousand," the announcer said. "Is the mystery woman in the back still in?"

She raised her paddle one last time. If Paisley went for four, Emily was out. She didn't have five grand to spare.

Paisley bid four thousand, and Sean ground his teeth. The muscles in his jaw flexed like they always did when he was frustrated. Emily's heart sank. He'd be taking Paisley Monroe out on a date. An image of her pressing her hot pink lips to Sean's face flashed in her mind, making her ears burn.

Madeline clutched her elbow. "Bid ten thousand and shut that tramp down."

"I don't have ten thousand dollars."

"I'll pay for it; you just bid."

The auctioneer peered into the crowd. "Five thousand from the mystery woman?"

Emily didn't raise her paddle. "You don't have to do that for me. This is my fault. I can live with him going on one date with her."

"Going once."

"Well, I can't." Madeline tried to lift Emily's arm. "Besides, I'm not doing it for you. I'm doing it for my future grandchildren."

"Going twice."

Emily stared the woman hard in the eyes. She seemed as serious as she could be. She gave her a nod, and Emily shoved through the crowd, waving the paddle in the air.

"Ten thousand dollars," she shouted at the top of her lungs. She elbowed her way through the throng of people and stumbled into the aisle. "I bid ten thousand dollars."

She caught Sean's gaze, but he didn't smile. His face remained expressionless as the auctioneer waited for Paisley to make a move. Paisley bickered with an older man, most likely her father, but he shook his head. She crossed her arms over her chest and stuck her bottom lip out. She was done.

"Sold to the mystery bidder." The auctioneer rapped her gavel on the podium, and everyone in the audience stared at Emily.

She forced a smile and ducked her head, her heart racing at the sudden onslaught of attention. As she lifted her gaze to meet Sean's, the corner of his mouth twitched. He hopped off the stage and made his way past the front row and up the aisle toward her.

Time seemed to stand still as the image of Trish's fantasy prediction flashed through her mind. He was moving toward her, but his arms weren't outstretched, and he certainly wasn't smiling. Had she made her grand gesture for nothing? Had she wasted Madeline's money only to be rejected in front of hundreds of people?

He stopped two feet in front of her, his gaze heavy, brows knit. She fought the urge to throw herself into his arms and reminded herself to breathe. Why didn't he say something? Her lip trembled, and tears stung her eyes, but she held them back. She hadn't thought this through. Now she had to beg for forgiveness in front of the entire community.

"Sean, I'm sorry. I was wrong and stupid, and I miss you. I shouldn't have broken up with you. I just…Will you please give me another chance?"

He shook his head. Oh, god, he was rejecting her. Her legs turned to noodles, and her stomach churned.

"Emily, I can't change who I am."

"I don't want you to. I love you. Every part. Just the way you are."

Still no smile. She'd never seen him so serious. "And the box?"

"It's gone. Natasha took it this morning. And I talked to Jessica. Well, she talked some sense into me, anyway. I was wrong, Sean. I don't want you to change."

He only stared at her.

"I understand if you don't want to take me back. I put your life in danger. You deserve better—"

He took her face in his hands and pressed his lips to hers. Fire shot through her veins as he stepped closer, closing the space between them until his firm chest pressed against hers. She wrapped her arms around his waist and let the rest of the world slip away. The audience was silent, but they could have been screaming for all she cared. She wouldn't have heard them over the fireworks exploding in her mind. Sean was in her arms, and that was all that mattered.

He linked his fingers behind her neck and pressed his forehead to hers. "Of course I want you back."

"Are you sure?"

A warm tear rolled down her cheek, and he wiped it away with his thumb. "This is true love. You think this happens every day?"

She threw her arms around his neck. "I love you, Sean."

"I love you too."

"Well, ladies," the announcer interrupted their reunion, "I can't guarantee a ten-thousand-dollar bid will end this way for you, but it's worth a shot, isn't it? Let's get the next bachelor out here and see if we can find his true love."

The crowd focused their attention on the stage, and Sean took her by the hand, leading her up the aisle. Sydney gave them a thumbs up from the sound booth, and Trish waved from behind the registration table. The crowd parted for them as they headed toward the exit door.

Sean stopped and pulled her into his arms. "I can't believe you paid ten thousand dollars for a date with me."

"Well, technically your mom paid for it. I just waved the paddle."

He arched an eyebrow. "Did she?"

"She said something about it being an investment in her future grandchildren."

He chuckled. "I'm an only child."

She slid her arms around his waist, pressing her hips to his. "I guess we're her only hope."

"I guess we are. Want to get out of here?"

"I'd love to."

"Hey, Momma?"

Madeline sashayed over and kissed them both on the cheek. "I've got this shindig under control, kids. You two go home and make me some grandbabies while I'm still young enough to enjoy them."

Sean's cheeks flushed with color. "Momma…"

"Oh, hush, you were both thinking it. I just said it out loud. Now get on out of here. Scoot." She ushered them out the door and closed it behind them.

The sun dipped behind the building, casting long shadows across the street. A musician played a saxophone a block away, the soft tunes drifting in the autumn air, creating an intimate soundtrack for their reunion. Sean swept her into his arms as he swayed to the music, and she melted into his embrace.

He gazed into her eyes and tucked a strand of hair behind her ear. "What do you want to do now?"

"I want you to take me home and love me forever."

With a sly grin, he stepped back and dropped into a formal bow. "As you wish."

*R*oxy bolted out the car door as soon as Sean opened it and bounded toward his mother's house. Sometimes he swore that dog liked his mom more than him. It definitely liked his wife more, but he was okay with that.

He offered Emily a hand and helped her out of the car. By the time they reached the front porch, his mom was on her knees, scratching the pit bull behind the ears. Roxy planted a sloppy kiss on her cheek, and she stood up laughing, wiping the slobber from her face.

"Happy birthday, Son." She kissed him on the cheek and pulled Emily into a hug. "And how are you, dear?"

"Never better."

She ushered them into the sitting room and tossed a piece of rawhide to Roxy. "That ought to keep her busy for a while."

He laughed. "Maybe for five minutes."

Emily looked at his great-great-grandmother's spirit and smiled. "Hello, Lenore. Lovely day, isn't it?"

Sean couldn't help but grin at his beautiful wife.

She'd gone from being terrified at the mere mention of ghosts to talking to them like they were old friends. The power of her gift still astonished him. She was getting better at communicating with the deceased than he was, and she'd only been practicing a few months. In fact, in the short amount of time she'd been investigating with his team, she'd already discovered what happened to little Alice and Jonathan from the hotel ballroom. Their father had been a doctor with an office located in one of the upper floors of the building. Left unattended in one of the exam rooms, the children drank some sort of medicine and passed away from poisoning. And Eli…well, he was a work in progress, but he didn't frighten Emily anymore.

Madeline uncorked a bottle of wine. "Who's drinking with me this evening?"

He raised his hand. "I'll have a glass."

"None for me, thank you." Emily flashed him a knowing smile, and he moved to hug her from behind.

"Are you sure, Emily? I have white if you don't want red." Her gaze fell to her son's hands resting on Emily's lower stomach. "Is that? Are you?" Her mouth dropped open.

He laughed. "Momma, meet Sable Lenore LeBlanc. She'll be making her appearance in about seven months."

His mom clasped her hands together under her chin, tears welling in her eyes. "Seven months? How do you know the sex already?"

Emily rubbed her hands over his. "Sydney told us. The next one will be a boy."

"Oh!" His mom hugged them both, sandwiching Emily in the middle. "Life could not get any more perfect than this. Excuse me, I have to go make a few phone calls." She danced into the kitchen, and Emily twisted in his arms to face him.

"She's right, you know. I can't imagine a more perfect life than this one."

"If we're to take Sydney at her word, it's only going to get better."

She smiled and ran a playful finger down his chest. "Good. Because I won't accept anything less than fireworks."

"Neither will I." He pressed his lips to her forehead and tightened his arms around her. Lenore lifted a translucent hand and faded out of sight, taking the soft buzz of her spirit energy with her.

Emily glanced at the empty chair and returned her gaze to his. "Do you think she'll be back?"

"No. I think she's finally moved on. She's been fading for a while."

She pressed her lips together and nodded, a tinge of sadness softening her eyes as if she'd miss his great-great-grandmother. "Moving on is a good thing."

He brushed his fingers across her cheek. "So are fresh starts."

"I'm glad I made mine with you."

"So am I, Buttercup. So am I."

ALSO BY CARRIE PULKINEN

**Crescent City Wolf Pack Series**

Werewolves Only

Beneath a Blue Moon

Bound by Blood

**Spirit Chasers Series**

To Catch a Spirit

To Stop a Shadow

To Free a Phantom

**Stand Alone Books**

The Rest of Forever

Reawakened

Bewitching the Vampire

**Young Adult**

Soul Catchers

## ABOUT THE AUTHOR

Carrie Pulkinen is a paranormal romance author who has always been fascinated with things that go bump in the night. Of course, when you grow up next door to a cemetery, the dead (and the undead) are hard to ignore. Pair that with her passion for writing and her love of a good happily-ever-after, and becoming a paranormal romance author seems like the only logical career choice.

Before she decided to turn her love of the written word into a career, Carrie spent the first part of her professional life as a high school journalism and yearbook teacher. She loves good chocolate and bad puns, and in her free time, she likes to read, drink wine, and travel with her family.

*Connect with Carrie online:*
www.CarriePulkinen.com

CPSIA information can be obtained
at www.ICGtesting.com
Printed in the USA
LVHW090912160419
614194LV00013B/29/P